'*Sinners Never Die* should, in the leavening of time, find its way to the small but choice selection of mystery classics. I doubt if you'll ever forget it. A rare and fine experience.'

Dorothy B. Hughes

'A beautiful job, in which the warmth of community comes through (despite alien locale and nasty narrator) to combine with a pure gift of story-telling reminiscent of Wilkie Collins.'

*San Francisco Chronicle*

'*Sinners Never Die* is a bold and succesful innovation in contemporary mystery fiction. Meticulously Victorian in writing, setting and characterisation, the story holds tense interest to the end. Sterling job creating sanctimonious villain and fitting him into expertly planned drama.'

*Chicago Tribune*

'*Sinners Never Die* is to the ordinary run of mystery stories what *The Oxbow Incident* is to the ordinary run of Westerns.'

*Springfield Evening Union*

'The story is full of surprises, considerable violence and wry humour – something different in mystery yarns.'

*New York Herald Tribune*

**WAKEFIELD CRIME CLASSICS**

**SINNERS NEVER DIE**

———

A.E. Martin was born in Adelaide in 1885 and died in Sydney in 1955. As a young man he travelled the fairgrounds of Europe with Houdini as his mentor, and later worked in Australia as an entrepreneur and publicist in theatre, circuses, the movies and vaudeville.

He grew up in the outback town of Orroroo, where they used to say that when the post-master was late opening his window, it was because he was reading everyone's mail.

A.E. Martin drew on his experiences of both small-town and show-business life in *Sinners Never Die*, which was listed as one of the 'Ten Best' of 1944 by every major mystery reviewer in the United States.

# SINNERS Never DIE

## A. E. MARTIN

Series editors Michael J. Tolley and Peter Moss

Wakefield Press
Box 2266
Kent Town
South Australia 5071

First published by Simon and Schuster, New York, 1944
Published in Wakefield Crime Classics November 1992

Edited by Jane Arms
Designed by Design Bite, Melbourne
Printed and bound by Hyde Park Press, Adelaide

Cataloguing-in-publication data

Martin, A.E. (Archibald Edward)
Sinners Never Die
ISBN 1 86254 290 2.
I. Title (Series: Wakefield Crime Classics).
A823.3

I am accustomed to having my own way and I find hospital discipline irksome. It is a sorry situation in which to find oneself at eighty – to be reduced to this irritating impotency. At my age, surely, one might expect the maximum of attention; yet I have more than once had to complain to the matron. I still have the means, thank heaven, to pay for a private room but, for all the service I get, I might be the veriest pauper.

I have insisted on the removal of several of my nurses since I entered the hospital, and I hope the painted little creature who deigns to attend upon me at present will prove better than her predecessors. Her name, she informed me, was Eileen, but I would have none of that.

'I shall call you Jane,' I told her and, contrary to my expectation, she agreed.

'Righto,' she said. 'Plain Jane it is.'

She has the exasperating habit of forgetfulness. She has, for instance, forgotten to tell me the name of the woman patient who has expressed a desire to meet me. It is a small matter, perhaps, but I find it very annoying. Goodness knows, I have few enough visitors these times, and the days have become unutterably wearisome.

My eyesight is poor so I cannot read, but I manage a little solitaire. And there is the radio! My nurse, with the impertinence of her class, has, without my permission, switched it on. Well, I can switch it off! I like switching it off. It gives me a gratifying sense of power to dismiss the musicians at will, snub genius, and silence the notorious.

'The virtuoso of the mouth organ' is on the air, but I lean forward and twist the dial. And he has gone! But I can still hear the notes of the instrument – not the music of Larry Adler, but of that Larry who looked through the delivery window of my little post office one morning fifty years ago and asked, 'Any letters from me sweetheart today, Mr Ford?' – the Larry who played his mouth organ at the concert when old Sam Cotter rose from the front seats and faced the cheering audience, his very beard rigid with indignation, and shouted –

But let me try and recall in some sort of order those happenings which, today, seem, even to me who lived through them, almost incredible. To those who live among modern miracles they may seem incredible, too, but it should be remembered they were far away days, and our little town had at that time never seen a motorcar or a motion picture, never dreamed of wireless. It was such a little town, so far from anywhere that mattered.

I often wondered why it existed at all, and yet there were many of these places scattered throughout Australia, a few hundred souls clinging together as a small community, living on each other apparently, but actually, I suppose, dependent on the surrounding farmers, sons of those pioneers who had come, mostly from England, in incredibly small ships after long and perilous voyages, to find themselves on inhospitable shores without any of the decencies of civilisation.

They had travelled inland then, by pack horse and dray, suffering the most damnable hardships, made homes for themselves in the wilderness, building with their own hands and with primitive tools the first drab houses, felling trees and tilling the stubborn land and always at the mercy of hostile natives. With the herd instinct of the working classes one attracted the other and a community would gradually grow. They would breed like rabbits and, somehow, the brats not only lived but actually thrived and before long there'd be a fuss pother and the authorities would send a schoolmaster. After that there'd come a post office like mine, with a shop or two and a mill and, by-and-by, what had been a bush shanty would become a hotel like Marven's Royal, which was still the only hostelry in our town and which had been developed from a stopping place on a lonely track where, on a time, bushrangers had caroused before being caught and decently hanged.

Some of the old-timers had been sly dogs. Old Edward Price, for instance, who had reached the locality first and greedily grabbed the best land. His son, Garnet, was now reaping the reward of his father's shrewdness, deriving a splendid income while the surrounding farmers slaved to extract a pittance from the parched earth, making barely enough in the good seasons to pay their debts to old Cotter, the storekeeper, who gave them credit through the bad times and lent them the money (at extortionate interest, no doubt) to pay for what they needed to keep their homesteads together.

I close my eyes and peer again through the tiny window of my post office to see Larry Ward's laughing, impudent face; and Timothy Speek, the blind man, and his wife Helen; Garnet Price with his fierce black eyes, his hands thrust deep into the pockets of his riding breeches, a whip looped over his arm; and Sam Cotter with his pointed grey beard – and Eileen Mahoney, lovely as that March morning I can never forget.

'Any letter from me sweetheart today, Mr Ford?'

I had been expecting Larry to call, and steeled myself to meet him easily and smile back at him, but, when I heard the tap on the wooden frame of the window and threw it open to see him standing there, hatless and handsome, his dark hair ruffled as usual, his shirt open at the neck, his blue eyes twinkling, I suppose my courage failed me, and for a moment I must have stared at him a little stupidly, for he shifted on his feet before he spoke again.

'Ah, now, come, Mr Ford; don't tease a poor lad. Give me me letter.'

That brought me to myself and the thing I had in hand.

'There is no letter for you,' I said.

Just for an instant he waited, too surprised to speak; then he shook his head in that way he had.

'Come, Mr Ford,' he said, smiling. 'I know it is here. It was promised me. Like a kind man give another look. It's slipped down somewhere, maybe; behind the pile ye've got for Sam Cotter, or the National Bank, perhaps?'

I shook my head. 'There's no letter, Larry,' I repeated, firmly.

For the first time his eyes stopped smiling. 'But, Mr Ford,' he pleaded, 'it's just got to be there. Ye could easily mislay it, couldn't ye, or mix it up with others? I wish ye'd look again – as a favour, sir.'

'All right,' I said, and left the window and moved from his view. But I didn't search. Why should I? I waited a minute or so and I could picture him standing, all the careless gaiety gone out of him in his anxiety and disappointment. I remember I thought how strange it was that I could feel no pity in my heart for him, though but a few short hours before I had called myself his friend. I returned to the window.

'Sorry, Larry,' I spoke shortly. 'There's no letter.'

He stared at me unbelievingly and, for a brief moment, I feared he guessed something of the truth; but his eyes fell, and, staring at the ground and without a word, he turned and walked slowly away.

Only then did I notice that Timothy Speek was standing on the post-office verandah. The blind man walked towards my window, but his unseeing eyes were gazing after Larry.

'And who would *he* be expecting to write *him* a letter?' he was saying, and it seemed half to himself. When he came to the window I noticed he was carrying a paper bag of sweets in his hand. Despite his infirmity Speek needed no guide through our streets. In ten years of blindness he must have memorised every corner and fence, gate, and gutter. With stick tapping and his long coat flapping about his knees he found his way to the post office day after day at the same hour, although it was seldom he collected any mail, and then went on to gossip with this one and that with such regularity that people would set their clocks by his comings and goings.

Perhaps, in his sightless solitude, Timothy Speek craved companionship, yet one seldom saw him with his handsome wife. I had never met a man with such appetite for small talk, nor one given so greatly to the spreading of scandal, but, as my years of service lengthened so that I sometimes wondered whether the Department had utterly forgotten me, it seemed that the little tidbits he retailed were growing less innocuous. His tongue acquired an acidity which at first repelled, but came to fascinate, me.

'But fancy me standing here and telling you this,' he would say after he had passed on to me some gossip he had picked up on his rounds. 'You with secrets all about you.'

'Secrets?' I queried when he first spoke in this way.

'Aye,' he laughed. 'Secrets packed away and sealed down in envelopes. Aye, if all the letters that you hand through your window could cry aloud their contents, Mr Ford, we'd be hearing some pretty things, that we should.'

As he turned from watching Larry and the filmy blueness of his eyes met mine, he chuckled. He popped a sweetmeat into his mouth and offered the bag to me.

'And so you had no letter for the poor lad?' he said contemptuously, munching, and caressing his thick, short beard. I did not reply, for I was in no mood for talk, but he went on, 'It might be a letter from Eileen Mahoney he'd be expecting.'

'Indeed,' I said, but my heart stopped a beat.

'Aye,' he went on, 'to tell him she was leaving the town. She drove off with her father at daybreak for Baloola to catch the train for the city. But you'd know, of course. Didn't you send Mahoney his telegram?'

'Really, Mr Speek,' I said. 'You know I'm not supposed to discuss these things.'

'Oh,' he said, and stopped, and his lips curled back until I saw two big front teeth gleam white against the black of his beard. His eyes never left my face. 'No,' he went on, 'of course not.' His fingers fumbled in the bag for another sweet, and he laughed. 'You're the great guardian of secrets, Mr Ford, but half the town knows a telegram went to old Mahoney last night late, and within an hour I'll be bound half the town will know what was in it.'

'I suppose you're right,' I said. 'After all, it's a small place and nothing much ever happens. People must have something to talk about.'

He leaned forward and spoke eagerly. 'You're right, Mr Ford. It keeps 'em alive. It's father and mother and food and drink to 'em. It's water in a parched land.' He broke off but continued more quietly, and, if he could have seen, I am sure he would have looked at me shrewdly. 'Aye, Mr Ford,' he continued, 'you're a lucky man to be locked up all alone in your office there with all the innocent little tidbits – aye, and reading all the postcards, too, I shouldn't wonder.' He chuckled.

'Really, Mr Speek,' I remonstrated. 'You surely don't think – '

He put out a protesting hand. 'No, no, of course not, my friend,' he said. 'But I wouldn't blame you if you did. No, indeed.' For a second he looked almost wistful, then shrugged his shoulders. 'As for Larry Ward,' he continued, 'maybe Eileen Mahoney's old man has nipped *that* romance in the bud. And just as well. Aye, just as well, Mr Ford, for the feller's a philanderer, if ever there was. A no-gooder like his father before him.'

Two little women tripped together on to the verandah, one of them holding a child of ten by the hand. They stood, side by side, waiting pointedly for Speek to leave the window. Though obviously sisters and of the same build and height, the younger was definitely the prettier if the word could be used to describe spinsters I considered long past their youth. Curiously it was the blind man who spoke first.

'Good morning, ladies,' he cried with a clumsy bow and a sweep of his broad, black hat. Then he turned again to me and slapped his palm down upon the window ledge.

'Any letters for the Misses Garner, Mr Ford?' he called heartily and strode off, chuckling as at some secret thought, his stick tapping on the stone floor of the verandah.

As I moved away to the letter racks, the voices of the women came to me, low-pitched but perfectly distinct.

'Agatha! I *hate* that man.'

'Sh-h.' I imagined the other putting a restraining hand on her sister's arm. 'Polly! Mr Ford will hear you.'

'I don't care. I *hate* him. Oh, Agatha, sometimes when he looks at me with those awful eyes I think he *knows*.'

I glanced down at the meagre mail in my hands – all local, unsealed accounts, and an invitation in a square envelope from the tennis club committee (I had had one myself), and I thought suddenly of the registered envelope that came for one of these faded little spinsters as regularly as clockwork at the beginning of each month.

For the first time I found myself wondering what it contained.

Hidden by a partition from any one who might come to the counter of the main office (which was open except at mail-delivery times when I closed the door and transacted business through the letter window), I sat down and took from my pocket the note Eileen had scribbled to Larry and posted to him the night before.

I spread it before me and let the words eat like acid into my tortured soul. For a whole sleepless night they had burned themselves into my brain. I knew them by heart, yet I needs must read them over and over, hoping against hope that I might find in them some grain of comfort for myself, but knowing full well that I was only adding to my agony – an agony which had begun the evening before when I had seen Eileen slip the letter into the box and run quickly towards the home where she was packing against the morrow's journey. I had entered my office, lit the table lamp, and easily identified it.

When I saw it was addressed to Larry, the suspicion within me quickened to certainty and such a torment of jealousy surged through me that I almost wept. Until that afternoon I had never thought of Larry as a rival. Social position and solid respectability counted for much in those days, and Larry's gay irresponsibility and impecuniosity were not the stuff, according to my lights, of which suitable husbands were made. Larry and Eileen forsooth! A moth desiring a star!

And then, in the middle of one of my solitary walks, I had seen the carving on the tree trunk. It was but a chance in a thousand that any except those who knew its whereabouts would have found it. I was forcing a path for myself through the thick undergrowth, finding a new way to reach the creek that trickled past the town, when I slipped and thrust out my hand to steady myself against the bole of a great gum. As I withdrew I saw that my palm had been covering some lettering carved on the trunk so low down that whoever had made the signs must have been sitting hidden even from any in the near vicinity.

Just two Christian names:

LARRY

EILEEN

but, as I realized their significance, jealousy thrust at me, filling my whole being with an awful numbness.

If I had had a knife, I would have scraped the wretched letters from the trunk, but I had to leave them, and I made my way back to the town, my heart aching dully, my reason striving to find an alibi for what I had seen. I tried to tell myself it was the work of some youthful mischief-maker. Or Larry's wishful thinking – a hope carved on a tree trunk. Nothing more. And Eileen never within a mile of the place. I had seen such things before – carved initials entwined in crude hearts, silent memorials of spasmodic courtships that never progressed further than furtive kissings in secluded corners.

No lovers' lanes for me, no lucerne patches, no unchaperoned walks! I prided myself I was a gentleman. I did my courting as I conceived a gentleman should, with dignity and according to the laws of etiquette. My jealousy took a new turn and rage and resentment filled my heart – rage that Larry Ward should dare drag Eileen down to his level, resentment that she should have slipped from that pedestal of Christian virtue and maidenly modesty on which I had set her.

So filled with my thoughts that I scarcely knew which way I was walking, I pushed through the bushes and came at last almost to the edge of the road. Ahead of me I saw a bridled horse, browsing, and, hidden from the road by a tree but plainly visible to me, a man and woman standing locked in embrace. The man I recognised as Garnet Price, but the woman's back was towards me. Her bonnet had fallen over her shoulder, and I saw that it had a green feather and that her hair was golden in the setting sun.

Unseen by either, I turned away and forced another path for myself towards the town and came to the post office in time to see Eileen Mahoney dropping her letter into the mailbox. There were several youngsters playing about the verandah and I brusquely ordered them off. They were obdurate, for they were in the middle of some game, but scattered at last, shouting rudely at me from safe distances. I stood for a moment after they had gone, trying to decide what to do; then made up my mind, unlocked my office, and went straight to the mailbox.

When I found the letter and stood with the envelope in my hand, I remembered things about Larry – his twinkling eyes, his careless air, his perennial good humour, and I knew then that he would be the most formidable rival of all. What if Eileen's father rejected him? Even in those days young women occasionally flouted their parents' wishes. What if he had no solidity, no money, no prospects? Was Eileen the girl to be swayed by such considerations?

All my dreams, all those great things I had planned for our future, came tumbling about me as I held that accursed envelope between my fingers. I saw again the carving on the tree, I thought of the two of them hidden there alone, laughing, exchanging God knows what secrets in their damnable intimacy, and already I *knew* the nature of that which I would find in the letter. And yet I had to know for sure and know all. I *had* to turn the knife in the wound.

I lit the little spirit stove I kept handy to make myself tea and waited till the kettle boiled. I held the envelope in the steam from the spout until the gum was moistened, and, with a thin pencil, carefully rolled back the flap, then drew out the letter and spread it before me.

My nerves were on edge, and I fancied I heard a sound. Hastily hiding the letter under a blotter, I went to the front door and peered out, but there was no one to be seen. I returned to the office, locking the door behind me, and drew out the letter. It was no more than a pencilled scribble but, even today, I can shut my eyes and it is before me again in letters of fire.

*Larry – Dad has a telegram to say he is to see a specialist in the city at once and I am all of a dither packing, for we leave at daybreak tomorrow. So you see it was just as well I said I'd write to you, Larry, and tell you what you want to know, for it may be weeks before I return, and after what happened this afternoon it isn't fair to keep you waiting, and so I'm letting you know now, Larry, that the man I am going to marry is*

and here, either by accident or design I know not, the first page of writing ended and Eileen had turned the leaf and continued:

*none other than Larry Ward. Surely you must have guessed what was in my heart. Oh, Larry, I love the man so much that my heart is bursting with the sorrow of leaving him. Promise you'll keep my grand news to yourself, Larry, and when I come back you can tell me in your own kind way that I'm right to be marrying the man – Eileen*

Throughout that horrid night the names on the tree had beaten into my brain. Eileen and Larry. Eileen and Larry. Eileen and Larry – a devil's tattoo that bred in me wrath indescribable and a bitter hatred of this shabby shop boy who had dared lift his unworthy eyes to the woman I had chosen for my mate. I wished to God I could put the clock back to that age of chivalry when, like a presumptuous varlet sullying the presence of a great lady, he might be whipped and driven naked from the town. As morning came I determined that Eileen's indiscretion should never reach his hand so that he might cease to befoul her with his importunities.

I had burned my boats. As far as the post office was concerned, there need be no such thing as this letter from Eileen Mahoney to Larry Ward. Eileen would be away for some time, and, if I wished, I could intercept any letters they might write to each other. Destroy them, even. If I could only keep them apart, their foolish dream would fade. These thoughts elbowed and jostled through my mind as I read through Eileen's letter for the twentieth time.

I heard a step in the office, and, hurriedly slipping the letter into its envelope, I hid it in my pocket. Helen Speek was standing at the counter. She was a handsome woman, no more than twenty-eight, I should say, with large, sombre eyes, and one of those mouths that inevitably lead men to certain conclusions. There had been gossip about her, but this was a town of whispers and I knew no more than scandalous tongues had hinted. Her husband had never mentioned her in my presence, and yet, I thought, as I looked at her now while she stood with fingers drumming impatiently on the counter, she was a woman a man might speak of with pride.

As I came forward, she stepped back a pace or two and

cast a quick, furtive glance through the open doorway; then she spoke rapidly, as if what she had to say had to be gotten over quickly.

'Will you do me a favour, Mr Ford? If a letter – a letter or a packet – comes for me, please don't give it to my husband.'

She stared at me with big, sullen eyes as I explained that, officially, letters addressed to her were her property and, if she wished, she alone might collect them.

'I didn't know,' she said. 'Thank you Mr Ford. But my husband mustn't even know if any come.' She waited a second and then added in a rush, 'He's a crabbed man, Mr Ford. He begrudges me everything – even the littlest things.'

I made no comment, but I could easily understand what she must have endured during the years of her husband's blindness, which had come on him less than twelve months after their marriage. I had not known him all this time, of course, but I had seen and heard enough of him to realise that when his sight went, a bitterness that had steadily grown in intensity had entered his heart.

'Thank you,' she said again. 'Please keep them – it – here if it should come.'

I patted her hand where it rested on the counter, and she withdrew it quickly.

'It's a pleasure,' I said, rather huffily, I am afraid.

She walked to the door, and, as she turned, I saw a green feather on her bonnet. I remembered the golden hair, and I knew that the blind man's wife was the woman I had seen near the creek locked in the arms of Garnet Price.

Luke Barmby, a God-fearing man if ever there was, walked fifty paces ahead of me along our main street as I went to my lunch. Carefully, lest he be contaminated by the proximity of alcohol, he ignored the friendly verandah of the Royal Hotel and stepped out on the roadway. The public house safely passed, he rejoined the footpath and continued his way to a home more or less crowded with cantankerous children.

As I entered the hotel and walked by the private bar on my way to the dining-room, I caught a glimpse of Larry Ward, a glass of beer before him, talking to Mrs Marven, the widowed proprietor.

She smiled a welcome to me and, later on, in the dining room, said, 'Poor Larry. He's not himself.'

I looked up from my soup enquiringly.

'I suppose it's an affair of the heart,' she said. 'It usually is.'

'I hope,' I said, with a weak attempt at a smile, 'he isn't taking to drink.'

'Of course not,' she said quickly. 'Though he did have two, which is one more than his normal.' She paused and a thoughtful expression came into her face; then she shook her head. 'No,' she went on, 'Larry's too sensible a lad for that sort of foolishness.'

Mrs Marven, of course, never spoke unkindly of any-one. I had found her tolerant to a fault. She even found excuses for Luke Barmby, who so ostentatiously ignored her hotel and had, it was said, thrashed one of his children for speaking to her. She had cried when she heard that and, when I had voiced some indignation over the incident, she had patted my arm.

'That's kind of you, Mr Ford,' she said, 'but you mustn't blame him. The weeds have got into his system. Some day, somehow, he'll get the garden tidy.' She sighed. 'Poor little children!' she added, and went on almost in the same breath. 'After all, I mustn't be hard on him or who'll be burying me when my time comes?'

Luke, among other things, was the local undertaker. I almost decided to snub the man when we next met, but remembered in time that he had a certain influence in the town and, after all, had acted according to his lights. Mrs Marven, though a very likeable woman, was a little irrespon-sible and at times spoke in a manner that made me feel faintly uneasy. One Sunday, for instance, I remember well. It had come on to rain rather heavily as we were about to set off for church. I would have stayed home but was singing in the choir, and they rather relied on me. She stood at the front door watching the downpour, then she took off her bonnet and said, 'God wouldn't want me to spoil a bonnie new bonnet like that, now, would he? I'll stay home and pray a little in the kitchen while I make you a pudding that'll taste like manna from heaven.' As we moved off she called to us from the door, 'Now you forget about the pudding, you heathens, and keep your mind on God.'

I am sure Luke Barmby would have burned her at the stake.

I had only just finished lunch when the accident occurred and they carried the little Barmby boy into Mrs Marven's bar-parlour. As it was told me, Larry was driving Sam Cotter's grocery delivery past the hotel when the Barmby child ran from the roadside and was knocked down. Larry had a spirited cob in the shafts and was either unable to pull away from the racing youngster or was so busy with his own thoughts that he just didn't see him.

Fortunately, somebody had spotted Dr Hansen entering Cotter's store, and he was soon on the scene. We stood round in a semi-circle, anxiously watching while he made his examination, and breathed a sigh of relief when he looked up, smiling.

'Nothing serious,' he said. 'Must have just touched him. Lucky.' The doctor rose to his feet as the child opened bewildered eyes. 'You'll be all right, sonny,' he said.

Larry gave a great sigh. Mrs Marven smiled happily. She patted the boy's head and embraced us all in a gesture. 'I think, after that, we need a drink.'

She voiced everyone's sentiments, for the lad had looked very white and still as he was carried in, and I know I, for one, was afraid he had been killed outright and, for a fleeting moment, wondered what they would do with Larry if this were so. We all moved towards the bar, and there was Luke Barmby standing in the parlour doorway.

'Who brought my child into this abode of iniquity?' he

demanded in a voice shaking with anger. We were all thunderstruck, and no one answered him. I saw the colour drain from Mrs Marven's face, and Larry's fists clenched as he took a step forward. The doctor brushed him aside.

'Come, come, now, Mr Barmby,' he said. 'Your child is not hurt. This was the nearest place – '

Barmby interrupted him rudely, pushing his way past him to the couch. He turned on us, his eyes blazing. 'I would sooner see my son dead,' he cried, 'than in this evil house.' Stooping, he picked the boy up in his arms and carried him towards the door. As he passed Larry he paused and stared him in the face. 'As for the drunken lout that nearly killed him,' he said, 'he will hear more of this.'

He strode out, leaving us dumbfounded. Larry made to follow him, but Mrs Marven restrained him. 'Don't, Larry,' she pleaded.

She sat down on the couch and Dr Hansen put a consoling hand on her shoulder. She looked up at him, her eyes full of tears. 'Doctor, dear,' she said, 'will you see Mrs Barmby like a good doctor and tell her he mustn't? I couldn't bear to think of that baby being thrashed because of me.'

Larry refused a drink, after all. He loosed the cob and drove away in his delivery cart, and I noticed he held the animal well in check. Outside Barmby's place I could see Luke talking vehemently to a small, silent, but interested group. Heads turned and gazed curiously as Larry drove past.

That evening we were to hold a concert in aid of the school prize fund, and it was during the late afternoon when I, as secretary, was conferring over last moment details with Hennessy, the teacher and organiser, that Larry rushed in on us, flushed and excited.

'I've come to tell ye that I cannot play at the concert tonight, Mr Hennessy,' he said. 'I'm finished with this damned town and everybody in it.' He pulled himself up short and amended his words. 'I don't mean that for you, Mr

Hennessy, or for Mr Ford either,' he went on as the school-master removed his pipe and gazed at him in astonishment, 'but things have happened today till I can't stand any more.'

Hennessy soothed him and gradually the story came out.

'It's all so *silly*,' Larry cried, and made an exasperated motion, swishing the hat he held in his hand. 'What demon's loose to torment me this day?' he asked, and then he told us how he had driven from Mrs Marven's hotel after the accident and called at Timothy Speek's place to deliver a grocery order from Sam Cotter's store where he worked. He had tethered the horse and carried the box of groceries to the back door and Helen Speek had begun to check them over.

'I don't know what came over me then, Mr Hennessy,' Larry explained, 'but all of a sudden I felt queer. I suppose it was the shock still upon me after upsetting Barmby's lad, but suddenly I fell against Mrs Speek, and she saw there was something wrong.'

She led him into her parlour and told him to lie on the sofa and rest and brought him a glass of water. She'd hardly spoken, he told us, for Helen Speek was a woman of few words, as all the town knew, and, when he'd finished drinking, he sat up and she sat down beside him, putting her hand on his forehead.

'It's biliousness, maybe,' she declared. 'It can take you that way.'

'I'd better be moving,' Larry said.

'Rest awhile till you're yourself again,' she advised him.

There was no more to it than that, according to Larry Ward, but the next thing they knew Timothy Speek was standing at the side door, leaning on his stick. He had come on them so silently that they saw him before they heard him, and they stared back at him dumbly for a moment, forgetting his blindness, so penetrating was the glare the sightless eyes directed upon them as they sat, side by side, on the sofa.

When at last Helen Speek's voice came, it was saying a foolish thing.

'Why, Timothy, I didn't expect you back – ' She broke off helplessly.

'Aye,' her husband said, and he sucked in a great breath and went on. 'I wasn't expected. It were not my time to return. The blind man was on his rounds, tap, tap, tapping about the town, feeling the way with his stick. Folks were setting their clocks by him. Aye! and his wife entertaining in his absence!' He emphasised 'entertaining' till it was a slur and an insult.

Mrs Speek walked towards him and his eyes turned unerringly to her. She said, 'You should be ashamed.'

'*I* should be ashamed?' He laughed and wagged his head from side to side. 'Aye, Helen, but you say some queer things, lass. But come now, introduce me to this gentleman with the two fit eyes who comes creeping to the wife while the blind man is away.'

'Don't say such things,' Helen Speek cried. 'Don't keep on *saying* such things.'

Timothy laughed again.

'Be generous, wife,' he urged. 'They've taken me eyes. Leave me me tongue.'

'Your tongue's sour; it's always sour,' she cried vehemently, and turned to Larry, standing white and impotent behind her. 'Larry, you'd better go.'

Speek threw his head back and laughed again and then his blind eyes went straight to the boy. '*Larry!*' he cried. 'Well, well, well, now 'tis surely a harem you're aiming at.'

Larry took a step towards him. 'I don't know what you mean, Mr Speek,' he said indignantly. 'I don't know what this is about. I called with the groceries and – '

'And crept right past the kitchen into the parlour.' Speek's voice rose, penetrating, growing in bitterness as he went on. 'And sat down on the sofa with her, maybe, and held her hands, maybe, cosseting and cuddling her, laughing at the blind man, lusting after his wife.'

'*Stop*,' Larry shouted. 'You're mad.' He turned to Mrs Speek in bewilderment.

'Larry, please go. I'm used to this.'

'Larry,' Speek mimicked. 'Aye, but before I interrupted you, maybe it wasn't just Larry.' His voice rose again. 'It was some word you've never had for me, some endearment you've stored in your wanton heart for a lover but never for a poor devil of a blind husband.' He brought his stick down on the floor with a bang as Larry sprang at him and gripped his arms.

Speek stared with visionless eyes. 'So,' he sneered quietly. 'You'd lay hands on me? You'd strike a blind man?'

Larry's grip tightened and the words hissed from his mouth. 'You're vile. I wonder God lets you live.'

The other man never flinched. Their two faces almost touched, and Speek must have felt the boy's hard breathing hot on his cheeks, for he said, 'And you with your foul breath poisoning the home of the afflicted! Who are you, Larry Ward, to speak of God? You who come adultering fresh from the arms of Eileen Mahoney.'

It was meant to hurt Helen, of course. For an instant the boy shut his eyes, he told us, and fought for self-control.

'Aye,' Speek went on, relentlessly, 'but she found you no great lover, it seems. She jilted ye, so ye picked up with the next – '

Larry claimed the word was unpardonable. He loosed his hold on the arms of the blind man and smashed his fist into his face. Speek fell and lay still. His wife gazed down at him, watching the red from his nose bloodying his mouth and chin. She turned without a word and left the room, returning at once with a bowl of water. There was no haste in her movements, no sign of resentment or concern on her sullen features. Her eyes never altered their expression as she bathed Speek's face, but her lips moved slightly as if she were shaping soundless words.

She rose at length and picked Larry's hat from the sofa and

handed it to him and made a slight gesture with her head towards the door.

'What else could I do, Mr Ford?' Larry asked, anxiously, as he finished. 'I was beside meself.' As I didn't answer, he turned to the schoolmaster. 'Ye're not blaming me, Mr Hennessy, sir? What would ye have done?'

Hennessy took his pipe from his lips with exasperating slowness and carefully knocked out the ashes before he answered.

'Who knows, Larry?' he replied quietly. 'But, in confidence, just between us three, I'm afraid I'd have done the same.'

I was shocked. It had seemed to me that any man, and especially a young man, should have refrained from striking one without sight, whatever the provocation. Besides, I wondered whether Larry's story was altogether true. I remembered Helen Speek down by the creek, locked in the arms of Garnet Price, and her anxious request about her letters. Maybe there was something to Speek's suspicions. Later, when Larry Ward had gone, Hennessy said, 'You've only to look at the lad to know he's telling the truth,' and it was with some difficulty that I refrained from voicing my opinion.

I could no longer see Larry as a carefree youth. Speek had called him a philanderer, a no-gooder, and I persuaded myself that he was weak and unreliable. Though far from subscribing to the doctrines of teetotalism, I had a hearty contempt for any man who flew to alcohol to alleviate his troubles. I recalled with interest Mrs Marven's hesitation when I had expressed the hope that Larry wasn't taking to drink.

I said nothing to Hennessy, of course, but joined with him in persuading Ward to help us at the concert. It would have been a great disappointment to the schoolmaster if he had failed us, for Larry was, in a rugged, unschooled way, an artist of sorts, thanks to the guidance of Hennessy, who was himself no mean musician.

When Hennessy first suggested that we should ask Larry

to play his mouth organ at the concert, my aesthetic soul revolted. I had always considered the mouth organ an instrument for stableboys particularly and members of the lower classes generally, but the schoolmaster had brushed my protest aside. He was a man, as I see it now, much ahead of his day, and he had a flair for organising so that the modest local entertainments we held from time to time invariably included one or two little surprises to relieve the monotony.

Our talent never reached a high standard, and I believe Hennessy would have taken the keenest delight in drowning a few of our performers and their offspring, who, with grim insistence, gave their services for sweet charity's sake. It was not, however, a town in which a schoolmaster could afford to offend, and he suffered in silence and carried on steadfastly.

'Larry will bring the house down,' he prophesied. 'I'll get him to start off with some simple melodies they all know and then startle them with *Rigoletto*.'

'Grand opera on the harmonica?' I smiled indulgently.

'You'll see,' Hennessy said. 'We're rehearsing hard, and I'll accompany him on the piano. I tell you, Harry, the boy's got real music in him.'

The long and short of it was that the schoolmaster's persuasive manner won from Larry a promise that he would play at the concert, though it abated none of his wrath and, as we left Hennessy's place and I parted with him at the gate, he reaffirmed his intention of leaving the town.

'I think you're right, Larry,' I said. 'This place is too small for you. I'd clear out myself if I were in your place.'

'It isn't as easy as all that, Mr Ford,' he replied.

'Money?'

'Oh, sure,' he said with a bitter laugh. 'That wouldn't be worryin' the likes of me. I'm a millionaire.'

'I'd be glad to help you get away, Larry,' I said.

He put his hand on my shoulder. 'Thanks, Mr Ford.' 'You're a good friend to me.' Then he added, rather curiously, 'It's a wonder ye haven't married.'

I was taken aback.

'A friend of mine – a lady friend – always would be saying to me about ye, Mr Ford, "Now, *there's* a man who should have a good wife and home and family instead of living his years in a hotel".'

Eileen Mahoney! I knew almost as if he had told me her name. For an instant, hope flickered in my heart. I looked at him steadily. 'Perhaps I may marry, Larry,' I told him, 'and sooner than you think. But I believe a man has no right to ask a woman – any woman – to be his wife until he has won a place for himself in the world and has the means to support her in comfort. A woman expects that. Take my own case. I have worked hard. I have been provident. I am only a few years older than you. And yet, already, I have a thousand pounds invested – a thousand pounds that I can make over to my wife on our wedding day.'

Larry looked downcast and said, 'Ye think ye must have money?'

'Of course – and position.'

He smiled ruefully. 'Then to add to me other discomforts, Mr Ford,' he said, 'I fear I'll be dying a bachelor.'

As I walked along the main street, I met the two Garners. Little Miss Agatha stopped me, concern in her voice.

'Oh, Mr Ford,' she cried breathlessly. 'Is it true that Larry Ward became intoxicated and nearly killed Mr Speek?'

The blind man, I realised, had wasted no time in resuming his rounds. Before I could answer, Garnet Price rode up and sprang from his horse, throwing the reins over the post. Miss Agatha turned to him and repeated her query.

'Nearly killed Timothy Speek!' Price roared at the top of his voice. 'No, I hadn't heard it. Did he now?' He ruminated a moment, then struck his high boot with his riding whip. 'Mind you, Miss Garner,' he went on, 'I don't think he did, but, by hookey, it would have been a grand idea.

CHAPTER 2

The rain which had been reported in the district as heavy, but of which we had had none locally, began to fall lightly towards six o'clock, but it kept away from our concert, and Hennessy was beaming when at eight Polly Garner stepped smiling in front of a crowded audience to play the overture.

My job was at the back of the curtain and, through the peephole, I saw Sam Cotter, local magistrate and president of the school board, moving pompously at the head of his family into the best seats. I saw Mrs Marven with Teecher the bank clerk, who boarded at her hotel, and remember wondering to whom she had given the other ten tickets she had bought from persistent children. On the opposite side were Luke Barmby and his wife; but I did not see Dr Hansen or Garnet Price. As the overture commenced I watched Timothy Speek being led to a seat halfway down the hall. His wife was not with him and, as far as I could see, there was no sign that he had received any injury in the affray with Larry.

Following the overture the school band played ruthlessly upon piccolos. Owing, no doubt, to excitement, they were never much in tune, but the parents applauded lustily. Then the curtain fell and rose again with Hennessy sitting in an armchair, from which position he recited – a revolutionary idea if ever there was in those days when every elocutionist was expected to stand and face the audience and announce the title of his piece before clearing his throat and boring everyone to tears. I have never been able to memorise verse and I found Hennessy's effort depressing.

The two Misses Garner floated down the grand canal in song, and Haggart, the draper, who was regarded with amused tolerance as the town Lothario, held a sheet of music at arm's length and warbled in a hard, unemotional voice a love song with the most pulsating lyrics, pulling meanwhile at his straggling moustache in a veritable frenzy of self-consciousness. I rather thought Hennessy had made a mistake in placing him in this part of the programme because I had to follow with a ballad almost before the ironic and scattered handclapping had died away. I was in good voice but I was surprised and hurt by the comparatively lukewarm appreciation that rewarded my efforts. I could only surmise that my item was over their heads.

So it went on until it was time for the last performer before the interval. Hennessy stepped out and told them that the act would be a little unusual, but he was sure that they would like it nonetheless for that. He had great pleasure in announcing that Mr Larry Ward would entertain them.

There was a rustle and much whispering among the audience but, significantly, no applause, for I believe that most of those present were already agog with the gossip about Larry's trouble with Speek. Through the peephole I saw Sam Cotter frown and say something to his wife.

My eyes flashed to Timothy Speek. I could see him plainly. He was sitting on an aisle seat and had half turned in his chair with his feet thrust out into the passageway. He leaned on his stick and his visionless eyes were gazing intently at the stage. A few rows in front of him Luke Barmby had partly risen in his seat and his wife was clutching his arm and trying to pull him down again.

The curtain was raised to show the full extent of the stage, and I sensed the expectation of the audience. Before they saw Larry they heard him playing his mouth organ. He started with a ripple of notes, up and down the scales, as if experimenting with his instrument. From my point of vantage I noted Sam Cotter's look of astonishment, and then the broad, pleased smile of Mrs Marven. From the lads seated on the piled-up forms at the rear of the hall came a little laughter.

Larry walked on to the stage, swinging into a lilting old waltz tune. He never looked at the audience, and I must admit he played well. Even I caught the rhythm and, against my will, felt myself moving to its lilt. Without effort or pause he merged the notes and before we knew it, he was in the middle of another popular air – one of those cheap, tuneful, sentimental songs sung in that day at bachelor gatherings when the wine was in and the wit was out:

> *We fought, he fell, I left him there;*
> *In rage and fear I fled.*
> *Tum-tum-tee-tum, tum-tum-tee-tum,*
> *I knew not he was dead.*

On he went from tune to tune until he came to a rollicking air known to all the lads at the back, who, unable to contain themselves longer, joined lustily in the chorus.

> *Oh, poor Mary Ann,*
> *When she got to the top,*
> *Her heart went flipperty flop,*
> *For the Wheel began to stop.*
> *The man in the moon began to laugh*
> *And Mary began to squeal –*
> *And she lost her reputation*
> *On the great big Wheel.*

He walked off the stage playing the last notes as he disappeared from the view of his audience. Immediately from the back there was pandemonium. The applause was deafening. Larry stood alongside me, flushed with excitement and a little breathless with his efforts. Hennessy, wearing a fatuous grin, patted him on the shoulder.

I said nothing, pretending to be busy, but I thought with

sudden apprehension that this triumph might well go to Larry's head. He'd take new heart and stay on and face whatever was coming to him and, by and by, Eileen would come back.

I wished the applause would cease but, instead, it grew in volume. I pulled Eileen's letter from my pocket, sealed and addressed as it had been when she dropped it into the mailbox the night before. Who was to know I had read it and doctored those pencilled lines? I gave it to Larry with a smile.

'Here's what you were looking for, Larry,' I said, above the din. 'Must have been posted from Baloola.'

He grabbed it with hasty thanks and tore it open, a new light in his eye, and I turned from him, unwilling to watch as he read.

I saw Hennessy beaming as he prepared to walk on to the stage and make an announcement about the opera selection and again I put my eye to the peephole. Sam Cotter's wife was talking excitedly to her husband, the young Cotters, very stiff in their best clothes, sitting silently, but with wide, puzzled eyes directed upon their parents. Mrs Marven was applauding ecstatically.

From the back the ovation continued without interruption. After all, it was not so much for Larry as for his music. It was the music they understood, that they could sway to, stamp their feet to, sing to, quite unlike the drawing-room songs, indifferently sung, they'd listened to for so long and borne with so much patience. The lads at the back shouted, 'Encore' again and again and continued their thunderous stamping. I looked inquiringly at Hennessy.

'Let them carry on a bit while the boy gets a breather,' he shouted, grinning.

But all at once the applause ceased with surprising abruptness, and we heard Sam Cotter's voice. Something was happening in front. I turned to the peephole again and saw Cotter standing up, his face thrust forward so that it seemed his still white beard was pointing accusingly at the back rows.

'Order,' he cried. '*Order*,' and so vehemently that there was no opposition. The old man turned again to the stage. 'Mr Hennessy,' he called, and the schoolmaster stepped out, wondering. 'Mr Hennessy,' Cotter called up to him, 'we will hear the next performer.'

Hennessy leaned over the edge of the stage and spoke quietly.

'Larry is to play again, Mr Cotter,' he said, and added in a loud whisper, '*grand opera!*'

'Grand fiddlesticks,' the old man retorted rudely. 'We don't wish to hear any more. Enough of this vulgarity.'

In that little hall you could hear every word. Hennessy's face must have flushed and he looked, uncertainly, past Cotter to the seats beyond. There was a murmur. They were to be baulked of their entertainment, but they were not men enough to voice a protest. Not so Mrs Marven. She began to clap her hands and the sound was startling as it broke the silence that had grown while Hennessy stood, perplexed and hesitating.

'Bring Larry back,' she cried. 'Encore, Larry, encore.'

Suddenly Luke Barmby was on his feet, his wife tugging at his arm in an effort to stay him.

'We want no more bar-room bawdiness,' he roared.

'*Order*.' It was Cotter again, feeling, perhaps, that authority was being usurped.

Another voice joined in, penetrating, bitter. Timothy Speek was standing in the aisle, pointing his stick to the spot where, doubtless, he imagined Larry was standing.

'And we want no lecher to play for us.'

An awful quiet descended on the hall. Sam Cotter's mouth fell open and he gaped helplessly; then Mrs Marven rose and began to walk down the aisle toward the entrance, the bank clerk at her heels.

'I'm going outside where I can breathe,' she said pointedly and, as she passed Cotter, she gave him a look that would have withered a lesser bigot. For an instant, it seemed to me, the old man wavered and was about to say something. After all, Mrs Marven's weekly grocery order was no mean one. But, before he could frame any words, she had swept past him to where Luke Barmby and Timothy Speek were still on their feet. She paused before them and looked each of them up and down contemptuously.

'When I see men like you,' she said quietly but so that all could hear, 'I want to spit,' and she walked on and out, the bank clerk fellow following sheepishly at her heels.

Hennessy beckoned to me.

'Let the curtain down, Ford,' he said in a toneless voice and, when I had done so, he asked, 'Where's Larry?' But Larry had gone. I picked up the letter he had dropped on the floor and thrust it into my pocket. I thought it was fortunate in a way that he had left it.

Few managed to get home dry-shod from the concert, for soon after Mrs Marven left the hall, the rain came rattling on the iron roof, completely drowning the voices of the players in the comic piece we had chosen to conclude the entertainment. Right in the middle of what Hennessy had prophesied would be the most talked-of incident in the comedy, old Sam Cotter popped up again and shouted that he considered it useless to continue, and that the balance of the programme should be abandoned.

I don't know what Hennessy thought, but I believe the rest of those acting the farce were rather relieved than otherwise. Perhaps our audience's appetite had been spoiled by the altercation following Larry's appearance, or maybe the din made by the rain on the roof made hearing too difficult; in either case it had been singularly apathetic, and even the best of our sallies had failed to raise any laughter.

The deluge continued, and I got back to the Royal Hotel, wet, tired, and dispirited, to find Mrs Marven in her bar – for those were the days of late closing – chirpy as ever, conducting herself as if nothing untoward had happened, and playing host to three old fellows who leaned on the counter, gripping the handles of their pewter mugs, and listening spellbound to what she was saying.

She lifted her plump arm and patted her hair with simulated vanity.

'When I was sixteen, boys,' she said, although there was not a man there under sixty-five, 'I was a very bee-utiful girl, and ran way from home to join a circus. You should have seen me a-riding bareback on a barebacked horse.'

She looked archly at the old men and went on. 'And, of course, on the flying trapeze, in pink tights – well!' She left it to their imagination, and they grinned delightedly while old Plank struck his tankard on the counter with an, 'I'll be danged. Pink tights, d'ye hear?'

'It was at the circus,' Mrs Marven continued, fluttering her eyelids, 'that I met Marven. He was the thin man in the freak show.' There was a roar of laughter at this, for the old men could remember the late Mr Marven who weighed seventeen stone. 'Of course,' she finished, 'I could have married the man with the flea circus, but, ugh!' she shrugged her ample shoulders.

'Flea circus!' Old Plant nudged his neighbour. 'D'ye hear? Flea circus!'

They rocked with laughter, and Plank, tears in his eyes, proclaimed that it called for another pot.

I felt faintly nauseated that a woman should use her late husband as a peg for a bar-room story. Maybe my nerves were on edge. In any case I did not wait to call good night but went on up to bed. But not to sleep! I tried to read, but the rain rattled with ever-increasing fury on the galvanised-iron roof, and I found it impossible to concentrate. I gave up at last, and, extinguishing my candle, lay tossing and turning. When at last I got off, it seemed only a matter of minutes before I was awakened by a knocking on the door and Hennessy's voice calling.

'Harry. Wake up.'

I lit my candle and glanced at my watch to find it was nearly two o'clock. I sprang out of bed and opened the door.

Hennessy stood in the passage, water streaming from his sodden hat, a lighted lantern swinging in his hand.

'Larry's missing,' he said shortly. 'I'm organising a search. Get on some clothes.'

As I dressed hastily he told me that the woman with whom Larry boarded had awakened the schoolmaster at his home, worried because the boy had not returned. She had been at the concert and she linked his disappearance with the incident at the hall.

'He's a strange lad sometimes,' she'd said to Hennessy, 'but it's not like him to stay out so late and have me worrying. With this storm and all I'm frightened. Mebbe he's taken what happened to heart, poor boy.'

Hennessy reassured her and began to rouse his friends. One of them had a story of Dr Hansen returning in his buggy from an outlying farm. The creek was in flood and he'd only managed the crossing by jumping waist-high into the water and alternately coaxing and pulling his horse across. As he climbed into the buggy again and drove toward the town a man had rushed along the road toward him. The doctor had pulled up and shouted, but the man ran by like one demented. That was an hour ago. The man might very well have been Larry, the doctor agreed, although in the teeming rain he couldn't be sure.

The schoolmaster detailed some helpers to call at various houses in case the missing man might have sheltered in one or other of them, but he was plainly worried. He'd roused Burke, the police officer, but it was characteristic of Hennessy that he should assume the leadership. Burke, in any case, was hardly the man to take the initiative in an emergency, for he was a heavy, slow-moving, slow-thinking fellow. The three of us took the path to the creek, the rain beating in our faces and soaking my coat through in a few minutes.

What a few hours before had been no more than a trickle was now a torrent of tumultuous water, unutterably dismal, and sinister. The creek crossing was quite impossible. Hennessy stood uncertainly. I shouted in his ear and we turned right and began to make our way slowly along the bank, flashing our lanterns and calling, '*Larry*.'

All at once I recalled the tree on which I had seen the carved names. We must have come close to it, but it was dangerously near, if not actually in, the flood waters.

'I saw him about here one afternoon,' I shouted into Hennessy's ear and led the way, and, as I pushed through the growth, I could feel the water swirl over my ankles. There was a steep grade and Hennessy cried a warning to be careful. We made slow progress and, in a little while, the water was up to our knees and we were still some distance from the tree. We paused and Hennessy directed us to hold our lanterns high and halloa together.

'*Larry.*'

There was no response except the roar of the flooded creek. For a few moments, however, the rain moderated and in the brief lull we shouted again and again. Then Hennessy said, 'Good God! Listen.'

Very faintly, but unmistakably, I heard it. The notes of a mouth organ! They came from the direction of the tree on which I had seen the names carved and which must, by then, have been submerged to its lowest branches. The music was not clear, for the notes were interrupted by the turmoil of the water and the sharp crackle of snapping boughs, so that they reached us jerkily. But I thought I recognised the fragmentary air, though I doubt if the others did. It was *Eileen Alannah*, but it was only momentary and my mind may have been playing tricks.

Constable Burke shouted, 'It's him, by gum.'

We stood waving our lanterns and shouting, the water by now so high that it was difficult to keep our footing. By common consent we fell silent, listening again.

Over the swirl of the water and the hiss of rain there came to us through the blackness the sound of laughter, crazy, high-pitched, and suddenly cut off as if a hand had covered the mouth that uttered it.

'God!' Burke dropped his lantern, and before he could recover it, it was swept away. For a while we could see it bobbing about, travelling into the gloom, and then apparently it was caught in a new eddy and with a sudden rush joined the main stream, and we watched it dancing like a will-o'-the-wisp on the water till it became smaller and smaller and at length disappeared altogether. No human sound reached our ears.

Hennessy made as if to go forward, but the constable restrained him.

'It's no good, sir,' he said. 'It isn't safe. If he was out there he hasn't a dog's chance, poor devil. Unless he's up the tree,' he added, 'and we couldn't reach him till dawn in any case. I'll come back then.'

We turned and with difficulty forced our way up and back to the higher ground, Hennessy pausing repeatedly and peering behind him into the darkness, holding his light high, and I could see the rain streaming over his deathly white face.

Before I went to bed that night I destroyed Eileen's letter to Larry. Eileen's letter! Before I burned it I read it through again, right down the first page to the fateful words:

*the man I am going to marry is*

I turned the page and read on:

*none other than Harry Ford.*

How fortunate, I thought, that our names had been so similar and that Eileen in her haste had scribbled in pencil. How easily I had effected the slight alterations.

As I scrutinised the changes I had made I could not but admire my work, for it would have been impossible to detect the alteration. Only one other person in the world was to know there had been any change in the original text. I had been sure that when Larry read it he would be more than ever determined to leave the town. Well, he had left, and gone further than he intended. Poor devil! At any rate, I consoled myself, I'd done my best to find him and quite likely caught a shocking cold into the bargain.

We searched again at dawn, although, had I not promised Hennessy, I would gladly have remained in bed, for I was alone at the post-office, and I could not afford to be sick. The local rain had abated, but the creek was more swollen than ever and had become a terrifying sight. We satisfied ourselves that Larry was not sheltered in the high branches of the trees about the spot where we had heard the music and the laugh that still lingered with faint unpleasantness in my memory.

I suggested that the unhappy lad had probably started to drink, following the affair in the hall, but Hennessy rather rudely shut me up and made no demur when, a little later, I excused myself, saying that I had some things to attend to. I was hurrying back from the creek and passing the post office in the deserted main street, for it was still very early and there were no shops open, when Helen Speek came hurrying toward me. She was hatless and breathless.

'I saw you from my gate, Mr Ford,' she said in a rush, 'and I hoped you'd help me.'

Her face was flushed, the colour in her cheeks heightened by the freshness of the morning, and with her mop of golden hair she really looked a picture. It occurred to me that a woman like this was wasted on a creature like Speek.

'There'll be a packet waiting for me,' she went on, speaking rapidly. 'Would you be so good – could I get it now?'

It was unorthodox, of course. Office hours began at nine. Still it was only a matter of opening the door and a refusal might have detained me longer.

'I cannot refuse beauty in distress,' I said, smiling at her boldly. I felt that with a woman of her reputation I could permit myself a mild flirtation, especially as no one was likely to see or hear us.

I slipped into the office and she followed me. I found the package she expected, for there were very few mail articles. It was a small, rectangular box of some sort wrapped in brown paper and addressed plainly in block letters. I came from behind the counter and gave it to her, and she thrust it beneath her shawl and was turning to go.

'Is that all the thanks I get?' I asked pointedly, putting my hand on her arm. After all, I had gone out of my way to oblige her.

She looked at me, surprise in her eyes, then pulled her shawl about her and without another word hurried to the door. Annoyed at her churlishness, I locked the office and when I gained the street she was already some distance away and walking fast. I had come hurrying through the doorway and anyone watching must have gained the impression that I was pursuing her. I heard a little cough and turned to see Craven, the caretaker of the local hall. He bade me good morning politely enough, but from the grin on his face I knew he was wondering. Impatiently, I dismissed the incident from my mind and went home to a hot bath and bacon and eggs.

Mrs Marven had not come down and Rosie, the housemaid, was tearful as she served me. She was a pert young thing of eighteen, inclined to step out of her station at times, and I never encouraged her talkativeness.

'Have they found him, Mr Ford?' she enquired.

'Found who?' I asked, buttering toast, though I knew very well whom she meant.

'Why, Larry, sir,' she went on.

'Oh, I guess he'll turn up,' I said shortly.

'I do hope so, Mr Ford,' the girl said as she took my empty plate. 'He was such a lovely boy.'

Teecher, the bank fellow, came down late as usual and greeted me with, 'Too bad about Larry. Fine chap.'

I found their comments exasperating. I had been out half the night looking for the man and had given up my morning sleep-in and was in no mood to join in a paean of praise simply because Larry Ward might or might not be drowned.

I was surprised to see Garnet Price come in to breakfast. 'Couldn't get across the creek,' he explained briefly. 'Had to stay. I'll be here tonight, too, by the look of things.'

I remembered he had not been at the concert, nor, I thought swiftly, had Helen Speek. I wondered had they profited by Speek's absence. As I spread marmalade on toast, I said without looking up, 'Enjoy the concert?'

'Eh?' He started. 'Oh, 'fraid concerts not much in my line. Now, what I like's a good circus with plenty of horses and trick riding. And clowns! Never got over my fondness for clowns, Ford. Remember once the old man gave permission for a circus to make its winter quarters on our land. What a time we had! There was an old boy – well, he seemed old to us boys – Charlie Baldwin; taught us how to throw lariats and train horses to do tricks. D'you know, Ford, he'd give the damn horse a signal simply by blowing out his belly? In the evening he'd come over to the house and show the old man card tricks and win all his money.'

He went on interminably with a rigmarole about wirewalkers and acrobats and the like till I marvelled that a man of his education and position should allow himself to rhapsodise over the vagaries of a lot of filthy gypsies. I got up in the middle of one of his stories, saying I had to get to the office, and left him to bore Teecher with the rest of the yarn.

That morning Timothy Speek called at my office, the everlasting paper bag of sweets in his hand. He proffered it, and when I refused, took one himself and began to talk with his mouth full in a way that irritated me almost beyond endurance.

He couldn't resist mentioning Larry Ward. 'He'll turn up like a bad penny,' he said vindictively. 'By the way, Mr Ford,' he continued, munching, 'I wonder, if you were free, whether you would help me tonight with a little document? You're the only one in this town I can trust, and – but if you'd rather not – '

'What kind of document?'

'It's about my will, Mr Ford. I haven't altered it for years. It needs a codicil. It should be very simple. You see, all I've got is left to my dear wife. That's natural, isn't it?'

I murmured assent. I could hardly comment, but I was interested. Speek had placed a certain sardonic emphasis on the 'dear'.

He went on. 'I just wish to tighten it up. I want Helen to keep on remembering me after I'm gone. I'd like to feel that we were still very close together. It can be done in half a dozen lines if they're carefully written. I'll make a rough draft, Mr Ford, and you can lick it into shape. Of course there'll be your fee – '

I waved this aside, but he protested that there was no lawyer in the town, and, if there was, he'd have to fee him, so why not pay me? I had augmented my salary to some extent helping in this way and felt that I was doing a service putting my talents at the disposal of the less enlightened who would, in most cases, have had to travel to Baloola for legal assistance and probably get themselves fleeced into the bargain.

'I daresay I can help you, Speek,' I said, 'if the document is as simple as you think.'

'Oh, it'll be simple enough,' he laughed. 'I'll wait for you at nine.'

At midday there was still no news of Larry. Dr Hansen and Garnet Price were eating as I entered the dining room, and Mrs Marven looked up and asked me if there was anything fresh.

'It's a thundering pity that a lad like that should be taken,' the doctor said as I shook my head.

'There's Providence for you!' Price exclaimed in that forthright way of his, black eyes glaring at the doctor as if he were to blame. 'A fine boy swept to eternity and others in this town, who would be better dead, left to snivel their way through God knows how many more years.'

There was an uncomfortable silence, Price having spoken with unusual violence.

The doctor said mildly after a while, 'That always happens, Price. I'm afraid fate's left many a sinner on top and pushed others under the sod without giving them a decent chance. Still, we doctors aid and abet. I believe that fate had it in for a few that I knew and I was able to interfere with her plans and at least postpone them.'

Price gave the doctor a cunning look. 'I understand, Doc,' he said. 'Probably saved their lives against your will.'

The doctor shook his head. 'Oh, I wouldn't go so far as that, Price,' he said, 'but I admit I wondered whether the ethical thing was the right thing.'

Mrs Marven looked puzzled.

'What the doc means, Mrs Marven,' Price explained, 'is that he had saved the lives of some skunks instead of letting 'em die.' The doctor made a protesting gesture, but Price went on relentlessly. 'Confess, Doc, you've yanked out of the grave many a man you thought would be better in it. You ought to be ashamed of yourself.' He grinned across the table.

'Surely,' I put in, 'it's a doctor's duty to save life under any and all circumstances.'

'Duty me foot,' Price exclaimed vulgarly. 'If I were a doctor and I knew a man was a skunk making a hell on earth for the living, I'd let him die. And to hell with your ethics.'

'I think I would, too, terrible as it sounds,' Mrs Marven said softly and rather surprisingly.

'But,' I expostulated, shocked at the turn the conversation had taken, 'you would constitute the medical man judge. I don't think Dr Hansen would care for that responsibility.'

'I'm sure I shouldn't,' Hansen said and, with a glance at his watch, rose and put his hand on Price's shoulder. 'I'm afraid, Price,' he said, 'if ever you send for me, I'll have to do the best I can for you, bad as you are.'

Price rose too. 'Oh, I'll take a chance on you, Doc,' he said, laughing.

That night I wrote to Eileen's father telling him of Larry's disappearance and describing the incidents leading up to it. It was my duty, I felt, to acquaint him of the fact that Larry and Speek had had a vulgar brawl when Speek had found the boy visiting his wife in his absence. It seemed a pity, I wrote, that

Larry should have lost his head and struck the blind man, but possibly he was not himself as he had had a few drinks in the morning and had already got himself into trouble by nearly killing Luke Barmby's child.

We had done all we could, I told him, and, with others, I had searched along the flooded creek until exhausted. I paid a graceful tribute to the courage of Hennessy and Constable Burke and asked him not to mention these things to his daughter because it might upset her and that was the last thing I wanted.

'You know, Mr Mahoney,' I wrote, 'that Eileen is very dear to me and, when she returns, I will, with your permission, continue to pay her my respects. Although I believe that she had a girlish infatuation for Larry Ward, who has by God's will been taken from us, I believe that this folly will soon pass. I want to assure you that I feel no bitterness in my heart, for I well know the vagaries of a young woman's emotions. I feel that this bitter experience will have a steadying effect upon her which will be all to the good.

'I have been a very careful man, Mr Mahoney,' I concluded, 'and, in the event of our marriage, I shall insist on making a settlement upon your daughter which, I believe, you will not find ungenerous. In short, I propose to settle upon her the sum of one thousand pounds.'

I wrote a short letter to Eileen herself saying I was desolated by her absence and that I looked forward eagerly to her return.

I had just finished the letters when a boy brought a note from Hennessy. His wife, he said, was helping him mark some examination papers but he would be free at nine and would be glad if I could come round at that hour and run over the school-concert accounts with him.

Speek, I felt sure, would not mind if I called earlier than he had arranged, so, sometime after eight, I strolled slowly along to his house. It was quite dark, for we had no street lamps and there was no light visible that I could see, except the one hanging outside the hotel, and this only accentuated the general gloom. However, as I reached Speek's gate and looked down the long pathway to his side door, I saw a glimmer. Nearer the house was a trellis so thick that it practically formed a verandah. As I stepped under this and reached the doorway I heard a scream that must have been audible to anyone in the street, and I stepped into the light to see Timothy Speek raise his stick and strike his wife.

The blow caught her on the shoulder, and she cowered before him, wringing her hands. I stepped into the shadows on the far side of the door, unwilling to be a witness to any squalid domestic quarrel, and, as I did so, I heard hasty footsteps running down the graveled path and, in a moment, Garnet Price was at the door, gazing into the room.

He was standing so close to me that I could have touched him, but so intent was his gaze upon the scene in the room that he was quite unaware of my presence and saw nothing but the blind man's grip on Helen's arm and the stick he held so menacingly over her. For one moment he stood like a statue, then he leaped in and, with one hand, seized Speek's shoulder and whirled him about. The blind man's stick fell to the floor and immediately he began feeling for it with his foot. His sightless eyes fixed themselves on the intruder. He said, 'So, Mr Larry. You've come back. I might've known.'

I suppose Price was too astonished to speak, but Helen made a quick gesture, putting her fingers over her lips warningly.

'Aye!' The blind man waited again, breathing hard; then, after a silence which seemed never-ending, he went on. 'I thought you were drowned and gone to the devil, Larry Ward, but it takes more than a flood to keep a lecher from his wanton.'

He stooped and regained his stick and then went to a big chair set against a small table and seated himself leisurely.

'Come, now, sit you down, Larry boy,' he said, 'and let us talk this thing over.'

'There's nothing to talk over,' Helen said sullenly.

'Oh, but there is Helen – *dear*,' Speek said, turning to her and talking with silky softness. 'There's divorce, for instance.'

'Divorce!' Helen Speek was frankly incredulous. Then she repeated in another tone, 'Oh, *divorce*,' and laughed hollowly.

The blind man chuckled. 'I thought you'd be interested,' he said, and his fingers, drumming on the table, touched a box of chocolates that was lying there with the lid off. He picked it up and sniffed. 'What's here?' he asked. 'Chocolates, eh? A lover's gift!' He put the box to his nose again. 'Aye, very pretty.' He turned to Price. 'You don't mind, Larry?' he enquired, softly, but there was venom in his voice.

His fingers began fumbling among the chocolates, and I could see that Helen was watching him as if hypnotised. He picked two out. One he popped into his mouth, the other he placed up on the table beside him.

'Um!' He ate with exaggerated appreciation. 'And very nice, too, Larry. *And* expensive!' he continued, talking with his mouth full. 'Of course, working in a grocery store, you could easily steal them for your fancy lady. *Um!*' He chewed meditatively and swallowed.

Helen Speek's eyes had never left his face. Very quietly she stepped forward. With the fingers of one hand she deftly removed the chocolate on the table, with those of the other hand she substituted a sweet which she took from the box. I saw Price start, but her finger went to her lips again, cautioning him, and he remained silent. Speek stretched out his hand and his fingers played with the chocolate beside him.

'And, now, regarding the matter of divorce, Larry,' he said, and he lifted the sweetmeat to his lips, holding it before him, turning it about as if he could really see as well as smell it.

'Don't!' The word burst from Price, and a quick angry expression crossed Helen's face, and she strode quickly to him and put her hand over his mouth.

Speek nibbled the chocolate delicately, then held the remaining portion up and regarded it with his sightless eyes.

Suddenly he popped it into his mouth and chewed in an objectionable way as he spoke.

'"Don't" is good advice, Larry,' he cried, rising. The chocolate swallowed, the silkiness left his voice. He spoke sneeringly. 'There'll be no divorce, Larry. Your fancy lady will live on by me side, for I'm hale and hearty and full of vigour for all me blindness, and Doc Hansen has given me a tonic that'll brighten me up still more and make me good company for the lass. Aye, Larry, the blind man's rounds will cease. I'll stay by her side, hour after hour, day after day, night after night, week after week, watching her, Larry. D'you hear? D'you hear, wife? I'll change my habits, my dear. There'll be no more walks abroad for me – or you. I'll be home, home by your side' – he thrust his head out toward her and his last words were a snarl – 'giving you all the love and attention you'll ever know this side of the grave.'

He turned to where Price stood, Helen's hand still covering his mouth.

'And now, Larry Ward,' he went on, 'ye can go back to hell, where ye belong.'

He stood, leaning on his stick, and the others waited, too, and I thought it was like a play I had once seen where the actors struck an attitude and paused, making a picture till the curtain came down.

But there was no curtain to hide these players from me and, by and by, they must needs move, and Helen urged Price to the door and almost pushed him outside. I saw his white, strained face as he passed and then his black suit merged into the darkness under the trellis, and I heard his footsteps retreating, crunching the gravel as he hurried up the path.

When I peered into the room again, Speek was sitting in his armchair. I saw Helen move to the table, put the lid on the box of chocolates, and carry it off to some other part of the house.

Avoiding the light, for I had forgotten Speek's blindness, and keeping away from the gravel, I ran noiselessly into the dark street and immediately collided with a cloaked and hurrying figure. For a moment I thought it was a child, and then I knew it for Polly Garner, and I went on, annoyed that she should have recognised me, for my breeding needs must come out and instinctively I had begged her pardon.

Something told me that it would have been better if I had not been near Speek's home that night.

The incident worried me so that I almost forgot that I had promised to call on Hennessy, and I had to retrace my footsteps. Our business was soon concluded and I went back to the hotel. Mrs Marven, who was sitting knitting in the deserted bar, called a cheery good night, and I went upstairs to bed, read for an hour or so, and then fell asleep.

I don't know how long I had slept before I was awakened by an unusual noise. I sat up, listening, then put my ear to the wall dividing my room from Mrs Marven's. The sound was unmistakeable. A woman was weeping, but now and then I thought I heard another voice. After a little while the sobbing ceased, a door closed softly, and I fell asleep, wondering.

CHAPTER 3

Long before the dressing bell rang next morning, I was awakened by a knock on my door and found the hotel 'boots' grinning on the mat, an envelope in his grimy hand. He handed it to me with a disgustingly knowing look.

'I was told to give this to you personally and at once,' he informed me and shuffled off to retail God knows what gossip to the housemaid and cook.

I had a premonition of trouble as I broke the seal. The note was from Agatha Garner asking would I call and see her without delay. 'It is of the utmost importance,' she had added as a postscript. I dressed immediately and walked to her home and was glad that no one saw me enter the gate, for it was an unorthodox hour at which to make a call on a lady and might well have started tongues wagging.

Agatha was waiting at the door, and beckoned me into her little, overfurnished parlor.

'Mr Ford,' she began, breathlessly. 'I am at my wit's end. I am sure something dreadful has happened. My sister is in such a state. She came home last night frightened and hysterical. I've never seen her like it before and I wanted to send for the doctor but she wouldn't hear of it, and he's always so busy, isn't he? But she's been tossing and turning all night, and early this morning she asked me could I get you to come round. Whatever is it, Mr Ford?'

I felt some secret anxiety, but I said, 'I haven't the slightest idea, Miss Agatha. Where is Miss Polly?'

'She's dressing,' she told me, and no sooner had she spoken than the door opened and her sister joined us. She was red-eyed and looked far from well, and Agatha hurried to her side and led her to the sofa. They sat there together facing me, like two dolls, Agatha patting her sister's hand.

'Forgive me for asking you to call round like this, Mr Ford,' Miss Polly began with an effort at calmness, 'but I had to tell someone, and oh' – she broke off and began to sob – 'it's all some awful dream; it can't be true.'

Her sister looked at me meaningly as she soothed her.

'Take your time, Miss Polly,' I said kindly.

She pulled herself together. 'After I ran into you coming out of Mr Speek's house last night,' she said, 'I went on to old Mrs Codd's. She's been sick and I'd promised to take her some things. I was only there a little while. She wanted some smelling salts as her head was bad, and I told her I'd hurry home and get some. Then, when I was passing Speek's place, I saw a light, and I thought I'd borrow the salts from Helen.'

She paused a moment and then went on, 'I ran down the path to the side door. It was open, Mr Ford, and – and – Mr Speek was standing in the room all by himself, staring with those awful eyes and, oh, it was terrible! He had the most dreadful expression on his face. I could see he was ill, and I ran forward to help and caught his sleeve, but he sank back on his big chair, and I heard him say, "Ford! Poisoned" – just those two words. Then' – she gave a frightened look at her sister – 'then, Agatha, he – he – died.'

She began to sob anew. Miss Agatha's face had gone deathly white, but, in a flash, she was on her feet, shaking her sister's shoulder.

'Polly,' she cried. 'What are you saying? How do you know he died?'

'Oh, I *know*, I know,' Polly sobbed. 'It was terrible.'

'But why didn't you call someone – Helen?'

'I don't know; I was terrified. I just wanted to get away from that awful place. I ran out of the room. I don't know how I got home. I was frantic.'

Miss Agatha spoke to me. 'Mr Ford, we must go and tell Mr Burke.'

'Just a moment, Miss Agatha,' I said and turned to her sister. 'Now, think again, Miss Polly. You say you heard two words, "Ford" and "poisoned"?'

She nodded.

'Might he not have said, "Ward poisoned"?'

'Oh, no, no, *no*,' she cried vehemently. 'I am sure it was your name – and, afterwards, I – I remembered seeing you come running out of his place and I wondered whether you had seen – ' she broke off helplessly.

I was aware that Agatha was staring at me curiously, but I pretended not to notice. 'Did anyone see you when you left Speek's?' I asked Polly.

She shook her head. 'It was so dark.'

I breathed more easily. 'Let me think,' I said, and paced up and down. Miss Agatha interrupted my thoughts.

'Mr Ford,' she said, 'I don't think we should stay here another minute. We should all go and see Constable Burke and tell him what we know – at once.'

I paused in my stride and said earnestly, 'If what Miss Polly tells us is really a fact, why haven't we heard something? If it happened, it happened hours ago.'

'Perhaps Helen is away,' Miss Agatha suggested.

'No, she's home,' I said, and was sorry I had spoken.

'Then we'd better go and see Mr Burke without delay,' Agatha began, but I interrupted.

'Listen, Miss Agatha and Miss Polly, why should you be mixed up in this thing? Nobody knows what Miss Polly saw except you and me. If it is true, and I can still hardly credit it, it will mean endless worry and trouble for you both.'

They looked at me uncertainly.

'But – ' Agatha began.

'Believe me,' I urged, 'I speak for your own good. You cannot imagine how unpleasant it will be. There will be ceaseless questioning and public examination – policemen, lawyers, God knows what.'

Polly paled a little and was obviously distressed. She turned to her sister for guidance.

'But, Mr Ford,' Agatha said, 'it would be *wrong*.'

'Besides,' Polly added, 'he spoke of – poison.'

I made a gesture of exasperation. It was a mistake. With more patience I might have wheedled these little spinsters into a promise of silence; a little more tact and they would have been my friends, seeing my point of view, as eager as I was to escape scandal and avoid all the unpleasant publicity; but I took the wrong way and awakened in them a suspicion that I had some ulterior motive.

'It's too absurd,' I cried, 'to have us all pulled into this sordid thing, to have ourselves dragged through a filthy inquest, all because Miss Polly imagines she heard my name. Is it fair to me that she should repeat this silly tale that will give birth to all sorts of offensive rumours? You know the reputation Helen Speek has in some quarters.'

Agatha Garner said simply, 'I never believed those things.'

'Well, you might have,' I retorted tartly, 'if you knew what really happened between her and Larry Ward and the man you say is dead. I tell you, Miss Polly, the name you heard Speek utter was "Ward". You think you saw me outside the house and you have confused the two names.'

The little woman shook her head resolutely. Her composure was rapidly returning.

'It was *your* name, Mr Ford,' she said firmly, and I felt uneasy under her steady gaze. She turned to her sister. 'Get your hat, Agatha.'

'Wait,' I ordered. 'I am not going to permit my name to be trampled in the mud like this. If you care nothing for your own reputation, Miss Polly, I do for mine. This thing might jeopardise my whole future. I forbid you to spread this ridiculous story.'

Her tiny form stiffened.

'Listen, Miss Polly, I said, firmly, and gazing directly into her eyes, 'I – did – not – see you last night. I was nowhere near Speek's.'

They faced me, those little women, their hands instinctively seeking each other's.

'And,' I continued, 'I warn you both, supposing he is dead, against repeating what Miss Polly claims to have heard.'

'We will tell the truth, Mr Ford,' Agatha said coldly.

'All right,' I said, 'if you must, you must. But, remember, your sister has already directed suspicion on herself by her delay in reporting Speek's death.'

'It was a mistake,' Agatha said, 'but Mr Burke will understand. It would be silly to suspect Polly.'

'I don't know, Miss Agatha,' I replied. 'You must remember she hated Speek. I heard her tell you that myself.'

Agatha looked her astonishment, but Polly drew in her breath sharply.

I made a shot in the dark. 'Perhaps I know why,' I said quietly. 'You remember, Miss Polly, outside the post office you said to your sister, referring to Speek, " *I think he knows.*" Well, Speek *did* know. He told me all about it yesterday.'

The effect of this announcement was instantaneous. Polly burst into tears and threw herself on the sofa, and Agatha hurriedly put her arms about her. I picked up my hat and went to the door.

'You see how unutterably foolish it would be to wantonly drag yourselves into this thing,' I said. 'We had nothing to do with it. Our consciences are clear. Let us keep our own counsel. As far as you are concerned, if Speek is dead, his evil tongue can spread no more scandal. Only I know, and you may rely on my discretion. After all, is there any earthly reason why we should be dragged into this discreditable affair, to be examined about who we are, and what we are? Believe me, I've seen it happen. Innocent witnesses trying to speak the truth made to look worse than the criminal in the dock. No,

Miss Agatha, and you especially, Miss Polly, mark my words, stay out of this.'

I left them on that, confident of their silence, relieved that my efforts had eased the situation. But I was worried about the package I had given to Helen Speek and already regretted the innocent little familiarity I had permitted myself when she called. I thought of the solemn, sullen eyes of the woman. She was an unknown quantity. The less a man like me had to do with one of her sort the better. I remembered, too, the grin on the face of Craven, the hall caretaker.

When I got back to the hotel, Mrs Marven greeted me with some astounding news. 'Oh, Mr Ford,' she cried. 'Did you hear?' she lowered her voice. 'Timothy Speek's committed suicide.' She nodded gloomy confirmation and added, '*Shot himself through the head!*'

Mrs Marven had more to tell and, as she talked, I became more and more bewildered. It had been a quiet night, and, after I had gone up to bed, she did not have a single customer for, as she put it, it was seldom that a body was thirsty in that town after ten at night, by which hour I believe most folk were in bed and fast asleep. About eleven she had finished her knitting and was thinking of shutting up when Helen Speek came running in. She was in great distress.

'Please come, Marvie,' she called. 'Something dreadful has happened.'

The landlady hastily extinguished the bar lamps and joined her, Helen pouring out her story as she hurried through the dark street. They found Speek in his big armchair, shot through the head, the pistol in his hand. It must have been a nasty sight.

Helen, it appeared, had already been to Dr Hansen's but remembered as she got there that he was on a confinement case some miles out of town. She had run to Constable Burke's place, but he was absent, for the creek was still swollen and there had been many narrow escapes at farm-houses along its course. She had pinned a note on his door.

Mrs Marven closed the house and took Helen back to the hotel with her, gave her a stiff whisky, and put her into her own bed.

'It would have been silly and useless to wake you or Mr Teecher,' she said, 'so I sat down to wait for Burke, who would have to pass the hotel on his way to Speek's.' After a while she heard a horse and went outside to see the doctor in his buggy. She called to him and told him the news and together they went to the house of death. The tired constable arrived half an hour later and Mrs Marven prevailed upon him to let Helen have her sleep out.

'He was nothing loath, poor man,' she told me, 'for, like the doctor, he was worn out. I dosed them up with brandy, and they needed it. You know, Mr Ford,' she said, 'I felt sorry for that man. He must have been a terrible man to live with. Who knows, after all, perhaps his last deed was his best.'

I could never condone suicide, I told her.

'Oh,' she replied, 'I don't feel like that. I'll condone anything within reason, and Speek was suffering the torments of the damned. He was poisoned, Mr Ford.'

'Poisoned!' I said, aghast, and my mouth fell open.

'Poisoned with his own self-pity,' she explained. 'And the devil's own pet poison it is, too. It made him a nasty man. All the same, to shoot himself!'

She looked up at me and her eyes were soft with tears.

'It must have taken courage,' I said.

'I suppose so,' she said thoughtfully. 'I know I couldn't take that way out. I'm terrified of guns.'

Our city mail came via Baloola three times a week and was due that morning. It arrived late, partly owing to the floods and the detour that Peter Gallagher, the mail driver, had had to make, and partly, I suspected, because Peter had stopped at many places en route, glad of the chance to exchange gossip, for he was a garrulous old fellow who knew everybody's business but neglected his own to such an extent that I had had more than once to reprimand him for unpunctuality. This day, however, his excuse was at least plausible. I posted a notice on the delivery window to the effect that letters would be ready an hour later and started on the task of sorting.

Almost immediately I came across the registered article addressed to Polly Garner that came to hand with such regularity. I examined it closely and put it on one side to enter in my record book. There were fewer letters than usual in the mail and none addressed to Larry Ward, and I finished sorting earlier than I anticipated.

My mind kept reverting to the incidents of the previous night and to the inconsistencies of the stories told me that morning by Polly Garner and Mrs Marven. I recalled the rather unpleasant interview with the two little spinsters and my eye fell on the registered envelope that had just come in. Queerly enough, the words of Timothy Speek came to my mind at the same moment. 'Aye; ye're in a position of great power here, Mr Ford, sir, with secrets enough under y'r thumb to set a whole town by the ears.'

I thought with satisfaction, So I am, and cast a speculative glance over the letters I had sorted. What secrets they must hold! What latent mysteries would be uncovered if they were opened! How many family skeletons would be bared by one swift glance at their contents?

I remembered Helen Speek's anxiety that her mail should not fall into her husband's hands. What dark secret was she harbouring? I thought I knew. I looked carefully through the little pile of letters addressed to Garnet Price, but they appeared innocent enough – from business firms, harness and horse dealers and the like. I recalled the instant reaction of the Garner women to my shot in the dark about *their* secret, and my attention was focused once more on the registered letter for Polly.

They had been badly scared, and here, I believed, was the key to the reason for their terror. I reasoned swiftly. It might be necessary for me to *know*. They might challenge me. They had spirit of a sort. Yes, I concluded, it was *necessary* for me to know.

Skilfully I opened the envelope, glanced curiously at the cheque inside, and read the accompanying letter. I smiled grimly as I finished. Well, one never knew! I had a mental vision of the two women sitting facing me in their funny little front parlour. They were faded now, and ageing, but, at one time, I supposed, they must have been bright young things. Polly, unquestionably, had the remnants of good looks.

As I put the letter and cheque back into the envelope, carefully resealed it, and entered the document in the official records, I thought how lucky these women were that the letter had not fallen into the hands of some unprincipled cad who might have gone about smirking, smacking his lips over the pitiful story of frailty I had uncovered, tearing Polly's reputation to shreds. Speek, for instance, with his gluttony for gossip! Why, their lives wouldn't be worth living in this narrow little town. Well, they were safe enough with me, provided they held their tongues.

Later in the day, when they called to sign for the registered article, plainly ill at ease, I felt quite sorry for them and went out of my way to let Polly see that, whatever her past had been, I was not condemning her. As she signed I looked at her with a new curiosity. She still had her figure. In the light of what I knew I could imagine she might have been quite a pert little piece in her youth.

As her sister put down the pen, Agatha Garner looked about her cautiously to see that no one was listening and whispered, 'What does it all mean, Mr Ford?' She was puzzled about Speek shooting himself, of course.

'It means,' I said calmly, 'that Miss Polly made a pardonable error.'

Agatha started to say something, but Polly interrupted. 'I still think I should tell Mr Burke,' she said.

I flicked a finger at the registered letter I was still holding.

'I wouldn't,' I said significantly, and they went out without another word.

I had had some good news that morning from the Postal Department, which had at long last recognised my ability. In a few weeks' time I was to be transferred to a more important post at a higher salary. It was a position of trust and considerable responsibility, and it made me more than ever determined not to allow the Speek affair to interfere with my prospects.

How did I know what the inquest of Speek might bring forth? I knew a little of what his wife had been up to. I had seen her with Garnet Price. But there might be more scandal. I disbelieved Larry's story. If I came into the business even remotely, the Department might think – even Eileen might think – ! No, the more I thought of the woman, the less I wished my name associated with her. I was glad that I had warned Polly Garner a second time. After all, why should I chance being dragged through the mire to suit the warped whim of a hussy?

Timothy Speek's funeral was remembered longer than the man himself, the circumstances of his death occasioning interest that an orthodox demise would never have awakened. I shall always recall it because Luke Barmby was down with a cold and one of his sons, a gangling youth of eighteen, took his father's place as undertaker.

The rain had quite gone and the sun was shining brightly as if there had been no such thing as a flood, but the atmosphere was steamy and oppressive. I had accompanied Mrs Marven on a tour of inspection of the outhouses, looking for possible leakage in the roofing, when young Barmby's head appeared grinning over the stable half door.

'Why, Josephus!' Mrs Marven exclaimed, startled. 'What brings you here?' Luke Barmby had scattered Biblical names among his swarming offspring with rare prodigality. It was, I believe, the nearest he ever came to extravagance, for he had a frugal mind, and I had been responsible for the rather neat *bon mot* that the few boarders he took were slowly starving to death.

'Aw, go on, Mrs Marven,' the boy said, turning red. It was his way of resenting her use of his Christian name. 'Don't you be making me look silly.'

'All right,' she said brightly. 'What brings you here, *Joe*?'

The lad grinned. 'You won't tell the old man, Mrs Marven?'

'Not till I meet him at the blue-ribbon meeting.'

Josephus's head waggled from side to side. 'Aw, Mrs Marven, you're a trick,' he announced.

She turned to me. 'Now isn't that splendid, Mr Ford? I think that's very nice of you, Joe,' she went on, as if he had paid her the greatest compliment in the world. 'I didn't think you could say such charming things.'

Young Barmby went, if anything, a little pinker and was somewhat bewildered.

She said, 'But you didn't come over just to flatter me, did you, Joe?'

He shuffled his feet and at last he came out with it. 'It's like this, Mrs Marven. I thought you'd know, you see.' He suddenly produced over the stable door a worn top hat about which were draped two hideous crêpe bands.

'Oh!' Mrs Marven was startled.

'I was wondering,' the Barmby boy said, 'whether I could get out of wearing this at Speek's funeral – when I drive the coffin, I mean.' He regarded the hat critically. 'It don't fit,' he announced with great gravity, and added for emphasis, 'an' it blows orf.'

Mrs Marven did not smile. Instead she opened the stable door. 'Come in here, Joe,' she invited quietly, and, when he entered, 'Put it on,' she ordered.

He obeyed, standing sheepishly before her, the absurd hat resting like a pimple on his bulbous head, the crêpe bands floating over his coatless shoulders. 'It makes me feel a fool,' he said.

It seemed to me definitely out of place to discuss these matters in such surroundings, but Mrs Marven was unconcerned. She regarded the boy's appearance quite seriously and shook her head critically. 'It *is* a *wee* bit small, isn't it? And it would be very awkward if it blew off. I quite understand how you feel, Joe.'

'I knew you would, Mrs Marven.' He spoke eagerly, gaining confidence. 'Now, I was thinking – it's so hot, see – couldn't I wear my new white Panama and tie these around it?' He indicated the crepe bands.

'I think you're right, Joe,' she agreed after a moment's thought. 'You'd look much nicer. And I'll borrow a dark tie for you. Now you leave the hat and these crêpe things here and sneak home and bring me your straw hat and I'll fix everything up for you.'

'Golly, Mrs Marven,' the boy cried, 'that's great! I knew you'd understand.' He opened the stable door and stepped out. 'You won't blow the gaff.'

'Cross my heart,' she answered with a smile.

For an instant he stared at her gravely, then a grin spread over his face. 'By gee, you're a oner,' he cried and dashed off.

In such a manner were the minor details of Timothy Speek's obsequies arranged.

When Barmby had gone, Mrs Marven stood, meditating, the silk hat still in her hand. Then she said with a sidelong glance at me, 'I always fancied wearing one of these to a hunt. I wonder how I'd look.' She put it on her head and went to the harness-room door, upon which the ostler had hung a broken mirror, and regarded her image critically, but with favour. I was so shocked I found it difficult to speak as we walked back to the house.

All the shops put up at least one shutter as the cortege passed, led by Josephus Barmby driving the aged buggy from which the back seat had been removed to make room for the coffin. His straw hat was laundered and shampooed into a lily-white purity and decorated with the crêpe bands, but worn, unhappily, at an almost rakish angle.

On the casket reposed the wreath of artificial flowers that had lain for months in a glass container, marked 'Mourners' Requisites', at the end of Sam Cotter's grocery counter. Beside it was a modest posy of real flowers painstakingly collected by Mrs Marven, the district being by no means a gardener's paradise. Even so, there were those at the funeral rather shocked and sniffy because the blooms were not all white, and I admit to a fleeting feeling that the conventions were being outraged, though the woman meant well.

Mrs Speek, as principal mourner, rode next in the town's only four-wheeler, 'Marven's Royal Hotel' painted conspicuously upon its sides. To the disappointment of many, the flaps of the cab were down, but it was generally known that the widow was accompanied by a minister from Baloola who had driven the twenty miles to officiate. Our town was godly enough, but in my time it never attained to an affluence sufficient to support resident clergy.

The hotel bar door was closed and all the Venetian blinds carefully drawn, but Mrs Marven permitted herself a discreet peep through the slats as the procession passed, counting twenty-six vehicles following the 'hearse' before she re-opened, put Charlie, the 'boots', in charge, and hustled Rosie, the housemaid, to help her with the refreshments she was taking to the Speek home, where the mourners were to be regaled on their return from the ceremony.

'No one shall say,' she announced, 'that Helen Speek doesn't know how to do things.'

I thought it proper to pay my respects to the widow and went along and ate a small sandwich and drank a cup of tea. There was no room for criticism. There was a large sultana cake, a feathery sponge with butter filling, and one or two smaller and more sombre affairs, for there were not wanting those who regarded sponges as too frivolous for such an occasion, and who deemed it indecent to eat any but plain cake, or, at the most, cake with a little fruit. There were several kinds of sandwiches and plates of the best mixed biscuits besides tea, cocoa, and coffee at choice. Mrs Marven had debated the beer question and, to the disappointment of some, decided against it.

The mourners condoled with the widow in clumsy, conventional phrases, and she made her acknowledgments mostly in monosyllables, and, thereafter, their duty done, they settled down to steady and gloomy eating. When I met Helen, I took her hand and laid my other hand upon it without speaking, gently pressing her fingers to express my sympathy. She looked rather beautiful, I thought, in her mourning costume, which accentuated the fairness of her hair, and as I held her hand I was surprised at the satin softness of the skin.

There were many pregnant pauses in the conversation and, once, when old Joe Plank dropped his teaspoon with a clatter, all eyes were directed on him in a baleful glare that made him feel distinctly uncomfortable, until Mrs Marven recovered the spoon and returned it to him with a smile and some silliness about it spelling good luck.

Fully thirty people were draped uneasily about the room into which I had gazed at that strange scene enacted by Helen Speek and Garnet Price and the man now lying in the desolate cemetery two miles away. Seating accommodation had been requisitioned from other parts of the house, but I noticed that everyone carefully avoided Timothy's big chair. I saw no sign of Price, but Polly and Agatha Garner were there, and I was a little surprised to note how Polly, while steadfastly avoiding my eye, efficiently assisted in ministering to the needs of the mourners.

Mrs Marven stood staunchly by Helen until all had been provided with refreshments; then she took her cup and saucer and, with a deep sigh, settled herself comfortably in the armchair in which Speek had breathed his last, while most of those present watched her with round eyes, cakes and sandwiches momentarily suspended midway to their open mouths.

'Oh, dear,' she said to the company at large, 'when I've been on my feet for long I do enjoy a nice sitdown.'

The day before the inquiry into Timothy Speek's death I had word from Eileen's father. He thanked me for my letter and said he was sorry to hear about Larry. 'Although,' he wrote, 'I would not have consented willingly to a marriage between him and my daughter.' He told me that, unhappily, the specialists in the city could do no more for him than Dr Hansen and he was a 'doomed' man. He felt he would like to see Eileen comfortably settled before his call came.

'I know you will make her a good husband,' he wrote, 'and it comforts me to know that you have been so provident and can make her such a generous settlement, because, I must tell you frankly, I have little or no money of my own, and my property is mortgaged to the very hilt.'

He suggested that in my own good time I should write to Eileen and ask her to be my wife. 'I have,' he said, 'conveyed to her the news of Larry's disappearance, and she is, of course, grieved for the moment, but, in a while, kindly time will dissipate her sorrow and make her forget any little sentimental attachment she had for the poor drowned boy.'

He had added as a postscript, 'Eileen asks me to thank you for your very nice letter to her.'

I was considerably surprised and very disappointed by the revelation of Mahoney's financial position. I had always regarded him as a man of substance, and had hoped that what he had to bestow on Eileen would offset the thousand pounds I had suggested as a settlement upon our marriage. Our joint fortunes would have enabled us to embark on the sea of matrimony more than ordinarily well equipped.

I wished to lift my wife high above the social levels she had found in this small country town and had believed our allied resources would have made it possible for us to move in a more worthy sphere among new and influential friends, permitting Eileen to cut adrift from her present circle of acquaintances.

I was annoyed to think that Mahoney should have let us down so badly, but Eileen was, after all, a very beautiful girl. It would be a delight to train her, guiding her footsteps up the social ladder, correcting those little enthusiasms and exuberances to which she was girlishly prone. I determined to dismiss all thoughts of old Mahoney and his penury from my mind, and I sat down and wrote to Eileen forthwith, composing my letter with the greatest care.

*My dear Miss Eileen,*

*I hope you will not think it presumptuous of me, but your absence has served to strengthen the deep and faithful love I cherish for you and of which you must surely be aware. Now that I have your father's permission to speak to you on this matter, I can no longer be silent.*

*Your beauty, your sweetness of disposition, and the many amiable qualities which endear you to your friends have made you dearer to me than any or all of them. I love you as a man should love a woman he wishes to make his wife, and I am bold enough to hope that this avowal will cause you pleasure. I ask you to be my wife and assure you that the best efforts of my life shall be devoted to your happiness and comfort.*

*I am not a millionaire*

I paused as I wrote, for the words reminded me of something Larry had said, and amended the sentence:

*I may not be a man of great wealth but I have ample means, as your father will explain to you, and I can give you a position in society which, coupled with my enduring love, should, as the poet says,*

Make our lives together a thing of bliss
Like eternal summer, an enduring kiss.

*I look forward to your answer consenting to make me the happiest of men. In the meantime,*
  *I remain, dear Miss Eileen,*

*Your devoted,*


*Harry*

The verse which I copied from a Birthday Book seemed to me to strike a happy if somewhat daring note of intimacy.

I considered a postscript condoling with her about her father's health, but abandoned the idea as tending to bring a gloomy note into an otherwise light-hearted document. I made a nice clean copy of the draft and sent it off with the afternoon mail.

Larry's disappearance lost interest for the town, which was intrigued and excited by Timothy Speek's unusual death. No actual tidings of the lad were received, but a small boy walking to school on the edge of the flooded creek picked up a cap and ran to Hennessy with his find. The schoolmaster identified it as Larry's and was quite disconsolate.

The body, however, was not found, although the search was continued persistently, for there were many curious places in which a raging flood might deposit its victims. Indeed, a fortnight after the inundation, they located, tangled in the branches of a big gum tree, a calf that had thirsted to death though imprisoned but a few feet above the water.

As coroner, Sam Cotter set the day for the inquest; as storekeeper, he saw to it that it did not conflict with the regular weekly half holiday, for he was well aware that it would attract many from the outlying districts glad to enhance the day's excitement with a little pleasurable shopping.

Mrs Marven, busy all the morning in her bar, although she was to be one of the principal witnesses, observed that Speek had never done her a good turn in his life but made up for it by dying. It struck me as a rather heartless thing to say, and, even if true, something she should have kept to herself. While I sipped my sherry before lunch, I heard her relating one of her highly coloured stories to a group larger than usual and marvelled that she could be so flippant on such a day and with such an ordeal before her.

She put out her hand and pretended to tug the prodigious beard of Bob Ennerway, a small farmer whose inquisitiveness had brought him into town when he might have been much better employed working to pay off some of his debts.

'In town for a haircut, Dad?' she inquired genially. 'D'you know, boys, they remind me of a fellow I knew called Sampson. When I was a young and beautiful girl of seventeen I worked at a coffee palace in the city and this Sampson used always be trying to entice me to the cyclorama.'

She looked down modestly and then up again with a most disgusting air of slyness, and the fools in the bar dug each other in the ribs and waited expectantly.

'Well, this Sampson had a crop of whiskers that must have gone forty bushels to the acre. Now, after lunch one day the mistress missed one of her best silver forks. She searched high and low, but no fork! Then I up and spoke. "I'll find the missing fork, lady," I cried. So we go creeping, creeping, c-r-eep-ing.' (Mrs Marven stopped and illustrated her words, and the oafs around her imitated her attitude, their silly mouths gaping.) 'Up the stairs we stalked and into this Sampson's room. And there he was, fast asleep like little Goldilocks, acres of beard cascading over his chest, snoring fit to wake the dead. Suddenly I draw a comb from my pocket and before anyone can stop me I am frisking the old chap's whiskers. And, behold, out falls the fork from where it had clogged in Sampson's whiskers. And ever after that they used to call me Delilah.'

The loungers roared with laughter as usual and as I finished my aperitif I could hear old Plank banging his tankard on the counter and bawling, 'Delilah, see. Sampson and Delilah. D'ya hear that? Sampson and Delilah. It's in the Bible. Well, danged if that don't call for another round.'

Her story was quite untrue, of course, but I rather envied Mrs Marven her aptitude for suiting her conversation to her company. Throughout my life I have found it not only difficult but embarrassing to talk to the lower classes.

The inquest was held in the hall in which our concert had taken place a few nights previously. Again every seat was occupied but, this time, Sam Cotter took the centre of the stage, seated at a deal table and dressed in the conspicuously new suit he had worn to Speek's funeral, his collar inordinately high and stiff. He reeked with authority as he frowned across the table on which papers in prodigious quantities helped to create the magisterial atmosphere.

A jury of five had been sworn in. In that sparsely populated district the law permitted that number and never in my life saw I a less intelligent-looking group. All appeared ill at ease and kept twiddling their collars and coughing self-consciously, obviously as interested in the impression they were creating as in the solemn duties they had so lightly sworn to discharge. They were, indeed, the sort of men one hardly associated with and never, of course, recognised socially, and it was beyond my understanding how Burke had come to select them. The foreman, I noticed, was the chief hand at Garnet Price's farm.

By the time I had found a seat, the body had already been identified, and Helen Speek was seated at one end of the coroner's table, being questioned by Cotter.

'What time was it when you discovered that your husband was dead, Mrs Speek?'

'It was about a quarter to eleven.'

'Tell us about it.'

'My husband had killed himself.'

'What made you think that?'

'There was a pistol in his hand.'

'What did you do when you saw this?'

'I ran to Dr Hansen's, but he was away. I called at the police station to get Constable Burke, but he was absent also.'

'Then what did you do?'

'I ran to Mrs Marven's.'

'Why to Mrs Marven's?'

'I saw the light in the hotel – and, besides, she is my friend.'

Sam Cotter removed his spectacles and said with a smile that embraced the whole courtroom, 'I think we may fairly say that Mrs Marven is everyone's friend.' He beamed, and they took the cue. There was restrained laughter and, looking very pleased with himself, he continued his questioning. 'And what did Mrs Marven do?'

'She came back to my house with me. She was wonderful. She – '

'Never mind that, Mrs Speek. We will hear Mrs Marven later.' He wiped his spectacles. 'Tell the court, Mrs Speek. Did you get on well with your husband?'

Everyone there knew that she didn't, but they hung breathlessly on her answer.

'No.'

I thought Cotter looked a little taken back by this unequivocal reply and, personally, I thought the woman was a fool to be so honest about her feelings.

The coroner pursued his inquiry, 'Do you think your husband was jealous?'

Her eyes had been cast down, but at the question she lifted them and stared Cotter full in the face.

'Yes,' she said, 'he was jealous of me and of everybody and everything. He was a sour man.'

There was a titter, then silence as they awaited the answer to Cotter's next question.

'Was he jealous of anyone in particular?'

Helen Speek hesitated, and Cotter spoke again. 'Come, Mrs Speek, please answer.'

She looked about her and down into the packed hall where they were all waiting, expectant, avid, but she did not speak.

'Well, Mrs Speek?' Cotter's voice assumed a severer tone.

From the body of the court there was a sudden scuffling,

and Garnet Price was on his feet shouting, 'Oh, for God's sake, Cotter, hasn't she been through enough? Everyone knows that Speek and Larry Ward had a fight, if that's what you want to drag in.'

There was a mild uproar at the interruption, and Cotter banged his mallet on the table for order. He glared down at Price. 'Mr Price,' he said, 'I must conduct this inquiry as I think fit. Please sit down.'

The old man turned again to the witness. 'Was your husband jealous of Larry Ward?' he asked her sternly. As she did not answer, he explained more softly, 'It is necessary for this court to try and find out why the deceased died – what made him take his own life, as you say he did.'

Helen nodded. 'I understand, Mr Cotter,' she replied. 'But my husband had grown into a strange man. He had no cause to be jealous of Larry Ward. If you had spoken to me in the street, and he had known it, he would have been jealous of you, also.'

There was a peal of laughter, and Cotter went very red and banged his mallet wildly.

'I quite understand what you mean, Mrs Speek,' he said loftily. 'Tell the court, what was the reason for your husband's quarrel with Larry Ward?'

'There was no reason for a quarrel. I hadn't spoken more than fifty words in my life to the boy. He came to my house with the grocery order and felt ill. I made him sit down and gave him a drink of water. My husband came in suddenly, and without reason called me a hard name and Larry struck him.'

Cotter did not speak, and she went on in a low, monotonous voice, 'My husband was always suspicious, always prying into what I was saying, where I was going, who I was seeing. My life wasn't my own. He made himself more sour every day. He fancied he was the only one in the world with troubles.'

She stopped abruptly as if she were suddenly afraid of what she was saying. I thought how damaging to herself such a statement might have been in a city court with avaricious lawyers eager to twist it to suit their case. Here, in this little town, where everyone knew Speek and his ways and the manner of man he was, it had the opposite effect. It rang true.

Cotter turned over some papers.

'Would you say your husband took his life because of his blindness – because he had grown so sorry for himself that he could not bear it any longer?'

I believe the old man was putting words into her mouth, but she did not answer.

'Can you think of any other reason?'

She shook her head.

'Thank you, Mrs Speek. That will be all for the moment.'

Cotter forgot his authority and actually stood as the constable helped her down the steps into the body of the hall. 'Call Mrs Marven,' he ordered, and there was a stir of excitement. They expected comic relief, but they were disappointed. Mrs Marven proved the very soul of propriety in the witness chair, answering Cotter's enquiries with the utmost decorum. She didn't even smile when he asked her her full name and where she lived.

She described how Helen had called upon her in great distress at about eleven o'clock and how she had gone with her to Speek's home and found the deceased lying in his big chair, holding a pistol in his hand. The constable whispered something, and Cotter delicately removed a cloth on the table and picked up the revolver that had lain beneath it. A pleasurable shudder ran through the courtroom. Cotter held out the gun to Mrs Marven.

'Is this the pistol?' he asked.

For the first time in my life I saw the landlady confused.

'You may take it in your hands, Mrs Marven,' Cotter said.

She shook her head and turned away. 'Please, Mr Cotter,' she said faintly, 'I – I'm afraid of guns. I don't know why but they terrify me. I'd rather not.'

'Come, Mrs Marven, this can't hurt you. It isn't loaded.'

With obvious effort she turned her head and looked at the revolver, but did not attempt to take it. 'It looks like the one,' she said. 'But I wouldn't really know. I didn't look at it closely.'

Cotter released her from the box after she had spoken of taking Dr Hansen to Speek's house. He treated her with marked courtesy and I couldn't help think that, despite his onerous duties, his mind was on the next hotel grocery order.

Constable Burke again whispered in his ear and he recalled Helen Speek.

'Do you recognise this weapon?' he asked, showing her the gun.

She looked at it calmly enough. 'It belonged to my husband,' she told him.

'You are sure?'

'Of course. He showed it to me – many times. He used to sit cleaning it by the hour.'

'Why did he show it to you?'

From the body of the court Price shouted again, rising to his feet, 'Why, why, why?' he cried in exasperated tones. 'Why shouldn't he? He'd shown it to me and to almost everybody else in the town. Why in God's name do you have to keep on asking things you know? The man shot himself – the only decent thing he'd done in years. Why prolong this damn nonsense to satisfy a lot of miserable scandalmongers?'

---

Cotter rose, pale and trembling, banging his mallet, and by the time Price had had his say Constable Burke had tumbled heavily down the steps and was at his side. There had been some angry cries and someone at the back shouted, 'Put him out.' Price ignored the policeman and glowered round the hall.

'How can you sit here pretending you want justice for the dead, but hungering in your hearts for dirt to defame the living?' he cried. 'While he lived there wasn't one of you had a good word for Speek, blind as he was. We all knew him for a miserable, self-pitying, contemptible crawling apology for a man and the world's the better for his going. Don't you touch me, Burke,' he continued, turning to the constable. 'Don't you put your hand on me till Cotter says I'm in contempt of court. Then you try it.'

For a moment there was no sound. Old Cotter's mallet was still in his hand, but he made no attempt to use it or exercise his authority. Instead he said weakly, 'I think the court will adjourn till this afternoon at two o'clock.'

Garnet Price laughed contemptuously and strode out, and nobody followed till he had disappeared.

When the court re-assembled Cotter had prepared a little speech.

'We are to the best of our ability trying to establish the cause of death of one of our fellow townsmen, and to be reasonably sure that it was self-inflicted, and, if self-inflicted, we must try and find a motive that prompted such a desperate act and whether the deceased was of sound or unsound mind when he perpetrated it.'

It sounded to me as if he had hastily read up on coronial procedure in the recess but, whether this were so or not, he evinced an anxiety to get the business over and done with. Dr Hansen, just back from an out-of-town accident case, gave evidence that he had been taken to Speek's home by Mrs Marven. The deceased had a bullet wound in the head. It had obviously been fired at close quarters. The deceased had apparently placed the muzzle of the gun alongside his mouth, pointing upwards. Death would be instantaneous.

Constable Burke went into the box and deposed that he had returned from flood duty at midnight and found a message pinned to his door. He proceeded at once to Speek's place, where he saw Mrs Marven and Dr Hansen. The body was in the position described by the medical witness, the revolver still in the deceased's fingers.

Old Cotter pulled out his watch and consulted it gravely. Then he recalled Mrs Speek. 'Under the terms of your husband's will you are the sole beneficiary – is that correct?'

'Yes.'

'When was the will made?'

'I am not certain of the date. Some years ago.'

'Had your husband mentioned the will to you lately?'

'He spoke of it a little while ago.'

'Can you remember his actual words?'

'Yes,' she said, 'I think I can. He said, "I'm making a little change in my will. But don't be afraid. I'm leaving everything to you. I just want to tighten it up."'

Cotter asked, 'When did you last see your husband alive, Mrs Speek?'

She told him, as far as she could remember, about 8.30 pm on the night of his death, and I knew that must have been about the time I saw Garnet Price leave the house.

'Where was that?'

She told him.

'Then,' he said 'as far as you are aware you were the last person to see him alive?'

'As far as I know, yes.'

'It is possible, however, that someone might have seen him *after* you went to bed?'

'Yes, it is possible. I wouldn't know.'

'Was he expecting any visitors?'

My heart stopped a beat.

'Yes,' she replied. 'He told me Mr Ford was coming at nine o'clock.'

'Mr Ford, the postmaster?'

'Yes.'

'But you did not see Mr Ford?'

'No.'

'Nor hear him or anyone talking to your husband?'

'No.'

'Thank you, Mrs Speek, that will be all.'

Cotter conferred with Constable Burke while I waited uncomfortably. At length the old man peered over his spectacles.

'Is Mr Ford here?' he asked, and I stood up.

'You have heard the evidence, Mr Ford? Would you volunteer to go into the box? Failing that, I am afraid we must adjourn again to subpoena you.'

After all my trouble to keep out of the wretched affair it was the dead man himself who was dragging me in. As I walked toward the platform, I passed Garnet Price sitting by himself, his head on his chest as if asleep. It was plain he had no interest in my evidence. Helen Speek did not even look at me.

Why should I, I thought, for the sake of some nebulous question of ethics, plunge into this thing? If I admitted what I had seen, what a welter of questioning I would be loosing. I might be engulfed in a criminal trial that would drag on interminably, interfering with all my plans, preventing me most likely from taking up my new position. My motives might be questioned. I had been foolish enough to let Helen Speek into the post office in the early morning and give her that confounded package! Craven had seen her come out, too! The more I thought of the possibilities the less I liked them. After all, Speek was dead one way or another, and a good job, too.

I took the Bible from Constable Burke and swore I had not seen the blind man on the night of his death. I could not have been calling on him at nine because I had an appointment with Hennessy for that hour. That, of course, could easily be verified.

A few minutes later I heard the court's decision, 'suicide while temporarily insane', and Cotter thanking the jury. As the verdict was given I intercepted a look between Helen Speek and Garnet Price. It was but transitory and then Price had jumped up and was rudely pushing his way out of the hall, but in that hasty glance I had read relief and satisfaction, and I wondered what they would be thinking if I had told all I knew.

With the instincts of a gentleman, I had kept clear of this shabby business, but, as I reviewed past events and remembered Helen in Price's arms down by the creek, her agitated request and acceptance of the package I had given her at the post office, and her strange movements in that room of death when the blind man had mistaken Price for Larry Ward, I realised that I held these two in the hollow of my hand.

All the secrets of the town were not, as the late Mr Speek had suggested, sealed up in envelopes.

The excitement occasioned by the flood, the funeral, the inquest, and Larry's disappearance subsided, and the town settled down to its normal, humdrum way of life. The drone of the meagre mill machinery would come to me, faintly vying with the closer buzz of a late blowfly busy about the post office window; over the way, Haggart, the draper, would close his shop regularly at five minutes to one and return, picking his teeth, promptly at two.

I had plenty of time for reflection. Plenty of time to wonder by what queer trick of fate a man of my breeding had been set down in this cultureless town. I reflected how my poor mother must have bemoaned the day she relinquished her comfortable English way of life and voyaged with my father to this far land, bedazzled by high adventure, seeking romance and finding nothing but hardship and anxiety and few if any social equals.

I remembered the determination with which she had planned my destiny, insisting that I should have a private tutor, fighting my father's desire to take me away from civilisation into some wretched no man's land, maintaining that I should have those cultural opportunities that were my right of heritage. I recalled the letters she had written to friends in England, requesting their influence to get me settled into some lucrative official post where I could at least live like a gentleman and not as the boor my father intended.

He had gone off one day, crying out some nonsense about bringing her to a land of opportunity and that she was robbing me of a chance to be a man. I don't know what he expected, though I believe he was mad enough, self-willed enough, anyhow, to expect her to trail along with him on his wretched expeditions. How well I remembered myself as a little child sitting in her lap, playing with her rings, twisting them about her long, white fingers, thinking how beautiful they were. Later it seemed incredible that my father could have expected her to be a pioneer to stand by him, scrubbing and cutting wood, milking cows and bearing innumerable children to populate this empty land.

We never saw him again. He'd made some prodigious journey into country that, at that time, had never been explored, and he paid for his temerity, for the natives speared him in the back, and his foolhardiness cost the government a pretty penny in bringing the remains of his mutilated body back to civilisation and a decent Christian burial. He left little or nothing behind him, and I recall my mother waiting long and anxiously for replies to the letters she had dispatched to people she knew in the old country, asking for help to pay our passages home.

She would sit talking to me after I had come back from my day at the postal department, where I had started my career, painting a rosy picture of our future life in England. But the only replies to the letters were evasive in character, and no money came, and I think that broke her heart, for she died very quickly, thankful at least that she had established me in a position in which even if I were not paid as much as I earned, I received enough to keep myself.

I had long played with the idea of putting a monument on her grave and had even written the epitaph, but the cost seemed terrific and would have set me back tremendously and I wondered whether it mattered after all. It wouldn't bring back those cool, white, comforting hands.

I was delighted to have an immediate answer from Eileen. Her letter came together with a business communication, which I thrust into my pocket for later attention.

Eileen wrote:

*My dear Mr Ford,*

*I detest false delicacy and I cannot pretend I have been blind to the state of your feelings. My father has told me of your generous offer about a settlement. I have, however, been in such a rush and am so anxious about my father's health that I cannot write as generously as you might expect. I hope you will understand.*

*I feel that, in the goodness of your heart, you may have made me this offer at a time when you imagined I sorely needed comfort, and I respect you for that. Indeed, I respect you greatly and I look forward to seeing you when we return. Then, if the same thought is in your heart, I think I may find it in my heart to say, 'Yes.'*

*Yours sincerely,*

*Eileen*

She had a postscript.

*My father and I are anxious for news of Larry. We are aware you have all done everything possible, but there may still be a chance, don't you think so, Mr Ford? Would you please be kind enough to let us know anything you hear – good news or bad?*

I would have liked the letter better without the postscript; nevertheless, it had been written with modesty and had all the ladylike qualities I felt the woman I intended to marry should possess. Her handwriting had character, and I was glad that she had used notepaper fashionable at the moment in the best circles. The future looked rosy and I went to an excellent lunch with a hearty appetite.

Mrs Marven was standing on a stool in the public bar, tacking up a coloured almanac. I remembered it represented the infant Samuel praying.

'It's pretty, isn't it? she said, stepping down and surveying it critically. 'Good for the customers, too. It helps keep their tongues tidy.'

Providence must have been in an amiable mood that day since it permitted the postponement of the evil moment when I was to recollect that other letter that had come with the morning mail. I was at least given time to enjoy my lunch. Strange how my mind retains the little details of that meal, the last for which I was to have any great appetite for quite a time.

There had been a thick soup, seasoned, as I remember, so that I felt the heat of it making pleasurable little prickles under my hair, and afterwards a huge Cornish pasty apiece, each made by Mrs Marven's own capable hands – with the turnips, potatoes and onions revealed in broad thin slices when you severed the paste that was no more than a thin covering to hold together the delectable interior. To finish, there had been a fruit salad served picturesquely in high wine glasses with fresh cream.

I sat back with a sigh of satisfaction and complimented the beaming landlady, and, taking the unopened letter together with the one from Eileen from my pocket, tapped the latter significantly as I placed it on the table beside me.

'A perfect luncheon to top off a perfect morning,' I said.

'Good news?' Mrs Marven enquired, smiling.

'The best any man could have,' I replied, and, try as I could to control my features, I am afraid I grinned fatuously as I picked up a clean table knife and slit open the other envelope. I settled myself comfortably to read its contents. In a moment, however, I must have uttered an exclamation of dismay, for I vaguely remember Mrs Marven's cry. 'Good gracious, what is it?'

I did not answer, for as I read, my world tumbled about my ears. Ignoring everyone, I crushed the letter in my hand and, rising without a word of apology, dashed from the room, blind with fury, mad with frustration, my mind reeling at the rank injustice of this blow that had been dealt me.

In the solitude of my bedroom I re-read the letter, hoping against hope that in some phrase I might find a measure of comfort. But I found nothing but bleak words. There was no doubt about it. I was ruined. Every penny I had invested had gone. All my thrift, all my striving and saving counted for nothing. This came of trusting people, I reflected. I recalled little things about the secretary of our company. His eyes, for instance. A plausible rogue if ever there was! And now he had gone – bolted – and with him our money.

I had come to my lunch a man of substance. I left it penniless. All I had was my position and God knows how many years of hard struggle ahead.

There was Eileen to think of! Doubt assailed me. I had promised a marriage settlement of a thousand pounds – more than I had actually had at the moment, but the round figures had appealed to me as sounding so much better than a lesser amount. What would be Mr Mahoney's reaction? What would Eileen think now?

Surely neither of these people could be so base as to let a few paltry pounds shatter the happiness of a man! I told myself that Eileen was too noble to be swayed by such considerations, that she would marry me for what I was, not for mere money.

And, in any case, I had my position. I was somebody in this town and promotion lay ahead. Nevertheless, doubts continued to crowd in on me when I remembered Mahoney's attitude as disclosed in the letter in which he revealed himself as a sick man with no money of his own but desperately anxious to see his daughter comfortably settled before he died.

I washed my face and hands and assumed a careless air as I ran downstairs. I need not have bothered. I had pictured them in the hall, waiting in shocked expectancy, but there was no one there. Rose, the housemaid, called from the dining-room where she was tidying up after clearing away the luncheon debris.

'Oh, Mr Ford, you left this on the table.'

She handed me Eileen's letter, which I had forgotten, and I detected a smirk, which she instantly covered. Surely, I thought, she had not the impertinence to read it. I would not have put it past her. I put it in my pocket as if it were of no consequence and gave her a curt thank you.

When I reached the front door Mrs Marven was standing on the footpath, talking to Helen Speek. The ostler drove up in the best buggy drawn by a pair of chestnuts and Helen climbed in and was driven away, Mrs Marven waving goodbye. She turned and saw me standing on the step. I felt hurt. Apparently, she had forgotten all about my agitation at the luncheon table, for she made no reference to it whatever. Instead, there was real pleasure in her voice as she said brightly, 'Helen's off to Baloola to see the lawyer about Speek's estate. I feel so glad, Mr Ford.' She assumed a confidential tone. 'Her husband was ever so much better off than she expected. She'll be quite a rich woman. Isn't it nice?'

Coming on top of my own distressing news, Mrs Marven's revelation was not comforting. I am afraid I forgot my manners.

'Nice,' I repeated with a bitter laugh. As I walked away I could feel her eyes following me curiously.

It did not improve my temper to find Garnet Price waiting

outside the post office, which I reached five minutes after the regulation opening time.

'Now then, young fellow,' he cried, disguising his impatience with heavy humour. 'Can't have this, you know. This is the sort of thing that throws governments off the treasury bench.'

I ignored his satire and, opening the office, attended to his requirements. He filled in a telegraph form and regarded me with mock anxiety as I began checking the number of words. 'You look a bit pale about the gills,' he said. 'Don't go overdoing it. Better cut out the sherries.'

It was like his impertinence, and I did not reply. I took his money and when he had gone I read the message over again, and it seemed to me that fate was determined to rub salt in my wound. It was an instruction to a firm of stockbrokers and, at any other time, would have made little or no impression upon me; but, with my disaster fresh in my mind, it seemed wholly unfair that this man, who had engaged in an illicit association with Helen Speek, should be able to deal in gilt-edge securities in an offhand manner while I, with my honourable love for Eileen Mahoney, should have been robbed of all I had. I thought, too, of Eileen and the poor resources of her dying father and compared her lot with that of Helen Speek even now hurrying to find out how rich she had become.

It was more than unjust. It was damnable. It had no right to be. I sent feverish telegrams to the city but received scant consolation from the replies. There was no doubt my money had gone – vanished like the wind. The damned rogue who had absconded had completely disappeared, and the police with their usual inefficiency hadn't the faintest idea what had become of him. Even if discovered he would doubtless have long since dissipated our funds. When a second letter came from one of my business associates reproving me for the wording of my telegram (for I had, of course, expressed my opinions rather trenchantly) and impertinently advising me to take my medicine like a man, I was almost beside myself.

Nevertheless, to the best of my ability, I hid my feelings from Mrs Marven and the rest of them at the hotel, though I am afraid I must have appeared a little taciturn and unlike my usual self.

Eileen's father irritated me by writing, reiterating his catalogue of woe, stressing his poor health and lack of resources. A fine time of life, it seemed to me, for a man to start crying poverty. I had no patience with him. He hadn't always been sick. He was twice my age and had had years of opportunity to provide for himself and his daughter. He had treated Eileen very shabbily in my opinion, and now he was looking to me to make up for his shortcomings. I loved Eileen. I wanted her with all my heart, but, damn it, a father had some obligations.

These thoughts were in my mind one morning when Garnet Price, after collecting his mail, stood outside the delivery window, reading a letter he had just received. He turned to me with a grin and waved the letter.

'If you weren't shut up in your little prison, Ford,' he said, 'we could go and have a drink on the strength of this. Five hundred pounds and made without turning a hair or doing a stroke of work. That's the way to make money, old boy. Better than the government service, eh?'

Perhaps he had not intended to be rude, but I chose to let him see I resented his tone and slammed down the wooden shutter. His contemptuous laugh rang in my ears as he strode away.

I think it was from that laugh that my idea was born, for I suddenly saw, as plain as day, how, by acting boldly, I could recuperate my losses and not only wipe them out, but in all probability establish myself more firmly than ever.

The decision I had come to was strengthened by the change in Helen Speek, who began to spend more time with Mrs Marven and sometimes helped her about the house. The sullenness had gone out of her expression, colour had come to her cheeks, and, with her large eyes and thick mop of golden hair, I had to admit that she had become even more attractive.

Her furtiveness of speech left her and she joined in the general conversation quite naturally, and frequently, and, despite her mourning, actually aided and abetted Mrs Marven in that particular brand of discourse in which the landlady excelled and which I could not help but think belonged more to the barroom than to polite society.

Mrs Marven, of course, went out of her way to make her feel at home, and, with a sad lack of decorum, but doubtless meaning well, even celebrated her birthday. I got to the hotel one midday to find myself dragged into the commercial room where an unusual drink was thrust into my hand, while Dr Hansen proposed a toast.

I had never tasted such a beverage before but I know that, temporarily at least, it eased my mind and even gave me a sense of well-being in addition to a tremendous appetite. I discovered later that it was two parts of sherry to one of brandy mixed with the yolk of an egg and two spoonfuls of sugar, the lot strained and dusted over with nutmeg or cinnamon, or maybe both. Somehow Mrs Marven had managed to keep it icy cold (they were the days before crushed ice came to the country towns), and I observed that tongues were noticeably loosened almost immediately we had drunk the stuff, Price in his boisterous manner declaring that our hostess should be recognised by the queen in the next birthday honours.

We drank twice, during which Mrs Marven told us with frank delicacy that the concoction was called a 'bosom caresser', and Price made some risqué allusion that embarrassed me greatly.

We went in to luncheon, the others laughing, and all of us hungry, and that was just as well, for Helen, it appeared, was of Yorkshire descent, and Mrs Marven had been up early to do justice to the occasion. We sat down to a Yorkshire pie such as I had never seen before. A goose and a fowl had been sacrificed on the altar of gastronomy, and both boned, the latter stuffed with minced ham, veal, suet, lemon peel, various spices, sweet herbs and goose liver, with onion and a little cayenne worked into a paste with the yellow of two eggs. Mrs Marven had then sewn up the fowl, trussed it, and stewed it with the goose for twenty minutes in some beef and giblet stock mixed with a small glass of sherry and in a closed stewpan.

After that the fowl had been popped inside the goose and the latter placed in a pie mould lined with short paste. The goose had rested on a cushion of stuffing in the middle of the liquor in which he had been stewed, and was surrounded in the pie with slices of semicooked hare and wild turkey (the latter taking the place of the Yorkshire pheasant and partridge, Mrs Marven explained) alternating with more seasoning. Butter was spread before the pie was roofed in, and, I believe, the whole lot had then been baked for three hours.

It was served to us cold and as I ate I imagined myself at the head of my own table as host at just such a meal, but prepared, of course, by servants. It was all right for Mrs Marven in her capacity as hotel-keeper to do her own cooking, but I could not see my own wife engaged in a task so menial. No, I thought, as the birthday luncheon progressed, the meals in my home would be prepared by our domestics, and the cook, no doubt, duly complimented after we had bidden good-bye to our guests.

Mrs Marven's little party, however, was not greatly concerned with the niceties of polite society. When the meal finished, I observed Helen Speek with her arm about her hostess in an attitude that might, of course, have been one of affection, but which was as likely as not induced by an excess of alcohol. I have been told, though I have never experienced the sensation, that the sense of well-being which drink occasions is frequently accompanied by a fixed determination to see only the best in one's companions and that it blinds one to their obvious shortcomings. I feel grateful that I have always been able to take my liquor like a gentleman without permitting it to disturb my logic, and when Garnet Price called as I was departing, 'Well, good-bye, Ford, old boy,' I chose to ignore him, and, thanking Mrs Marven, bowed to the company as a whole and went out.

I had a feeling that my departure was followed by a personal discussion in the worst of bad taste.

Garnet Price had made a habit of coming to the hotel for meals. His attitude to Helen was outwardly circumspect, but covert glances that I intercepted now and then told me as plainly as if these two had spoken that they had a secret understanding. In company they had agreed to appear no more than commonly polite to each other till such time as convention permitted more familiarity.

Price, indeed, made not the slightest attempt to remain alone with the woman and, as a matter of fact, on several occasions jumped up and said he must be going when it appeared he might be left with her and none other present.

The more I considered the idea fermenting in my mind, the more justifiable it seemed, so that, when I received from my business associates a further communication to the effect that not only was there no possibility of retrieving anything from the ruins of our company but we might be called upon to find some money to straighten the matter out, I hesitated no longer.

All I had to decide was the right moment, and the right moment was, of course, when Garnet Price and Helen Speek and I were alone and unlikely to be interrupted. This was not easy to arrange. Price appeared determined to make his departure every time he saw a probability that he would be left with the woman, and, try as I might to manoeuvre them into the situation I required for my plan, I failed over and over again.

I had almost decided to speak to Mrs Speek alone when chance stepped in and gave me the opportunity I wished. Helen had been in for luncheon as usual but was not present at tea-time. Price, however, was there, but excused himself early, saying he had to get back to his farm. I heard him, with that loud voice of his, calling the ostler to bring his horse to the front of the hotel.

After the meal, I played a few games of euchre with Mrs Marven, the bank-clerk person, a visiting commercial, and Dr Hansen, who for once had an hour or so to himself.

'And you deserve it, Doctor,' Mrs Marven said. 'I wonder you don't go off your head, what with one thing and another. People ought to have more consideration than to go getting themselves sick at all hours of the night. If I was in Parliament I'd make a law, too, that no baby should start being born except in broad daylight and the whole job would have to be over and done with by dusk.'

I thought her indelicacy might offend and would have changed the subject, but Hansen laughed.

'Oh, it's all right to smile, Doc,' Mrs Marven went on, 'but it's not only you I'm thinking of. One of these nights you won't know whether you're on your head or your heels, and poor Mrs Barmby will be getting my indigestion drops, and I'll be having her baby.'

'Really, Mrs Marven,' I said, and I thought the doctor seemed a bit annoyed.

He said quietly, 'Very awkward for you, I'm sure, Mrs Marven.'

When the game was over, he bade us good-night and went home to what he hoped would be undisturbed slumber.

'Works too hard,' the landlady commented as she returned after seeing him off the premises. 'It isn't right.'

For a while I sat on reading in the commercial room and at length decided to take a short stroll before turning in. It was fairly late, that is late for that town, and dark. I was surprised, however, to see a light in Helen Speek's home, glimmering from the room in which the blind man had breathed his last. Some instinct told me that Price was there with Helen, that his talk about going home had been meant to deceive us. I remembered how he had called for his horse in an unnecessarily loud voice.

Very quietly I walked up the longest path to the side entrance, avoiding the gravel. The door was shut and the blind down but, stooping and peering, I managed to get a glimpse of the interior. Sure enough Price was there, sitting on the sofa alongside Helen. He was holding her hands and they were very close together as they gazed into each other's eyes.

Gripping the handle of the door firmly, I turned it slowly so that it made no sound, and gently pushed. It was not locked.

I stepped quietly into the room. 'Good evening,' I said.

Price sprang to his feet, an angry frown on his brow, and faced me. 'What the devil?' he began. But Helen was on her feet, too. She had paled but regained her composure quickly.

'Why, Mr Ford,' she said, coming toward me, 'I didn't hear you knock.'

'I didn't knock,' I said, 'because I wanted to catch you together.'

My choice of words was unfortunate. I had meant to convey that I wished to see them both at one and the same time, but Price preferred to read another meaning into them.

'And what do you mean by that?' he demanded truculently.

'Please don't get excited, Mr Price,' I said. 'I am here on a matter of business.' I turned to Helen. 'May I sit down?'

Silently she pushed a chair toward me.

'Please,' I said, indicating the sofa. 'You both looked so comfortable when I came in.'

Price glared, but Helen put her hand on his arm and they sat down and waited for me to explain my visit.

I put my hand in my pocket and pulled out some share scrip.

'I fancied,' I said, 'that you – that is one or both of you might care to buy these securities.' I held out the scrip to Price. He hesitated, but took it.

'What *is* this, Ford?' he asked suspiciously, but I was pleased to note that the truculence had gone from his voice and there was concern in his tone. 'It's a damn funny time to come talking share scrip, isn't it?'

'Oh, I don't know,' I returned lightly. 'It occurs to me that it is nice and quiet at this hour and that this is the very room in which this business should be transacted.'

'But,' he exclaimed in bewilderment, looking up from the document he held, 'this is scrip for – ' and he mentioned the name of the company in which I had lost my fortune. 'Why, dammit, man; it's worthless.' He turned to Helen and explained. 'The secretary defaulted. Got away with everything. The show's up the spout.'

He looked at me keenly. 'Surely you're not serious, Ford?'

'Oh, but I am,' I told him. 'I still have great faith in the shares.'

'Oh, come, Ford,' he said, 'you can't expect me to believe that.' He held the scrip out to me with an air of finality, but I thrust my hands in my breeches pockets and stared back at him.

'Don't be hasty, Mr Price,' I advised. 'Look at the scrip again, please; and you, too, Mrs Speek. You may remember promising to buy these shares on a former occasion – in this very room.'

Price stared incredulously, but I believe Helen had some premonition of what was coming. She said, faintly enough, however, 'I don't remember.'

'Why, the man's mad!' Price cried.

I shook my head. 'Let me refresh your memory.' I looked at Helen. 'It was the night – forgive me, Mrs Speek – the night your husband died. I recollect it quite well. It was before Mr Speek shot himself. He was standing just here.' I indicated a position near the small table. 'You, Mrs Speek, were here, and, Mr Price, you came in by this door and stood – here. Surely you remember?'

Both continued to stare at me, but neither spoke.

'You can't so easily have forgotten that night?' I urged.

'You're crazy,' Price shouted. 'I was never here the night Speek died.'

'Oh, come, come, Price,' I said, 'your memory's failing. Why, so many little details come to my mind! Let me see now. Oh, yes! Speek was talking about something. He'd mistaken you for Larry Ward.'

I expected a furious outburst and a flood of denials, but none was forthcoming, and I went on relentlessly. 'Let me think.' I shut my eyes and pretended to concentrate. 'Oh, yes! On this little table, I remember, there was a box of chocolates. Speek mentioned them. He suggested Larry had stolen them. He selected two. He ate one and put the other on the table at his side. Then, I recollect, Mrs Speek, you did a very strange thing. You took away the sweet he had placed before him and changed it with another you selected from the box. Being blind, your husband did not see.'

Helen sank down upon the sofa from which she had slowly risen as I began my reconstruction of the scene I had witnessed and gazed up at me with eyes that were full of fear. It gave me a feeling of confidence and a new sense of power. But Price suddenly galvanised into life.

'You're a perjuring bastard, Ford,' he shouted.

'Please, Price,' I said calmly, for I had been prepared for his violent outburst and could afford to ignore his insult. 'Don't shout or perhaps Mrs Speek may have to place her hand over your mouth – as she did on a former occasion.'

At this Helen began to sob and Price turned to her.

'Helen,' he cried wildly, 'let me take this thing away and kill it.'

She stood up and put both her arms around him.

'Don't, Garnet, please,' she cried sobbing. He held her closely and in a moment or two she grew calmer and gently released herself and took the scrip from his clutching hand. She addressed me almost calmly.

'I understand, Mr Ford – perfectly. You need money very badly. And you wish to sell your securities.'

'Exactly,' I bowed.

She waited, thinking, then asked quietly, 'How much, Mr Ford?'

'Why,' I said, trying to appear indifferent. 'You shall have them for what they cost me – a thousand pounds.'

Price exploded. 'A thousand fiddlesticks!' he cried. 'I tell you, Helen, the shares are valueless.'

'I am sure Mrs Speek doesn't think so,' I ventured.

'Helen!' Price turned to her excitedly. 'Speek shot himself and there's an end to it. He shot himself, didn't he?' he seized her arms and shook her roughly.

Turning away from him she gently pushed him from her.

'Not an end to it, Price,' I said. 'There are such things as exhumation.'

I think he was genuinely startled.

'Good God,' he cried, and his eyes again sought Helen's. She avoided them but put out her hand, and he seized it and held it in his rough grasp while she kept her eyes on me and spoke in the dull toneless voice I had known her use in the days when her husband lived.

'I will buy the shares, Mr Ford. You have my word. I will get in touch with you very soon. Good night.' She handed the scrip to me and, as I turned to leave, she added, 'I wish you to understand, Mr Ford, that I am speaking for myself. Mr Price is not concerned in this matter.'

I laughed at that, and Price said violently, 'But, by God I am, Helen. What concerns you concerns me.'

'Spoken like a gentleman,' I said.

'Please, dear.' She turned to him and I noted the familiarity, although I am sure they were both unaware of its implication. It struck me as rather humorous after all their previous efforts to conceal their feelings.

'I will expect to hear from you very soon, Mrs Speek,' I said. 'You will understand, I am sure, that one has a duty to society and these things cannot be delayed.'

I had said no more before Price seized my arm in a grip of iron and roughly propelled me to the door. He opened it with his free hand and I thought he was going to start a vulgar brawl. Instead he held me at arm's length and stared me up and down. I could see his lip curl back from his teeth as he spoke.

'D'you know what I think of you, Ford?' he asked, and gave me no time for reply but tightened the pressure on my arm till I winced with the pain, and added, 'You stink.'

With that he flung me away from him with such force that I stumbled and fell, badly grazing one of my hands and the wrist on the gravel. It was quite nasty and rather painful, and, when I got back to the hotel, I made some excuse to Mrs Marven and had her get some hot water and bathe it for me.

CHAPTER 5

I was by no means surprised at Price's attitude. Indeed, I had anticipated violence. As I went to bed that night I consoled myself with the thought that I had faced the matter out bravely enough and with the cool confidence that had convinced Helen. She in turn, I felt reasonably sure, would persuade Price that I held the whip and that it would be wise to jump at the crack.

And what, after all, was a thousand pounds between these two? Price was a wealthy man, and Helen had just inherited much more than she had any right to expect. Price was a proud and hasty man, but he might also, I figured, be a shrewd one. I was a little puzzled about his behaviour during our business talk. Did he know what Helen had been up to? In any case, I told myself, it didn't matter. Being the man he was, he would stick to her through thick and thin. I was sure of that. Hadn't he said, 'What concerns you concerns me.'

Whether he only suspected that Timothy Speek had been poisoned, or actually knew it and had had a part in the crime, I felt confident that he would realise the wisdom of the policy of silence I had suggested. I didn't let it keep me awake but went to sleep planning a new future with Eileen by my side.

I heard in a roundabout way that the Garners were selling their home and leaving the town and wondered whether this would affect me. Would they, at the last moment, tell what they knew? I thought not. The inquest was over and done with, and I could hardly see them raking up the past to be bullied with a thousand and one questions about why they had not spoken before. Even if Helen Speek and Price became aware of what Polly Garner had seen, it would make them more anxious if anything; and I could impress upon them that I alone knew how to keep the Garners silent. And I was convinced that I could make any inquisitive authority believe that the woman was mistaken and Speek's dying reference was to Ward, not Ford.

I hoped, however, that the whole regrettable affair would be kept decently dark, and if the Garners spoke at all it would be at a time when I wanted them to loosen their tongues and to such people as I wished to hear their story.

I had always connected the package I had given Helen Speek as having a definite bearing on the blind man's death. The box of chocolates I had seen on the table and that Helen had so carefully removed was approximately the size of the package she had received from me. But in the mail the morning after my interview regarding the disposal of my shares I found a similar article. It was wrapped and addressed in exactly the same way, the addressee's name in plain block letters as on the previous occasion.

There was, of course, nothing to do but open the thing. The box contained handkerchiefs and, contrary to postal regulations, a letter. It was couched in the politest terms, the labour of a lovesick swain too bashful to make a personal approach. To my astonishment it was from none other than Haggart, the draper, the little waxen-moustached fellow who had sung sentimental ballads so forlornly at our concert, the nonentity at whom everyone laughed and whose peccadilloes provided ceaseless town gossip, for he appeared to live in an everlasting state of unrequited love.

His letter said that, despite her admonition to refrain from sending her presents owing to her husband's objections, he felt he was justified in renewing his attentions because of her changed circumstances, and he hoped and so on and so on. I felt the matter had to be cleared up at once, and, when he called for his mail later in the day, I asked him to step into the inner office.

'Now, Mr Haggart,' I said severely, after offering him a chair, 'you will of course understand that I am speaking to you as a post office official. It is my duty to see that postal regulations are not contravened.'

I pushed the box of handkerchiefs across my desk.

'You sent that article package rate and enclosed a letter?'

He blushed like a schoolboy.

'Do not fear, Mr Haggart,' I said. 'Anything that goes through this post office is as secret as the grave; but it is my duty to deliver the package to – let me see,' I pretended I was uncertain of the address, 'oh, yes, Mrs H. Speek, but the recipient would have to pay letter postage and at double rate. Moreover, she would be entitled to know why, and that would be embarrassing for me, for she would become aware that I knew your sentiments toward her' – he went a deeper red – 'and it wouldn't be nice for you if she were to think you had so thoughtlessly put cheap-rate postage on your, er, token of friendship. Now would it?'

He shuffled. 'No, of course not, Mr Ford,' he admitted. 'What must I do?'

'If Mr Haggart, you will tell me as a post office official and quite in confidence that you have not sent similar parcels to Mrs Speek enclosing letters, I will reseal this article and you can repost it with the correct postage or take it away, for all I care. It is of no moment to me. But I must assure myself that this has not been a constant practice.'

'Oh, indeed, I can assure you of that, Mr Ford,' he replied eagerly. 'I did send her one other package with a note, but that was the only time. It was a box of chocolates.' He added rather wistfully, 'She never acknowledged it, but I suppose that is understandable. I posted it the night before her husband was found dead, poor fellow.'

'Very well, Mr Haggart,' I said, rising and dismissing him.

'We'll forget all about it. We're men of the world, I hope – so, mum's the word.'

I grinned at him and, a bit sheepishly, he left the office, carrying his love offering with him.

He had told me all I wished to know, but it would have given me more satisfaction had the chocolates come from a less obviously innocent source.

Till late that evening I sat in my favourite armchair in the commercial room, my book unopened on my knee, puzzling over the absurd Haggart and his chocolates and the box from which Timothy Speek had helped himself with such disastrous result. I was convinced that Speek had been poisoned. It was possible, I thought, that, when Polly Garner saw Speek, he had collapsed but had not immediately died, as she had suggested.

It might be that he had poisoned and shot himself, making doubly sure his attempt at suicide would succeed, but this argued a strength of character and courage hardly compatible with the man's nature. Or, perhaps, finding himself poisoned and unable to endure the agony, he had used the gun to end everything. That was more likely.

My conjectures were interrupted by Mrs Marven's voice calling from the landing on the first floor, 'Mr Ford! Are you there?'

I jumped up and went into the hall.

'Would you be a good man, Mr Ford,' she called, 'and, before you come up to bed, pop into the bar? I've left the key in my safe. Lock it like a dear and push the key under my door when you pass. There's no hurry. I'll throw down the bar key. Catch!'

The incident was on a par with many another, for she was a curiously careless woman about important things; I couldn't see myself leaving my safe unlocked and handing the key to a comparative stranger. I read for a little longer, then crossed the hall to the bar door. The house was silent.

I found the bar candlestick on the counter, where it was invariably placed with a box of matches against emergency, and went to the small iron safe. Its door was shut, the forgotten key in the lock. I swung it open and held the candle to illuminate the interior. There were the usual drawers, one containing a little pile of silver and some notes – the day's takings, I presumed; another with small change and a third with a collection of old-fashioned jewellery including a gold locket with a miniature of the late Marven. The thing was so ugly I wondered why on earth it had been kept all these years.

Stored in the safe there was also a number of oldish papers, insurances and the like, and, at the extreme end of the bundle, a thick parchment envelope. On its front was scribbled in Mrs Marven's characteristic scrawl:

WITH GREAT CARE

I wondered what it might be. It was lightly sealed, and I easily opened it by softening the gum very gradually in the heat of the candle flame. There were two tiny packets inside, and the seal of one was broken.

I took a used envelope from my pocket and poured a little of the white powdered contents into it and re-placed it in my pocket. Then I carefully re-sealed the parchment covering, restored everything as I found it, and locked and closed the bar.

The custom at the hotel was for the last person retiring to lock the front door, and, before proceeding to do so, I stepped outside for a breath of air. It was a fine, still evening with a splendid moon, and, as I stood gazing up at the majestic heavens, enraptured with the beauty and silence of the night, my reverie was interrupted by the antics of a small dog that ambled up and began jumping up at me, thrusting its dirty paws at my knees. I am not fond of dogs at any time and I tried to drive the creature away, but, with absurd insistence, it kept returning as if, in some ridiculous way, it imagined there was a bond between us, the only two abroad that lovely night.

On the spur of the moment I drew from my pocket the envelope containing the powder I had taken from Mrs Marven's safe. My mind was crowded with suspicion, and this seemed as good a time as any to make a test. The dog sniffed and licked up the powder, and I watched it run off in the direction of the school.

In any case, I thought to myself, the stuff was not immediately harmful to the cur, and, if it died later, I should doubtless hear about it in the morning. I stood for a little longer enjoying the freshness of the night air and watching the moon go gliding behind a cloud for all the world as if it were ashamed to be seen. I waited watching for its re-appearance, but it seemed determined to remain hidden, and I went inside, locked up, and climbed the stairs to my bedroom, pushing the safe key under Mrs Marven's door as I had promised.

By an ill-chance the dog turned out to be Hennessy's. He was fighting mad when I met him next day.

'Whoever did a thing like that should be skinned alive,' he cried furiously after he told me about the animal being found dead. Apparently it had managed to reach home just in time to die. It was a little difficult for me to understand his attitude, for I distinctly remembered him telling me that the dog was by no means a thoroughbred but some homeless mongrel that he had picked up God knows where.

At first opportunity I went for a walk along the creek which had begun to look more like its old self, though there was still considerably more water than normally. Curiosity prompted me to make my way towards the tree upon which the names 'Eileen' and 'Larry' were carved.

There was too much mud and slush for close approach, but I could make out that only one name remained, and I was reasonably sure that the 'Eileen' had been obliterated with a knife. In any case the letters were no longer legible. I presumed that Larry had rushed there from the concert and, in a frenzy, had symbolically erased the girl's name from his heart.

As I walked further, noting the little geographical alterations the flood had made in the course of the creek, it occurred to me that Larry might have deliberately drowned himself. I had, however, a more pressing problem and began to turn over in my mind the possibility of Mrs Marven being implicated with Helen Speek in the death of the latter's husband. After all, Mrs Marven and Helen were friends and had become more attached to each other in the last few days. If Price had not provided the means to poison Speek perhaps they had come from the hotel landlady. Judging by the fate of Hennessy's mongrel, these means were in her possession, though how on earth she could be so careless to leave her safe open and then ask me to lock up for her, I could not imagine.

She never imagined, of course, that I would be astute enough to look through it. She did not know that I had seen Speek, Helen, and Price together on the night of the blind man's death. She had no reason to distrust me. I suppose she had never dreamed that I would do more than turn the key in the lock and take it up to her when I went to bed.

More than once I had heard her ask people to perform little missions of trust, with a total disregard for their qualifications. Once she had actually asked Rosie, the housemaid, to count the day's receipts for her and lock them in the safe, simply because, as she put it, she felt too comfortable and wished to 'warm her tootsies' at the fire before she went to bed. She gave the girl the key and, when it was returned, asked her in front of us all, how much the money had been. When she was told she said, 'Dear, dear, I'll soon be bankrupt.' The amount the girl had named had sounded to me preposterously small, and I am quite sure that I should have questioned her honesty in the matter.

I found it difficult to believe that this plump, good-natured, and rather vulgar woman who spoke her mind with such disarming frankness could have been party to a cold-blooded crime, but, after consideration, I recalled that in criminal history there had been many instances of foul deeds brought home to the least suspected.

I thought again of the verdict of the coroner's court. It was legally recorded that Speek had committed suicide by shooting himself. Perhaps the poison I believed he had taken might have brought about the same result. If that were proved after an exhumation it would provide quite a pretty tangle. With a grim smile I permitted my thoughts to ramble through the realms of fancy. I saw a judge scratching his wig in perturbation. How was the guilt to be assessed? If A occasioned enough poison to enter B's stomach to bring about B's death, but B shot himself before that auspicious event, was it murder or suicide?

Fancy, of course! for there was to be no exhumation. If Helen and her lover refused to be reasonable and dared me to do my worst, I could not see myself playing the role of an informer, getting no more out of it than the unwelcome publicity and the cold comfort of knowing I had acted in the cause of justice. At the moment I had nothing to lose and everything to gain by my tactics. If Mrs Marven was implicated, so much the better. It would be easier for the three guilty persons to subscribe the thousand pounds of which I had been robbed.

As I walked towards the town I played with the idea of raising my price if I became reasonably sure that the landlady had had any part in the business, but shook my head resolutely. No! I had lost a thousand. It was equitable that I should have a thousand. No more, no less. I wanted to be fair.

At the creek crossing I met Dr Hansen driving home. He stopped his buggy and offered me a lift. He looked very listless and told me he had been up all the previous night.

'I won't object to you taking the reins, Ford,' he said. 'I feel all in.' He shut his eyes and fell asleep, and, noting the drawn, weary face, as I drove to the surgery I thought if ever Eileen and I had a son I would take good care he did not become a country doctor, working his head off for a lot of ignorant and selfish people who, for the most part, I suspected, never paid their bills. No! if the boy wished to be a doctor he should have a decent practice in the city with a fashionable clientele.

Driving into the town, I observed that old Craven, who in addition to being the hall caretaker was also the town bell-ringer and bill poster, had just pasted a showy placard on the side of the police station fence:

### CARLO BOLDINI

I read the name as we were carried past and wondered what it meant. I was soon to learn, for, although I had never heard of him till that moment, Signor Carlo Boldini was to play an important part in my life.

Next day Gallagher, the mail driver, surprised me with the news that Eileen and her father were in Baloola. They had come from the city by train, but the journey had been too much for the sick man and he had remained at a hotel in the railway town to rest up before continuing to his home. Naturally I was a little annoyed that I should receive this news second-hand and felt that both father and daughter had treated me with scant courtesy.

'He's a sick man,' Gallagher said. 'He's coming home to die is Mahoney, poor feller. 'Tis a pity for Miss Eileen.' He shook his head sadly. 'She'll need to get herself a husband soon,' he went on, and I looked up, suddenly suspicious and alarmed.

He noted nothing untoward in my expression, however, and rambled on, 'And her father a poor man!' he said woefully.

'But he must have *something*,' I suggested.

'There'll be nothing but doctor's bills left at that house, Mr Ford,' he replied. 'Oh, a pile of them, I'll be bound, and Doc Hansen's, if he ever sends it, at the bottom as usual.'

He saw that for once I was listening to him and made the most of his opportunity.

'They do say, Mr Ford, that every stick's mortgaged to Garnet Price like everything else round here, and when I say every stick,' he lowered his voice, 'I mean every stick. When the place is sold up, Price'll get the lot and his money back – if he's lucky.'

'What do you mean, if he's lucky?'

'Why, Mr Ford, the place'll never bring what the man's lent on it. He's been mighty generous to Mahoney. Price isn't as hard as some think him, sir. Oh, I know Garnet Price, that I do.' He began to laugh softly.

'I've always thought him a rather violent person,' I ventured.

'Oh, so he is, so he is. Oh, very violent!'

He laughed as if he were saying a funny thing. 'As soon as knock you down as look at you, that's young Price. I wanted a horse once, Mr Ford; needed it bad, and I made Price an offer. He asked more, but I said I couldn't go any higher. He said the horse was worth more, and he'd be what's-its-named if he'd take a penny less. He was very rude indeed. And next day he sent the horse over to my place as a present for the wife. The funny thing is it weren't the old woman's birthday for a full four months.'

He took out his pipe and began to fill it. He was in reminiscent mood and nothing could stop him.

'Why, once when he was a bit of a school kid, Mr Ford, I saw him thrash the life out of another lad – bigger'n him, too. And when he'd blacked his eye and bloodied his nose, what did he do? Picked him up and took him into Sam Cotter's store and bought him a lump of almond rock 's big as his fist, and a bottle o' lemonade into the bargain. That's Garnet Price for you, Mr Ford, for all his rough ways.'

'A regular paragon,' I commented.

'As for that, sir, I don't know,' Gallagher said gravely. 'I never did hear of Price going to any church, but his old man now and then used to be a Methodist.'

I let it pass, and he puffed his pipe and rambled on. 'No, he's got the whip hand with Mahoney, has Garnet, and with the daughter, too, when her father dies, but he'll never use the lash.'

I wished to hear no further eulogy of Price and turned to some business papers in token of dismissal, but the garrulous old fool hadn't done. He stood, puffing his pipe complacently, and went on, inviting questions. 'Nice goings-on at Baloola with this Boldini feller.'

'Boldini? Who's he?'

'Queer fish, all right, Mr Ford. I ain't seen him act, but I see his bills stuck up on Burke's fence. He's a mind reader.'

'Stuff and nonsense,' I retorted. 'What will they believe next?'

'Now *that* I don't know,' Gallagher said, as if he had knowledge of everything else. 'But I do know this, sir. Everybody's talking about him in Baloola. Jim Fenton's got it all set out in the *Banner*.'

He fished the rag from his pocket. Garnet Price, I knew, owned it lock, stock, and barrel, though I can't imagine he made anything out of it, for if ever there was a cheap sheet this was it. Fenton did the whole job from setting the type and working the handpress. A boy delivered the copies. I remember that in an effort to help I had sent Fenton an article once and was surprised when it did not appear. I watched for a few issues to see if he had printed it and then forgot about the thing. When I got home one day Mrs Marven said, 'I see you've been figuring in the *Banner* this week,' but instead of the article I had expected, there was an offensive little three-line paragraph saying I had been in Baloola for a haircut. This was true enough, for we had no barber in our town, but I considered the paragraph impertinent and offensive. I told Fenton so in no measured terms when I next saw him, and he muttered some sort of apology and referred to my article, claiming it had been held over for lack of space and making some vague reference to publishing it later.

I tossed the rag back to Gallagher. 'I suppose Fenton's been paid to print the stuff,' I said, but the old man looked dubious.

'I don't know,' he said. 'I only know this Boldini came

right into the town and told things about people he'd never seen in his life afore. How do you make that out?'

'Fake,' I said, shortly. 'Just another charlatan.'

'There's a lot o' things us don't understand, Mr Ford,' Gallagher said. 'Why, they say there's talk of horseless carriages runnin' about city streets. D'you believe that?'

'Why,' I said, 'that's a definite possibility, of course. But you'll never see it here. Horses will be taking the mail buggy between here and Baloola long after you and I are dead.'

'I do hope so, Mr Ford,' he observed gravely. 'I couldn't afford to lose me job, that I couldn't. Well, I'll be moving. You go and see this Boldini for yourself, Mr Ford. He's sure to pop into the post office with a free ticket.'

He went off unaware of the annoyance I felt at his impertinence in inferring I would bother my head about getting to see this charlatan's performance for nothing.

Mahoney came home the next afternoon, and I called in the evening. Things did not go as I expected. Instead of showing me into the parlour, Eileen took me to the sickroom immediately, as though I were more interested in the old man, and fussed about him so that I scarcely got a chance to speak to her at all, let alone privately.

She had lost some of her healthy bloom, and I felt impatient with this inefficient old man who had permitted his home to fall into the hands of Garnet Price and who was now monopolising the time of his daughter and robbing her of her charm. I sat twiddling my thumbs by the sickbed, listening to Mahoney's platitudes. It was all up with him, I gathered, and his death might be expected in a matter of weeks. The way he dwelt on the subject you'd have thought no one had ever died before.

It was gloomy enough, in all conscience, to have to listen to this without Mahoney persistently whining about what would have become of Eileen if I had not wanted her for a wife. I saw he was hinting about the settlement, and, driven by his promptings during Eileen's temporary absence from the bedchamber, I made some half-hearted reference to the matter. He seized on it with avidity.

Eileen came back into the room at the moment, and he turned to her eagerly.

'My dear,' he said, 'we've just been discussing the marriage settlement Mr Ford had promised. You know, my dear, how ill I am. I shall not be with you long.' (Would the man ever forget it?) 'And how happy it would make me to see you and Harry married before I go. Couldn't we arrange the whole thing now?'

I saw the flush mount on Eileen's cheek.

'But, Mr Mahoney,' I said. 'Miss Eileen has not yet actually consented to be my wife.'

'Not in words, maybe,' he replied, and beckoned his daughter. 'Give me your hand, dear.' He turned his eyes on me. 'And now yours, my boy.'

I had perforce to put mine in his, though it made me shudder, it was so skinny. The next instant, however, he had joined my hand with Eileen's, and I marvelled at its softness. It was the first time I had ever touched her, and I confess that I thrilled to the contact so that I almost forgave the old man his importunities.

'I want you both to promise me that you will marry very soon so that I may live to see you joined together,' Mahoney said.

I felt unutterably foolish standing there clasping Eileen's hand across the bed of this wretched old man, but what could I do? I knew that the moment the thing was arranged he would harp on about the settlement, yet I could not rudely break away and suggest delay. Eileen was apparently affected by the situation and the pleading of her father, for there were tears in her eyes although she did not look at me.

She nodded her head. 'If you wish it, father,' she said so softly that I could barely hear her.

He smiled up at her.

'As soon as Harry wishes?' he asked and as she nodded again he turned to me.

'Shall we say the twenty-third – that is, three weeks from today?' he asked, and I knew he must have had the details planned in his mind before I called.

'That will give us plenty of time to arrange everything,' he urged as I hesitated.

I nodded, too annoyed at the high-handed way the matter had been managed to speak. He let his skeleton hand drop and shut his eyes.

'Now I am happy,' he sighed quietly, and Eileen withdrew her hand from mine and began rearranging his pillows.

'You'd better go to sleep, Dad,' she said, 'You've had a heavy day.'

'Yes,' he agreed weakly. 'I'd better sleep.' He looked at me. 'Do you mind, my boy?'

I was so angered that I felt as far as I was concerned he could sleep forever, but my breeding came to the surface as usual and I hastily rose and apologised for staying and tiring him and bade him good night. Eileen accompanied me to the door. She did not speak, and, for the life of me, with all my social training and experience I was as tongue-tied in her presence that night as the veriest bumpkin. We stood silently on the doorstep.

'Well,' I blurted out at last. 'That's that.'

'Yes,' she said.

'The – the twenty-third, wasn't it?'

'Yes.'

She said nothing further and I made a half movement toward her, but she stepped back quickly, eluding my embrace.

'I think I hear father calling,' she said in embarrassment. 'Good night.' She stepped inside and practically shut the door in my face.

Altogether, I reflected as I walked home, an unsatisfactory evening. I had not only been stampeded into the settlement, but Eileen had by no means shown the enthusiasm I felt I was entitled to expect, nor even any real appreciation of my generosity. The evening, however, had at least emphasised one thing – the necessity for speedily making Helen Speek and her paramour toe the mark.

I was rather surprised to find Garnet Price waiting for me as I closed the office at luncheon time next day. With an air of friendliness he took my arm and, by its pressure, compelled me to walk more slowly than I would have chosen. My expression must have shown him that I resented his familiarity as an impertinence after the way he had treated me within the hearing of Helen Speek. I anticipated an apology, but none was forthcoming. Anyone would have thought, as we strolled together arm in arm, that we were on the best of terms.

'Look here, Ford,' he began, 'I wanted to have a quiet talk with you. I'm a bit worried. It isn't nice to hear a chap in your position talking like you did the other night. You must be in a hell of a hole, and I'm ready to help you; but it's got to be in a straightforward way.'

I said nothing, for I was suspicious of his affability and wondered about his motive.

'Now,' he went on, 'if you want money I'll lend it to you.'

'And the security?' I asked.

'Oh,' he replied lightly, 'I don't know your resources, of course; but if you've nothing tangible we can fix it up some way or another – promissory notes, for instance.'

So that was it!

Very cunning, I thought. But I couldn't see myself stepping into such an obvious trap – tying myself up to a man like Price. Supposing I signed his ridiculous notes, and, standing on my rights and as a price for my silence, I didn't redeem them on the due dates, what would be the position? He might insist on payment, and if I told what I knew he would claim that I had done so because I owed him money and was trying to evade my just debts. Just debts, indeed!

He noted my hesitation. 'Of course, Ford,' he said gently,

'they could be long-term notes and the interest rate would be very modest.'

We were nearing the hotel. I stopped, and, disengaging my arm, turned on him. 'You would actually expect me to repay your notes?'

'Why,' he said, in surprise, 'of course.'

'You poor fool,' I said and saw his tanned face flush. 'What do you take me for? You're frightened out of your wits and you come to me with this absurd proposition.'

I believe he only controlled himself with an effort, for Mrs Marven had stepped out of the hotel on to the verandah and was watching us.

'Listen,' he said tensely, 'I've never been afraid of anyone in my life. Remember that. I've spoken to you today to give you a chance to regain your self-respect.'

'*You* talk of self-respect!' I said bitterly. 'With Speek hardly cold in his grave!'

He gave me a queer look.

'I don't quite understand what's got into you, Ford,' he said, 'but I tell you this. There are many things you don't know. Don't rush into this terrible thing.'

'I know what I saw, Price,' I retorted, 'and I know what was done on the night Speek died. I'll sign nothing and I stand by my offer to sell my shares to you and Helen Speek or to one or the other of you, I don't mind which; and you'd better make up your minds to buy without further delay.'

'You're the fool, Ford,' he said more quietly than I had ever heard him speak. 'What Helen does is her own affair, but I tell you now, as far as I am concerned, you're a dirty, low skunk, and you can go to the devil. And remember, when you get there, the road was of your own choosing. Let's go to lunch.'

He turned abruptly, and the next moment was greeting Mrs Marven, who was engrossed in a handbill advertising the coming of Signor Carlo Boldini, 'The Master Mind-Reader'. She offered the paper to Price, who glanced through it, smiling.

'Why, Ford,' he said with a laugh, 'if the great Boldini were here now I wonder what he'd read in our minds.'

'I know,' Mrs Marven cried, 'and I'm no Boldini.'

I looked at her in astonishment, and Price raised his eyebrows quizzically.

'No?' he grinned. 'Not really?'

'Yes,' she said, 'you're wondering whether there's a pigeon pie for lunch. Well, there is.'

'What a woman!' Price shouted. 'Madam, my arm.'

Laughing, she took it and lifted her skirt delicately. With mock ceremony they preceded me to the dining room, Mrs Marven calling over her shoulder, 'So sorry, Sir Harry, I have no partner for you. Lady Lah-dee-dah has sent an apology.'

'Dear, dear!' said Garnet Price in an affected voice, 'Washing day, I presume?'

They laughed together foolishly, but, as I followed, I was convinced that Price was putting up the bluff of his life, for Helen Speek had called at the post office that morning and, while inquiring for letters, had whispered me an invitation to call and see her that night at ten o'clock.

Mrs Marven was very merry during luncheon. With Price and the sheepish bank clerk, Teecher, and one or two others who dropped in, she kept up a continuous flow of inanities which, with all the things I had on my mind, almost drove me crazy.

Price entertained the company with his everlasting reminiscences of the circus that had once planted itself on his father's property, telling how he had been head over heels in love with a tightrope dancer till one night he had peeped into her dressing tent and seen her in the act of retiring, her beautiful blonde wig hanging on a peg and her own hair drooping in two unbeautiful braids over her ears. This bit of vulgarity raised roars of laughter, and Mrs Marven told him, when he complained that romance had gone from life at that moment, that it served him jolly well right.

How strange, I thought, that Price could talk in this flippant manner at such a time. How curious that Mrs

Marven should show no sign of anxiety. They were either very clever or very callous. Price, I considered, might be both, but I still could not bring myself to believe that Mrs Marven was hard-hearted.

And then I suddenly recollected something I had read about the peculiar indifference of poisoners to the fate of their victims. There was one, I recalled, who had poisoned the maid at an inn because her thick ankles offended his sense of the aesthetic. Was it not also a fact that even the most brutal murderers were sometimes deeply attached to children and dumb animals?

I had once had a rather interesting talk with Dr Hansen – many months before Speek died – and it came back to me vividly. He had especially mentioned poison as a woman's weapon. He had told me that a Roman emperor had publicly executed no less than one hundred and seventy wives on the one day and en masse, all for poisoning their husbands; and that an Italian woman in the seventeenth century confessed to poisoning six hundred people.

I looked about me at the laughing faces and wondered whether they'd be smacking their lips over Mrs Marven's pigeon pie if they knew what was in the parchment envelope hidden in her safe.

Mrs Marven, it seemed, had made her pie in a dish lined with highly seasoned veal forcemeat with slices of bacon and veal shortbread. There were also a few tiny mushrooms and the veal gravy added flavour. As she explained this, it occurred to me that in living at the hotel I really took my life in my hands. One day, perhaps – I brushed the hideous thought away. After all, she would hardly wish to poison all her guests.

But the idea persisted. All these little culinary embellishments that she brought to her dishes. Might it not be possible to serve me with something that was not given to those eating at the same table? We would all have partaken of the same pie, yet they would live, and I would die, and it would all be very mysterious, just as Speek's death was mysterious. The idea was not a nice one to contemplate and so upset me for the moment that I carefully pushed on one side of my plate a couple of button mushrooms, and ate the rest of my pigeon pie without relish.

Talk naturally turned to the coming performance of Signor Carlo Boldini, for visits by professional entertainers were few and far between. The Bellringers and one or two standard shows came to our town now and again, but, for the most part, we had to rely on Hennessy's amusing little efforts.

'If Boldini reads what's in my mind,' Price said with a laugh and a glance at me, 'he might have me arrested.'

The bank clerk gave it as his opinion that mind-reading was all nonsense, and for once I agreed with him.

'Oh, I don't know,' Mrs Marven said. 'I think it can be done. Why, only last night old Mr Plank came into the bar and said to me, "Now Mrs M., I know what you're thinking. You're thinking I'm going to ask for more credit. And, believe it or not, so I was."' We all smiled and she went on, 'But I don't say I hold with mind-reading. It would be a terrible thing if we all knew each other's thoughts.' She had spoken in an unusually serious tone, and there was a momentary silence broken by Price's explosive laugh.

'You're right, Mrs Marven,' he cried. 'You're not only a beautiful woman, you're a wise one, a wonderful cook, and you're a widow, ma'am, and, if you knew what everybody here was thinking about you at this moment your blushes would set the curtains afire.'

After all, I suppose, these conversational vulgarities might be all right when addressed to one of Mrs Marven's station and calling, but I was nauseated at the innuendo and glad to think that before long I would be taking my wife away from this atmosphere to a town where we could establish our own home and live our lives with a proper regard for social values.

After lunch, as we sat smoking on the front verandah, a little man on the roadway bade us a polite good day as he passed. We gazed after him speculatively, for any stranger in the town excited comment, and Price said, 'Don't remember him.'

Mrs Marven joined us at the moment, and Price gesticulated with his cigar.

'Who's your friend?' he asked.

Mrs Marven looked toward the little man who was now turning in at Constable Burke's gate.

'I don't know his name,' she said, 'but he's boarding with Luke Barmby.' She shook her head sadly. 'Poor man,' she added.

'Poor man is right,' Garnet Price agreed.

Haggart, the draper, called at the post office and bought a money order. I was no longer interested in the man with his silly moustache and air of braggadocio, but, despite our previous conversation, or perhaps because of it, he chose to take me into his confidence.

'I'm sending for a present,' he said with a disgusting wink. 'Something special.' He lowered his voice. 'Not for you-know-who. No, sir. No more in that quarter for Henery D. Haggart, Esquire – not with a man like Garnet Price hanging around.' He had the effrontery to lean across the counter and poke me with his finger as he leered, 'You and I know, Mr Ford, there's as good fish in the sea as ever came out of it.'

'I suppose you're right,' I agreed coldly as I handed him the money order, and noticed that Luke Barmby's new boarder had come silently into the office and was standing at Haggart's elbow and just behind him. He was a man of no more than five feet two and of indefinite age, sparely built, and with shrewd blue eyes that darted hither and thither, taking in everything not only while he listened but while he spoke, as if he were engaged in a mental inventory.

'Good afternoon, sir,' he said, and made Haggart jump so that he dropped the addressed envelope he was holding. The newcomer, with a hasty apology, bent to retrieve it, and, almost before his hand reached it, he uttered an exclamation of pain and pressed his other hand to his hip and remained in the stooped positon so long I thought he must be suffering seriously.

'Lumbago,' he explained, and gradually straightened up. 'Gets me like that suddenly. Your letter, sir.' He handed Haggart the envelope, and the draper took it and departed.

'Nasty thing, lumbago,' the little man said. 'Still, we mustn't grumble. Think of all the trouble in the world. People crippled, and deaf and dumb and blind.' He paused as if something had just come into his mind. 'Blind,' he repeated, shaking his head mournfully. 'I wouldn't like to be blind. Anything but that. Not knowing what was going on around you, guessing at who you were speaking to. No, I wouldn't like that.' He fumbled in his pocket and produced a wallet. 'Six two-penny stamps, please.'

As he took them and stowed them carefully away he said, 'No, I wouldn't like to be blind. Terrible thing. No wonder that poor fellow Speek poisoned himself the other day.'

'Speek shot himself,' I said, but the carelessly spoken words had given me quite a shock.

'Oh, was that it? I heard he'd done himself in.' He regarded me with his piercing eyes. 'Didn't I see you outside the hotel a while back, sir?' he asked.

'Possibly,' I said. 'I live there.'

'I should have put up at the Royal,' he told me, 'but I was recommended to Barmby's. I'm afraid that Mr Barmby doesn't think highly of the landlady.' He gave me a knowing look, but I was not to be drawn.

'Mrs Marven is a very respectable woman,' I volunteered.

'Marven!' He repeated the name. '*Marven*! Not the wife of Bill Marven – little chap about my size?'

'On the contrary,' I said coldly, 'Mr Marven weighed seventeen stone, his first name was James, and his wife has been a widow for six years.' I had spoken tersely, hoping to stop further questioning, but he was in no way abashed.

'Well,' he said, 'if it had been old Bill I'd have hopped over to the pub pronto – recommendation or no recommendation.'

I was to see more of the little man that day. A telegram came in with porterage paid, which meant that someone had to ride to a farm a few miles out of town. It was a pleasant late afternoon and I decided to earn the money myself. I obtained a horse from Mrs Marven's stable.

The way led past the dreary site where Speek lay buried and, as I rode by, I saw a horse tethered at the cemetery gate and a man moving slowly among the graves. He held a book of some sort in his hand and intermittently paused and, as far as I could see, made an entry. The day was darkening, but I was quite sure I recognised Luke Barmby's new boarder.

CHAPTER 6

It turned out a glorious night and, at a circumspect hour, I again called upon my fiancée and her father. The old man had had his evening meal and was sleeping, thank heaven, and, although I could not claim Eileen was overjoyed to see me, she at least gave me the opportunity to talk to her alone. We sat in opposite chairs in the parlour across the hallway from the sick chamber, the door discreetly ajar. It was very evident that there was something on her mind and she was not long in coming to the point.

'I wanted to tell you something, Mr Ford,' she said hesitantly, 'something you have got to know before we're married.'

'You may be sure you may speak in confidence, Eileen,' I said, and I was relieved to find that she accepted my free use of her name as if it were the most natural thing in the world.

'It – it concerns Larry Ward,' she said. She gave me a fleeting glance and doubtless saw the quick stiffening of my jaw, for she turned away instantly.

'Larry?' I tried to sound indifferent. I had hoped we had heard the last of him.

She said softly, 'Larry and I should have been married.'

Suspicion thrust deeply into my heart at her words as it had the day I saw those names carved on the bole of the tree. Uneasily I recalled old Gallagher's words, 'She'll be needing a husband soon.' I waited till I could properly control my voice.

'I don't quite understand,' I said. 'I guessed you were friends – '

'We were more than friends, Mr Ford,' she interrupted, and I felt a sinking in my heart. 'The day before I went away he asked me to marry him. I was worried about Father. I knew how desperately ill he was, and I knew he wouldn't like the idea of Larry and me marrying. You know, Mr Ford, the poor boy had nothing; he was not the sort to save.'

'I know,' I said. 'He told me.'

'He told you?'

'He said that he had nothing – that a man should have money and position, some solidity before he married. He told me he was leaving town.'

'He told you that?' She seemed surprised. 'It doesn't sound like Larry. When did he tell you, Mr Ford?'

'The day he disappeared,' I informed her. 'He came and saw Hennessy and me just after his trouble with Speek.'

Her face flushed a little, and she turned her head away as she said, 'I've heard about that, but I can't believe that Larry would strike a blind man.'

'Yet he did,' I said. 'He confessed. He was very frank about it.'

'Oh,' she cried, 'then something terrible must have been said.'

I felt it was no use sparing her further. Sooner or later she must know. 'Speek had found Larry with his wife.'

'Oh, it's preposterous,' she cried indignantly. 'It's all so – so *silly*.'

How curious, I thought, that she should have used Larry's own words.

'Helen Speek is a very handsome woman,' I said.

'But,' she cried, 'Helen is so much older. Why, Larry's only a boy. Oh, I can't – I'll never believe it.'

'Eileen,' I said kindly, 'I am older than you. I am a man of the world. I know how these things happen. Larry was young, impetuous. Temptation was thrust in his way. He was left

alone with an attractive, experienced woman. He had acciden-
tally knocked down Luke Barmby's child and had had a drink
or two. He wasn't himself.'

'Please!' she put out her hand to stop me.

'Believe me, my dear,' I said. 'I do not want to hurt you.'

'I know,' she said weakly. 'You have been very good. I do
appreciate it, but – I like to think of Larry as I knew him. You
see, Mr Ford, I wouldn't say yes the afternoon he asked me to
marry him, though I had already said it in my heart. It didn't
seem the time to think of my own happiness when Father had
just had such terrible news. I promised Larry faithfully I
would write to him. I meant to try and persuade Father to like
Larry so that he would give his consent, but he was so sick
and wretched. I wrote to Larry as I had promised and I
couldn't bear to keep him waiting for my answer till I came
back from the city. I told him I would marry him. He must
have got the letter the day those dreadful things happened.'

'He did,' I told her. 'I remember quite well.'

'That's why I can't believe them,' she went on. 'I'd told
him I – I loved him, and yet – ' She broke off, tears in her eyes.

'Eileen, my dear,' I said, seating myself beside her and taking her hand, 'please don't needlessly distress yourself. The
poor boy is dead, and the past cannot be recalled. Let us think
of the future.'

She did not withdraw her hand. She said, 'You're right, of
course. I'll try and forget it all. But I couldn't go on without
telling you.'

'My dear,' I said, 'I think all the more of you for doing so.
Now, come, smile.'

I had the satisfaction of seeing her lips part and was about
to put my arm about her when Mahoney called from the
room opposite. She turned to the door at once.

'Father wants me.'

In a moment, and much to my chagrin, she had gone, but
returned immediately to say Mahoney would like to see me.
Annoyed that our tête-à-tête had been so inopportunely

interrupted, I cannot say I greeted him cheerfully. Nevertheless, he chose to be quite jolly.

'How are you, my boy?' he asked as Eileen left us. 'It's nice to see you again. I'm glad you've come round tonight. Daley, the lawyer from Baloola, is coming over on Wednesday to fix things up for me. Can't delay too long, you know.' He smiled wanly. 'I thought it might be a good opportunity to have the marriage settlement drawn up at the same time.'

Wednesday was not far off and I was confident my business with Helen would be wound up by then. Eileen, I felt, was thawing, and that had heartened me. I said it was all the same to me, and just then there was a knock upon the front door and in a few moments Eileen ushered in Polly and Agatha Garner. The little women were slightly embarrassed by my presence. They explained that they had merely called to enquire about Mahoney's health and to ask if they could be of any assistance and said that they wouldn't stay; but the sick man insisted that they sit down and talk to him.

They did so, and he said fatuously, 'As a matter of fact, Miss Polly and Miss Agatha, I think Eileen and this young man here will be very glad to have you watch over me for a while so that they may be alone together.'

He winked at them, and as they looked their astonishment, Eileen said, 'Oh, Father!'

Mahoney nodded sagely. 'You might as well know now as later,' he said. 'These two young people have decided to get married.'

'*No!*' Polly Garner uttered the exclamation and jumped up, overturning a vase from a table by the bedside.

'Ah, you are surprised,' the old man said as I hastened to help Eileen restore the flowers.

'Surprised!' Polly exclaimed hesitating. 'Oh, yes!'

Agatha said, 'It's such a shock. We had no idea.' She put her arm about Eileen and said, 'I do hope you'll be happy, dear.'

'I think it's a splendid match,' Mahoney said complacently.

The women twittered about Eileen and drew her from the room, saying good-bye to her father. He gazed after them.

'Poor old things,' he said. 'It must be pretty hard, Harry, for a woman to go through life without a husband or child. I think we're too prone to condemn frailty in women. Maidenly virtue is beyond price, of course, but there are times – ' He broke off, then continued, 'You must excuse me, my boy, but, since I learned what is before me, I've begun to see many things in a different light.'

As I walked to keep my appointment with Helen Speek I wondered whether the old man's words had any significance.

Punctually at ten I was at Mrs Speek's gate and glanced warily about me. I wanted to be sure I was not seen. But there were no lights in any of the houses round about, and I walked up the long gravelled path on which I had skinned my wrist so painfully. Though the thing was practically healed, the recollection of Price's behaviour hardened me in my resolve as I knocked gently on the side door. It was opened immediately by Helen.

'Good evening, Mrs Speek.'

She did not return my greeting and closed the door quickly after I had entered. I waited for her invitation to be seated. Instead she said, 'There is no reason to prolong this interview, Mr Ford. I had expected to give you something tonight, but there are bank formalities, it seems. I know very little about these things, but Mr Teecher has promised me that something can be arranged tomorrow. Half at least.'

I was disappointed, but I said, 'All right. You must pay me in notes, of course, and please have them in small denominations. Fivers and tenners will do. I do not want a cheque.'

'I'll arrange that,' she promised.

'Very well,' I said. 'You will please parcel the notes up and address them to some fictitious person and bring them to me at the post office no later than tomorrow, as if you were registering a package. Do you understand? I do not care to be seen calling upon you.'

She said briefly that she understood.

'And the other half, I suppose, will be paid by Price?'

An angry frown creased her brow. 'I have told you he has nothing to do with this,' she said.

I laughed. 'Of course not,' I said. 'Nevertheless,' I added, pointedly repeating Price's words, 'what concerns you concerns him. Where is the estimable Mr Price?'

'I don't know,' she said. 'I heard he had gone to Baloola.'

'Well,' I said, 'You would know better than I.' She changed colour at that, and I continued. 'I will not be content with half, Mrs Speek; be assured of that. The shares are worth the full thousand. The whole must be paid before Wednesday.'

Her eyes regarded me speculatively. 'What sort of a man are you, Mr Ford?' she asked.

I returned her stare. 'What sort of a woman are *you*, Mrs Speek?'

She turned with an impatient gesture and opened the door.

'Good night,' she said, dismissing me abruptly. I picked up my hat from Timothy Speek's big easy chair. The contempt in her voice had nettled me. I looked down at the little table. 'Dear, dear,' I said, 'no chocolates?'

The colour rushed to her face and tears of mortification started in her eyes, while she bit her lip to prevent herself uttering the words that trembled there. She opened the door wider and shut it swiftly after I went out.

Helen Speek had not appeared up to the time I went to lunch next day, and I saw nothing of Garnet Price. Luke Barmby's new boarder turned up enquiring for mail, and I learned that his name was Butters. One of his letters was enclosed in a flamboyant envelope, the words 'Carlo Boldini, the Master Mind' flourished along its upper edge in scarlet with black initials. There had been many similar in the morning mail from Baloola, and I supposed the Master Mind was publicising his coming visit.

Butters looked at the envelope curiously. 'Boldini?' he said raising his eyebrows. 'There's a man for you, Mr Ford.' He had, I supposed, learned my name from the Barmbys. 'Did me a great turn once, did Mr Boldini.'

'Indeed,' I said and saw I was in for his story whether I wished it or not.

'Yes, sir,' he said. 'When my old man died we couldn't locate the will. Then along came this Boldini. Well, Mr Ford, being in mourning, it wasn't proper for me to go to his public performance, so I went to see him privately and he was very decent. He was so.'

He paused as if mentally reconstructing the scene. 'He told me to bring him something my father had owned, so I took him a pen with which he used to write his letters. I thought maybe it was the very pen with which he'd signed his will. I gave it to Boldini, and he held it in his hand so tight that it broke in two, and he shut his eyes and trembled till I thought he was gong into a fit. And then he told me where to search, and it was such an unlikely place that I almost laughed. But I went home and looked, and there, sure enough, was the will.'

'Very interesting,' I said. 'Probably a lucky guess.'

He pursed his lips. 'No, I don't think so, Mr Ford. I've heard of so many strange things he's done since then.'

'And,' I asked, smiling, 'I suppose he charged you some little fee?'

'No,' he replied. 'When he told me where to look for the will, of course I didn't have any faith in him, but I offered him some small sum for his trouble. But he wouldn't hear of it.'

'But after you found the will,' I suggested, 'he surely expected some recompense.'

He regarded me with unsmiling eyes. 'No, sir,' he said. 'Wouldn't take a penny. Said it was a pleasure.'

'It sounds most extraordinary,' I said. 'I daresay there's some logical explanation.'

'Maybe,' he said. 'I'm not clever at these things. It all seems very wonderful to me. Of course, I'm not saying that *all* he does is important as it was in my case, but it's entertaining – such as guessing a man's second name. D'you ever consider what a few people know their friends' second names, Mr Ford? But Boldini guesses 'em as if he'd christened 'em himself.'

'Guesses, I suppose, is right,' I suggested. 'After all, there are so many common combinations of names. He wouldn't find it so easy with mine, I'm afraid. It begins with an X.'

'X?' he queried. 'I've never heard of a name beginning with X. I didn't think you could begin a name with X. However would you spell it?'

'Xavier,' I told him and spelled it out.

'Good Lord!' he said. 'That is a one. Rum way of spelling it, too, in my opinion. No, I rather think you'd have this Boldini stonkered there, sir. D'you mind if I sit down and read my letters?'

I told him to make himself at home, and he studied his mail while I attended to various callers, gossiping a little with this one and that, listening to their domestic troubles and their unimportant comings and goings. I found them singularly boring on this morning, when, every moment, I expected Helen Speek to come in with her packet of notes. Butters sat on, smiling, faintly amused at the bits of gossip, putting in a word here and there in a friendly way, but at length he got up and came over and to my surprise offered his hand.

'I have to move on,' he explained. 'I expected to be in town longer, but I've just had news that makes it imperative for me to go. I suppose Mrs Barmby won't like it. I told her I'd be here a week at least.' He thanked me politely for my courtesy and left.

Mrs Marven had a small private office at one end of the bar in which she could entertain any special friend who might pop in and at the same time keep an eye on her customers. It had a door leading into what we knew as the second dining-room, where labourers, hawkers, and a few of the poorer farmers ate at half the price charged in the first dining room, though, quite unfairly, I thought, the food was the same as that served to her better class patrons. Another door, almost adjoining the entrance to the parlour, led into the laneway to the stables.

Just before lunch I recalled that I had some instruction or other to give to the ostler, and, returning from this mission and contrary to my usual custom, I entered the hotel by the side door. As I stepped in quietly, I heard Mrs Marven's voice from the parlour. She sounded excited and a little angry.

'You must not,' she was saying. 'You *dare* not.'

I heard someone crying and then, as she spoke, recognised Helen Speek's voice.

'I can't go on. He thinks it's true. I know he does. I don't even know where he is.'

'But, Helen, if you tell Burke everything, you will ruin us all. Think of Garnet.'

'I am thinking of him. He is dragging himself more and more into this.'

'Well, think of me, then. I can't allow you to do this. You mustn't, do you hear?'

I had never heard Mrs Marven use this tone before and listened intently, but at that moment, as bad luck would have it, someone came into the public bar and knocked loudly on the counter. I heard the landlady say, 'Pull yourself together, Helen,' and Helen's rejoinder, 'I can't, Marvie. I'm frightened.'

I waited for a moment. I could hear Helen snivelling and I guessed she was drying her eyes. I stepped back quickly into the laneway, walked quietly to the front entrance, entered the hotel in the regular way, and, stopping at the small side bar, called for my usual sherry.

Mrs Marven served me, but she was obviously upset. She excused herself after a moment's conversation, saying Helen was not very well, and, as I stood sipping my drink, I saw her go to the safe and open it. To my astonishment and alarm she brought out the parchment envelope the contents of which poor Hennessy's dog had already sampled. She drew from it a smaller packet, some of the contents of which she emptied into a tumbler. She put the packet into the parchment envelope again and returned it to the safe, which she locked.

As I lingered, pretending to drink, I watched her fill the tumbler with some liquid or other and carry it into the little parlour. I heard her say to Helen in a firm commanding voice, 'You'd better drink this, and no more nonsense.'

Just then old Plank came surging through the door of the public bar. 'Are you there, Mrs Marven?' he bellowed.

As she emerged, I quickly strode through the swing doors behind me and into the hallway beyond, then sped through the empty second dining-room to the door of the little private parlour. Helen had the glass in her hand and it was already halfway to her lips. I snatched it from her, threw the contents into the fireplace behind me, and gave her back the glass. It was all done on the spur of the moment and in a flash.

I heard old Plank roaring some vulgarity to Mrs Marven, and I whispered, 'Don't be a fool.' I remember Helen's eyes, wide with astonishment, and then I turned and ran swiftly through the dining room to the stairs and up to my room.

I was trembling when I got there. I wondered what it all meant. I thought of Hennessy's poisoned dog and how it had had time to reach home before it died. Most of all I thought that I had to protect Helen – at least until she'd brought me my money.

It was some time before I could pull myself together sufficiently to go down to luncheon. Helen, Mrs Marven explained, had a bad headache and had gone home to lie down. She hardly spoke during the meal, which was unusual for her, and I noticed that she scarcely touched any food. I, myself, as a matter of fact, had very little appetite and felt almost sick when Teecher, the bank fellow, asked for a second helping of some dish or other. There was still no sign of Price.

As the afternoon wore on and Helen failed to appear, I became more and more exasperated, and, by the time the office clock showed the hour of five, it was small wonder that my nerves were on edge. I had grown apprehensive, too, and it was with a sigh of relief that I saw her enter at long last, but my heart stopped a beat when I observed immediately behind her the bulky figure and bovine features of Burke, the constable.

They came forward together, and Burke said with clumsy courtesy, 'After you, Mrs Speek.'

She gave him a half smile and handed me a small package. I would have preferred our little business transacted in private, but my fleeting irritation and suspicion of Burke was soon dissipated by a second glance at his heavy, unintelligent face. Here was the typical country policeman, with courage no doubt, and a certain doggedness, but very little wit – a man whose very mediocrity would be his undoing and who would linger for years, unpromoted, in this Godforsaken hole.

Helen said, 'Would you register this, please?'

As I took the package, my hands trembled. I thought of Price's words, 'That's the way to make money, my boy,' and the recollection steadied me. I made a pretence of entering the details of the package in my records and told her that the postage would be sevenpence. She lifted her eyebrows at this information, somewhat surprised at my thoroughness, but opened her purse and handed me the money without comment.

'I hope you are quite recovered, Mrs Speek,' I said as I gathered the coins.

'Oh, yes, yes, quite; thank you.'

She was gone, and Burke, who had been staring away from us, pretending to examine a map on the wall in order not to hear Helen's conversation, and determined, I suppose, poor fellow, to have us believe he was a gentleman, said heavily, 'I didn't know she'd been ill.'

I smiled knowingly and shrugged my shoulders. 'Some call it ill,' I said.

He stared dully and I made a motion with my fingers as if lifting a glass to my lips.

'Oh,' he said when at last my meaning penetrated to his

brain. 'I didn't know. I've heard lots about her, but I never heard that.'

'Mum's the word,' I said.

'Of course,' he said hastily. 'Poor woman!'

I felt a little sorry for Helen Speek but, after all, one had to protect oneself, and at the back of my mind the thought persisted that at some time it might be her word against mine. I flattered myself that my reputation would not suffer in comparison. I sincerely hoped, however, that she would not be indiscreet, but would pay the balance for the shares promptly, and free us both from the little awkwardnesses which were bound to temper our association until the whole affair had been settled and done with and we could resume our normal lives.

The constable handed me a bulky official document for registration.

'That's the last of poor Larry Ward as far as I'm concerned,' he volunteered, and I gathered that the document was his report on the lad's disappearance. 'It's a mercy in a way that the boy had no relatives, though, if he had, they'd not be fighting over his will, supposing he'd left one, which I don't think he did, for death was far from his mind. He didn't have a feather to fly with, Mr Ford – no more than he stood up in. If we'd found the body, we'd have had to put it in a pauper's grave.'

I think I showed how shocked I was at his words, although naturally I was well aware of Larry's poverty.

'Oh, no, Mr Burke,' I protested and I was quite sincere when I added, 'I am sure his friends would have seen that didn't happen.' Hennessy, I knew, would have borne the major part of any expense, and I would have been perfectly agreeable to donating any sum within reason.

'Well,' the constable said as he turned to leave, 'that's the end of that bit of excitement. It isn't often that anything happens here for the law to get a grip on.'

After all, I mused when he had gone, life had its funny side.

As I picked up Helen's package I chuckled at the thought of Burke being an innocent spectator of our little drama.

My spirits rose next day. Helen produced the balance of the thousand pounds and completed our share deal; Price was still happily out of the way, and I wondered whether he had abandoned his mistress; Eileen's attitude towards me, if it did not indicate a warm attachment, was at least friendly, and I had no doubt whatever it would gradually ripen into tenderness. I had astutely recovered my financial position, and I signed the marriage settlement with a light heart after carefully scrutinising the document and assuring myself that I was protected in the event of my wife's decease.

Naturally, I avoided any transaction which might have awakened the curiosity of the fellow Teecher. There was only one bank in the town, and I made careful and intricate arrangements in other directions for the safe bestowal of the money Helen had paid me, but in such a way that it came to my credit in the local bank eventually, although the source from which I had received it was, of course, unknown. Moreover, to be doubly sure, I carefully filled in the transfer form on the back of the share scrip, but before I sent it to Helen Speek I called on Hennessy and asked him to witness the signature.

'I sold some scrip,' I said casually. 'Not much profit in it, I'm afraid.' Hennessy was not a practical businessman and had an incredible disinterest in other people's affairs. He signed without comment and with hardly a glance at the document, and I changed the subject immediately, but I felt I had registered the transaction in his mind as quite open and above board.

News of my engagement to Eileen became generally known, and I was congratulated by many, but the notice that I had carefully prepared and sent to the Baloola *Banner*, with some biographical reference to my mother's family and my father's distinguished pioneering service, was distorted out of all recognition. Indeed, hardly more than the bare facts were recorded, although there was plenty of adulation of Eileen and reference to her great popularity. I was dismissed as 'the lucky man' and 'the town postmaster'. Fenton, of course, had never forgiven me for what I had said about his rag.

Mrs Marven, to my surprise, was only lukewarm in her congratulations, and I began to speculate whether she suspected me of interfering with the drink she had prepared for Helen, who, as far as I could see, had not been at the hotel since the incident. I asked after her one evening.

'We haven't seen much of Mrs Speek,' I said lightly. 'Is she still unwell?'

'I haven't the slightest idea,' Mrs Marven replied, and, rising, abruptly left the room. Even the bank clerk lifted his eyebrows.

'These women,' I said and turned again to my book. He nodded but looked puzzled.

Mahoney, considering his ill-health, was in splendid spirits and threw off his graveyard gloom. The day the settlement was signed he suggested that Eileen and I should celebrate. She protested, but he explained that he'd arranged everything. Polly Garner was to come in and look after him, and my fiancée and I were to go to the local hall and see the performance of Signor Carlo Boldini. Mahoney had even bought the tickets. Considering what I had done, I thought it was up to him.

For all his publicity, it was by no means a large audience that greeted Boldini at his first show. Our chairs had been reserved for us, so I called on Eileen about twenty to eight and had a chat with her father, timing our arrival at the hall for a few minutes before the entertainment was scheduled to begin.

I had dressed with great care and with a natural anxiety to make a good impression, as it was to be my first public appearance with my fiancée, and I looked forward to it with pleasurable anticipation. I had more than my share of good looks, I told myself as I looked into my mirror, and, moreover, I had an air that might have been fairly described as patrician. We would make a handsome couple. I was surprised to find that Eileen wore no shawl and carried no fan, but smiled to myself as I thought of the pleasant little lessons in etiquette I would have to give her. I felt sure she would prove an apt pupil under my gentle guidance, and for the moment I was quite ready to forgive any social slips.

I had expected, naturally, that we would be ushered to our places. As most of the best people would be seated, I anticipated a little personal triumph as we made our way to the front. However, it was not to be. The young person who did the ushering had, in addition, to perform on the piano and was already sitting before it when we handed in our tickets. We had therefore, much to my annoyance, to make our own way up the aisle and find the chairs which had been allotted to us.

Eileen, instead of standing discreetly behind me until I had located the numbers, irritated me further by finding them for herself and calling in an unnecessarily loud voice, 'Here they are.' I was further disappointed upon looking about me after we were seated to see none of the people I had expected to be present. The Cotters were absent, and there was no sign of Dr Hansen, Mrs Marven, Helen Speek, or Garnet Price. I was, however, able to bow to Hennessy and his wife, who had seats near us.

After the overture, crudely played from the floor of the hall, the curtain went up in a series of jerks, the young person at the piano struck a few loud chords, and Signor Boldini came on. I should say, rather, he sailed on, in ill-fitting evening dress, his head well in front of his ample body, his hand raised and extended before him, already modestly quelling the none too vociferous applause that greeted his appearance.

He was a large man, and the broad, red cummerbund he wore accentuated his plumpness. His hair was black and oily, and his large moustache curled up belligerently. A picturesque mountebank if ever there was, I reflected, and sat back, prepared to be somewhat bored, but nevertheless faintly amused at the eager anticipation already registered upon the features of my fiancée.

I had scarcely made my mental estimate of the fellow when he surprised me by saying, 'Ladies and gentlemens, some of you 'raps are telling to yourself thees man iss a beeg sham. He iss a spoof! A beeg fake!' He looked down directly at me. 'Maybe, thees gentleman in the second row who iss sitting weeth the so beautiful lady, he iss saying to heemself, Oh, ho, here iss a mountebank fellow, but he cannot fool me. No!' He shook his head in an exaggerated manner and went on, 'So I must show thees gentleman, iss it not so?'

Very lightly for one of his bulk he ran down the few steps to the floor of the hall, chattering as he moved. 'He has brought thees lovely lady to see poor Boldini. That iss verra nice. Boldini loves the lovely ladies. That iss verra good, but, for why, ladies and gentlemens' – he paused beside me and made a lightning dart with his hands about my waistline, disturbing my coat – 'for why does he also bring a bunny rabbit?'

He retreated, holding aloft, for all to see, a struggling rabbit he pretended he had taken from under my coattails and which he carried up the steps to the stage and handed to the young person, who, with miraculous speed, had changed from her tawdry evening gown into the garb of a pageboy.

The audience roared. I was annoyed at the unwelcome attention, and my face flushed with the displeasure I felt. Eileen's peal of laughter echoed throughout the hall, adding to my embarrassment. I trusted people would not think, as I did, that she was behaving with undue levity for a girl with a dying father. I said, 'Sh-h-h,' but she gently sh-h-d me back with no deliberate rudeness but because her whole attention was directed upon Boldini, who stood smirking and acknowledging the applause after making himself a good fellow at my expense.

I trusted that I would not be made the victim of any further buffoonery and determined to make it quite clear that I would stand no more nonsense. He started talking again.

'Now, ladies and gentlemens, some of you iss verra sad for me, iss it not? Oh, thees poor mans, you say! Thees poor Boldini! How does he live? How can he buy heem hees macaroni? Look at thees so empty chairs that oughta be filled weeth the nice two bobs. How does thees poor mans get hees mon' when the peoples they do not come to see hees show? I will tell you a leetle secret. I, Boldini, weel show you how to make the mon'. So!'

He turned sideways to his audience, extending his arm, spreading his long, white fingers, twisting his hands this way and that and, miraculously, a half crown appeared. 'Half a crown!' he exclaimed contemptuously. 'It iss not enough. I try again. So! And I have plenty more half a crown.' Several more coins appeared and he threw them into a high hat held for him by the young person assisting him in his performance.

He gazed enquiringly into the audience. 'But for why should I not get some mon' from the good peoples here?' Taking the hat from the girl he ran down the steps again, the top hat in one hand, the fingers of the other waving in the air. He paused before Eileen. 'Oh, madam, excusa plees.' He leaned over and touched her head lightly and drew back with a coin between his fingers. 'See! I taka from your so beautiful hair a golden sovereign.' He dropped it into the hat and his fingers fluttered delicately over my head. 'Thees gentlemans he geevs me the sovereign also! Yes?' He pretended annoyance. 'No, it iss only the bob he geevs.'

Passing rapidly down the aisle, talking incessantly while his assistant played upon the piano, he extracted money from his patrons' hair and ears and coat collars, and at length seized upon old Plank, pretending to scoop a veritable harvest of silver from the fellow's bald head, a performance ludicrous in the extreme since Plank was notoriously poor, and I had made it a standing joke in the town that he had never, at one time, more than enough for beer and bread and frequently only enough for beer.

The magician held the hat high in the air and rattled its contents as he moved back toward the stage. He hesitated beside me and rattled the hat again.

'But what is that they say? It iss not real money?' He looked at me. 'Please?' he said, rattling the coins in the hat, 'they say it iss not real money. Would you be so kind, *signore*, and put your hand in thees hat and take out the mon'? Tell them it iss good mon'.'

I saw no harm in that. He had selected me as a committee of one to investigate his claims. I rose, stretched out my hand and thrust it into the hat, groping for the coins, but to my surprise I could find none, although a moment before I had distinctly heard them rattling together.

I stood, groping foolishly, and to my chagrin Boldini said, 'What iss that you say? There iss no mon'?' He turned the hat upside down, showing that it was empty. 'Oh, *mia dolorosa*,' he cried in mock despair. 'Thees gentlemans has taken all my mon'. Verra well, then! He taka my mon' I taka hees rabbit.'

Once more he thrust himself against me offensively and retreated with a struggling rabbit in his hand. I went purple with rage at this second indignity, but the fellow had gone in a flash and was again on the stage, and any protest I might have made was drowned in the flood of laughter from the audience.

The sleight-of-hand performance continued until the interval. Had it not been for the ridicule heaped upon me, I really believe I should have found some interest and enjoyment in the show, for many of the tricks had undoubted merit, and to that audience of bumpkins, who for the most part had never before seen a professional conjurer at work, it must have appeared little short of miraculous.

Boldini brought the first half of his programme to a conclusion by trussing up the young person dressed as a pageboy and packing her into a small trunk. With a few magic words he transported her to a closed and roped trunk some distance away. I admit that even I could not see how he did it, though doubtless it was simple enough and the obvious escaped me. It was, however, quite impressive in its way, and the effect was heightened in the vulgar mind by the second appearance of the imprisoned girl who, in transit from one trunk to another, had apparently found time to change her clothes and made an indecorous but happily brief appearance in green tights.

It gave me considerable pleasure to see the light in Eileen's eyes and the colour on her cheeks. She turned to me and impulsively put her hand on my arm. 'Wasn't it lovely?' she cried, and began to chatter in a most spirited manner about what we had seen. I had to restrain her enthusiasm.

'Hush, my dear,' I warned her. 'We are making ourselves conspicuous.'

She withdrew her hand at once and said, 'Oh!' and turned her attention to the slip on which was printed the items for the second part of the programme.

During the interval the stage had been hung with dark curtains. The young person appeared, this time in evening dress, and caused me some little embarrassment by gazing directly down and favouring me with a dazzling smile. She sang a sentimental song very indifferently, although Eileen applauded before I had time to express my disapproval and point out to her the poor diction and lack of voice control. I saw how necessary it would be for me to train her to subdue her feelings and to impress upon her that, from our class, commendation called for no more than a gentle tapping of one hand against the palm of the other, allowing the boisterous plaudits to emanate from the lower orders in the cheaper seats.

Boldini reappeared. His bright red cummerbund had gone and with it his gaiety. His voice had acquired a new and sonorous quality and he had assumed an air of quiet dignity contrasting greatly with his former deportment.

'And now, ladies and gentlemens,' he began, 'we must be verra serious because we come to the experiments of the mind. First I weel show you some simple things. *Signorina!*'

He beckoned his assistant. 'Be seated, I pray.' She sat down, and he bandaged her eyes. 'So! Now I come among you, and you shall show me something you have weeth you and my lee-tle lady she weel tell to you what it iss.'

He moved to the auditorium.

Eileen whispered to me to show him my watch and I could hardly refuse her request. Boldini held it in his hand and called, 'What have I in my hand?'

The answer came pat.

'A watch.'

'What kind of a watch?'

'It is a gold watch.'

'There are some initials on the back. Tell to me what are these initials?'

'H.'

'Correct. And now the second one?'

She hesitated.

'Come, oh, come, *signorina*, he called sharply. 'The second one?'

She hesitated a moment longer and then said 'X.'

'The third and last? What is the third letter please?'

'F,' she said promptly. Boldini handed me my watch.

'Iss that correct, *signore*?'

I nodded, but he did not pass on.

'Excuse me, *signore*,' he said, 'but X iss a verra curious ini-tial letter. I weel try another experiment.' He pressed his hand to his brow as if concentrating and called. 'Are you listening, *signorina*? You told to me one of thees gentleman's initials iss X. That iss a verra unusual initial. I wish you please to tell me for what it stands. Theenk now, theenk.'

He stood beside me, towering over Eileen, his hand point-ing, his eyes closed, his face contorted in an effort, I supposed, to propel his thoughts into the mind of the young person on the stage. Those who watched saw her twitch in her chair and pass her hand wearily over her head.

'Tell me, tell me, *tell me*,' Boldini cried dramatically.

'It is – *Xavier*,' she shouted suddenly and triumphantly. I was really startled. Eileen leaned toward me, her eyes popping out of her head.

'Isn't it wonderful?' she said.

All about us people were eagerly offering articles for identification and, with a patience that surprised me, Boldini carried on, apparently satisfying all the clamourers, but at length he returned to the platform and took the bandage from the young person's eyes. Together they bowed and made their exit amid a babble of excited comment.

The mind-reader was back again very soon, inviting some 'well-known gentleman' to assist him during the next portion of his performance, which, according to the programme, was to consist of further demonstrations of an unusual character. Hennessy immediately walked up the steps on the stage and was greeted with applause.

The schoolmaster was popular in his way. Even his pupils had a regard for the man, and I had often seen them clamouring about him as if he were an elder brother rather than a pedagogue. And this, too, despite the fact that he had robbed the youngsters of their pastime of bird-nesting, and had had the temerity to protest to the Committee of the Baloola Agricultural Society against the offering of prizes for the best collection of eggs. To some extent he had offset this by dispensing with the cane and actually claimed that he got better results from the brats without it.

Boldini spoke to Hennessy in undertones, and the schoolmaster nodded and addressed the audience.

'The Signor Boldini,' he said, 'invites you to come upon the stage when I will introduce you by name. He claims that as soon as he has touched your hands he will tell you something of your life, though he has never set eyes on you before. I suggest that those who wish to be – er – experimented upon should come up six at a time, and from their own lips those remaining in the audience will know whether or not Signor Boldini has revealed the truth or otherwise.'

It was a sensible arrangement, I considered, as, during the earlier portion of the second part of the programme, while Boldini was on the floor of the hall, I had got quite a crick in my neck twisting in my chair to watch him and was a little concerned that my cravat might have become disarranged. Half a dozen chairs, placed on the stage by old Craven, were soon occupied by members of the audience who were prepared to make themselves ridiculous in order to satisfy their curiosity. They all looked very nervous and uncomfortable.

Old Plank was the first to thrust himself forward. Hennessy said, 'This is Mr Plank.'

'Ah, Signor Plunk.' Boldini shook him warmly by the hand.

'Plank,' said Hennessy.

'Ah! Pla-ank! So!' Boldini continued to hold his hand. 'Let Boldini see what he can find weeth hees mind for Signor Pla-ank.' He shut his eyes, while the old man stood like a simpleton, his mouth agape, staring. At last the mind-reader spoke.

'It iss a leetle, leetle town that I see, and a verra dusty road. I see a leetle boy playing on that dusty road. He iss seeting down in the meedle of thees road. I see a *signora* in clothes verra old-fash'. I heara the voice of thees lady. It is saying, "Francis Pla-ank, do not sitta on thees dusty road. The carts they weel run over you." And I see thees leetle boy look up at thees lady and hear heem say, "No-a they won't. They always go round me".'

Boldini opened his eyes as if he had just awakened and put a hand on the old man's shoulder. 'Do you understand what I have been speaking at you, my friend?' he asked quietly.

Plank stared unbelievingly for a moment longer, then he slapped his thigh with a characteristic gesture, and turned to the audience. 'By dang,' he swore, 'if it ain't the very words my mother said to me sixty year ago. Well, by dang!'

There was plenty of applause, and then Hennessy introduced the next subject for experiment. It was a Mrs Ringer, an illiterate creature who earned a pittance helping with the washing at Mrs Marven's hotel and at the better class homes in the town. She had come forward from the rear seats, but Hennessy introduced her without a smile as if she had been a person of importance, and Boldini greeted her with a bow.

'The Signora Rosita Ringer,' he said, and took her hand between his own, almost caressingly. He shut his eyes and everyone watched silently and expectantly, while the absurd creature waited, awkward and blushing. It was probably the first time anyone there had ever heard her full name, for some card had once christened her Wringer Rosie on account of her laundry activities, and it had stuck. At last Boldini spoke.

'The *signora* has lost something. She iss verra sad. I see a verra sweet lady put gold in her hand. I see her hurry to her home. She opens the gate. She goes inside her home and then she is having the shock, oh me! oh my! She has lost the piece of gold.'

This was true enough, as I myself could vouch. I had heard the gossip at the dinner table. The bank clerk had, during small talk, told how he had learned that the washerwoman had lost a half sovereign that Mrs Marven had given her for a birthday present. Wringer Rosie stood on the stage like a surprised fish, gaping at Boldini, but the *signore* had not finished.

'But the *signora* must not be sorry. No! For what do you theenk? There iss for her the news verra good. She weel finda thees golden piece. And I, Boldini, will tell her where. Thees night she shall go home and taka the look in – ' He bent over the woman and whispered. Her eyes lit in amazement and she descended from the platform more or less in a dream, Boldini calling after her, 'When you find thees gold, *signora*, you must tella the news to everybody so he weel know that thees Boldini spik the trut' and iss not the beeg fake.'

I gazed curiously after the woman as she hurried down the aisle, and was not surprised to see her leave the hall. I smiled a little to myself, for I was sure she had determined to put Boldini to an immediate test, and I looked forward, a little vindictively, I am afraid, to his discomfiture when she returned. Apparently, he had not noticed her exit, for he was again busy on the stage. He told a Mrs Jennerson she would find a ring she had lost but not for six months (by which time, I thought, who would know Boldini's whereabouts?), and he was aware that George Horler had sprained his ankle on Guy Fawkes Day six years before.

When he took the hand of young Mrs Partridge, he gazed at her soulfully, then closed his eyes and said very gently, 'Do not worry, dear lady, about the leetle one that iss gone and who now sleeps so peacefully, for I see great joy for the future and anozzer leetle bambino on a September day.'

He swung his arms absurdly as if nursing a baby. It was true, of course, for the woman had not long since buried a child, and, as the whole town knew, was expecting another. I marvelled at the infernal indelicacy of the man and kept my eyes averted from Eileen, lest she be embarrassed. The Partridge woman, however, far from being displeased, acutally looked radiant.

So it went on, one after the other testifying to Boldini's powers. I was, I admit, quite at sea. Some of his assertions were palpably guesswork, but in the most cases he was able to tell those whose hands he held something true about their past, although he had arrived, so Gallagher informed me, in the middle morning by the Baloola coach, and had spent the whole afternoon getting his show ready at the hall with the aid and in the presence of old Craven.

We had seen nothing of him at the hotel, and Mrs Marven explained that he had asked that his meals be served in his bedroom. And yet, as soon as Hennessy introduced the people on the stage, he was not only able to give them details of their past lives, but, in some cases, tell them what they were proposing to do in the future. He had them all openmouthed with astonishment, and I began to wonder whether there might not be something to the fellow after all.

My conjectures were interrupted by a little disturbance at the door and, looking round, I beheld Wringer Rosie running up the aisle, waving her arm and crying, 'He was right! There it was! Just where he said it would be!' She reached the front rows and called up to Boldini. 'You were right, sir. It was there.'

He looked down at her, smiling, his white teeth gleaming under his heavy black moustache. 'Of course,' he said. 'Of course it was there. Boldini iss always right.'

She turned excitedly and held out her hand to Eileen, disclosing a half sovereign on her palm. 'Look, Miss Mahoney, it was there.' Eileen picked the coin up and examined it.

'Oh, that's wonderful, Mrs Ringer,' she said. 'I'm so glad.'

'Please, do you mind, miss?' the woman said, and, to my dismay, pushed past me and my fiancée and settled herself in a vacant seat alongside. I felt extremely uncomfortable but consoled myself with the knowledge that the performance would soon be over. In any case few appeared to have noticed the impertinence, and Eileen herself was not in the least put out.

As the creature settled herself in a chair, Boldini was saying to Hennessy, 'And now, *amico*, before we pray to the good Lord to save the gracious queen, per'aps you weel tell Boldini where it iss you hide the leetle cane weeth which you do not whacka the leetle boys?' There was a big laugh, and Hennessy smiled as Boldini went on. 'I maka the joke, but please, Signor Hennessy, aska me somet'ing for yourself.'

The schoolmaster stood smiling. 'Very well, *signore*,' he replied quietly. 'If you can – will you please tell me who poisoned my dog?'

I counted my heartbeats during the hush that ensued, and I awaited Boldini's reply. It was ridiculous. Not a soul besides me knew of the episode under the hotel verandah. All the same I felt uneasy and was sorry Hennessy had brought the matter up. I wondered how a man with so much to do could continue to bother his head about a dead dog.

I turned to Eileen. 'Shall we leave now and avoid crowding at the door?' I suggested. 'It will soon be over.'

She looked at me in astonishment. 'Go now? Oh, no, please,' she pleaded. 'I do want to hear it all.'

There was nothing to be done about it. I had to see it out. In any event, even if this mountebank knew, he couldn't, he daren't say so in a public hall. There was such a thing as libel, thank heaven.

Boldini had taken Hennessy's hand. '*Signore,*' he was saying, 'I see you are a man who loves leetle dogs. I too, love the dumb animals, and, so, I tell to you frankly I do not know who did thees nasty thing. But' – he thundered as he saw the look of disappointment in Hennessy's face – 'Boldini weel try and find out. If thees person iss in thees hall I shall find him.'

Uneasily I noted that Boldini had referred to a little dog.

He dropped the schoolmaster's hand and addressed the audience.

'Ladies and gentlemens, please. I promise nuzzing but I weel pass among you and I weel stand beside you and look at you in the faces and maybe touch you, but, please, I ask you do not taka the offend. Only the one who bringed about the death of thees leetle dog need to be feared. Yes, I tella you, I, Boldini, he can begin now to shaka in hees shoes thees verra minute, for if he iss here I shall find heem, never fear.'

There was a stillness after this pronouncement. The scene had assumed a dramatic intensity out of all proportion to the absurd problem Boldini had so fantastically set himself. Who, apart from Hennessy, cared a snap of the fingers for the dead animal? And yet all were sitting tensely erect in their seats, as if human life were at stake and depended on their quiet.

I glanced at Eileen and saw, in profile, her parted lips. Her eyes were riveted on the stage. She, too, had fallen under the spell of this charlatan.

'This is too absurd,' I said in an undertone, but, if she heard, she gave no sign. The washerwoman alongside her, however, had the audacity to cast an indignant glance my way and say, 'Sh-h-h', in a loud whisper.

Boldini again took Hennessy's hand.

'If he iss here that person,' he said, 'I weel find him, my friend. Please now to shut your eyes and theenk of your leetle dog. You must see heem in your mind, thees leetle fellow. Think of heem, picture heem padding along on hees leetle feets.'

The two men stood with hands clasped and eyes shut, an absurd sight. I wondered that a person of Hennessy's education could make such a spectacle of himself.

Boldini spoke in a sonorous voice. 'You see heem, eh? He runs about, iss it not? He pokes hees nose into the shop doors. He stands heemself outside the gates, hees leetle head cocked. P'raps he iss saying in hees mind, Iss there a welcome for leetle dogs inside? You see heem at the school. He makes the frolic among the leetle chil'ren. And now he iss on thees dusty road and he iss lonely p'raps because there iss no one to play weeth leetle dogs, for it iss the night. He takes the leetle stroll through the streets, all alone by heemself beneath the leetle twinkling stars. Alas. There iss no one for thees leetle dog to play weeth. He iss so lonely, thees leetle fellow. And then he finds *someone*.' The man's voice took on a new note and he continued dramatically, 'Someone who geevs heem poison. Come, my friend, we weel find this person. If he iss here we weel find him.'

It seemed to have grown insufferably hot all of a sudden, and I took out my handkerchief and wiped my brow as the pair came swiftly down the steps into the hall. I tried to tell myself it was all play-acting. Boldini, give him his due, was a good show-man. He had qualified his boast. 'If he is here,' he had said.

Of course, I reasoned, he will not be here. Boldini will say, 'I am sorry, my friends, the man is not here. We will try again at my next performance.' He'd achieve an advertisement. Next day everyone would be talking about the damned dog just as they would be talking of the wretched Wringer Rosie. The dead mongrel would fill the hall for him.

Boldini and Hennessy passed along the front row, the for-mer touching people as he went by and saying, 'No, no, not here,' and came at length to the second row and stood next to Eileen and me. Leaning over, he touched the Ringer woman lightly, smiled, and passed on. His fingers floated about Eileen, and I was vexed to see her smile at him; then his hand rested on my shoulder and stayed there.

His grip tightened until I could feel his fingers crushing the bone. He leaned over me. 'You lika the leetle dogs, *signore*?' he asked, and I shifted uneasily as his big, dark eyes gazed at me steadily. 'Please to tell Boldini.'

'Of course,' I replied, feeling hot under the collar, 'I like dogs.'

I thought Hennessy glanced at me curiously and then, to my intense relief, the pair passed on, moving speedily through the sparse audience, Boldini's hand flashing here and there, touching this person and that, crying 'No! Theenk, Hennessy, my friend. Keep your mind always on thees leetle dog and we weel find this man – if he iss here.'

He had arrived at the very back of the hall and, the danger past, I could now watch with interest. I was curious to see how he would wriggle out of his predicament when he had exhausted all possibilities.

He had soon reached the very rear of the hall and Eileen stood up so that she could see more easily. Others followed her example. To my disgust, I saw the Ringer woman, overcome with excitement, grip the arm of my fiancée, who was so interested in Boldini's quest that she made not the slightest effort to dislodge it.

The mind-reader's eyes were fixed on a row of louts sitting like hypnotised dummies. They had piled forms three high against the back wall and they looked down upon him as they sat swinging their legs; nevertheless, he dominated them and there was not a move or a murmur as he proclaimed theatrically, pointing a long white finger, 'If that man iss in thees hall he sits in thees row! A man who poisoned a poor leetle dog. Surely he will tell us? He weel confess here and now, "I did thees so wicked thing. I took thees poor, innocent life."' His voice quietened and became soft and persuasive. 'Or, p'raps he weel say, "I didn't know. It was an accident."' But he weel tell Boldini *now*.'

The lads moved uneasily and, all at once, there was a stir and young Joe Barmby had leaped down and was rushing for the exit. Hennessy put out his arm and detained him.

'Joe,' he cried.

Barmby struggled. 'Let me go,' he shouted wildly, 'let me go,' and suddenly became still and looked into Hennessy's face. 'It was me, Mr Hennessy,' he said, 'It was me. I didn't mean to do it. It was an accident. I wouldn't do a thing like that, really. I wouldn't poison a little dog, Mr Hennessy, I wouldn't.'

The schoolmaster released him without a word, and the boy turned desperately to Boldini. 'Tell him,' he cried. '*You* know. You know I wouldn't do a thing like that a-purpose.'

Boldini put his hand on the youth's shoulder. 'Yes,' he said quietly, 'I know.'

Young Barmby's mouth fell open. He gazed at the mountebank as if he were God. Boldini spoke to Hennessy so softly that I could barely hear him and then only because everyone in the hall seemed to be stupefied into silence.

'It was an accident, *amico*. What happened thees boy shall tell to you – but not here. Not now. Tomorrow he shall go to you and tell you what happened to the leetle dog.' He turned to young Barmby again. 'Is it not so?' he asked, and as the youth nodded eagerly, he added, 'and tomorrow night you shall come here and see Boldini – in the front seats – the best seats because you have been so brave and told to us the trut'. So, you see, Boldini believes and so will Signor Hennessy.'

There were tears in Joe Barmby's eyes, and he brushed them away with the sleeve of his coat, looking unutterably mournful. He gave one hasty, appealing glance at Hennessy, and then wheeled and strode quickly to the door and disappeared.

'Let him go,' Boldini said, as Hennessy made a move to follow. 'It iss better so.'

I sat down again.

'And that's that,' I said with a sigh of relief, and, as I resumed my seat, realised the implications of Barmby's confession. After all, then, I had not poisoned the dog. Therefore the stuff I had taken from Mrs Marven's safe had been harmless, and the drink she had prepared for Helen Speek quite innocent.

Busy with my thoughts, I had for the moment forgotten Eileen. Boldini and Hennessy had already regained the stage, and, suddenly, she was pushing past me and hurrying up the steps to join them.

I rose to my feet in consternation and followed her to find her saying excitedly, 'Please. I want to ask you a great favour.'

Boldini bowed. 'Of course, *signorina*.'

'Eileen,' I began, in an effort to prevent her making a further exhibition of herself, but she brushed me aside with an impatient gesture.

She said in a low voice, 'Mr Boldini, a little while ago a young man disappeared from this town. It was at the time of the flood. They say he was drowned, but – his body has never been discoverd. Could you – '

'Eileen,' I broke in, 'this is preposterous.'

'Not preposterous, *signore*,' Boldini said, as Eileen looked at him appealingly. Hennessy came to her aid.

'What Miss Mahoney wishes to know, I think,' he said, 'what I, and I am sure Mr Ford, also, and all his friends wish to know is what became of him. His name was Larry Ward.'

Boldini's heavy eyebrows knitted.

'What name, *signore*?'

'Larry Ward,' Hennessy repeated.

Boldini reflected a moment; then he bowed to Eileen and addressed the audience.

'Ladies and gentlemens, you would like to know about thees Larry Ward?'

There was a chorus of assent.

'Then,' he went on, 'I weel tell you – but not now. Boldini iss tired. The strain iss verra great. And it iss late, my friends.' He passed his hand wearily over his brow. 'Tomorrow night I weel tell to you of thees Larry Ward. But tonight some one of you must leave weeth me some leetle souvenir that thees young man has give to heem. That iss verra necessary.'

I saw at once that he was seeking a way out but at the same time arousing a curiosity that would help to fill his coffers at the next performance, for none was likely to have come there prepared for such a demand and bringing a souvenir of the late lamented.

I was astonished, however, to see Eileen tugging at a ring on her hand, a tawdry little silver affair that I had asked her to discard when I had given her our engagement token. She handed the trinket to Boldini.

'This belonged to him,' she said. 'He gave it to me.'

Boldini took it gravely, twirled it about in his slender fingers as if assessing its value, and then transferred it to his pocket.

'This is utterly absurd,' I protested angrily. 'Entertainment is all very well, but I protest against the dragging in of private affairs. This is unwarranted. It is ridculous to permit this mountebank – '

Hennessy put his hand on my arm. 'Steady, Ford,' he said.

But I was beside myself. 'It is preposterous and unprincipled,' I cried, glaring at Boldini.

Flame seemed to leap suddenly from the man's eyes. For an instant I believed he would spring upon me but, instead, he wrapped his arms about his gross body with a peculiar action and, throwing back his head, roared with laughter.

'Preposterous!' he cried. 'He says the g-great Boldini iss preposterous, eh? Oh, verra good. Verra funny!' He ceased laughing and leaned toward me. 'The *signore* says I am preposterous,' he cried. 'But it iss not so! It iss the *signore* heemself who iss preposterous – thees funny man who brings the leetle rabbits to the show.'

With a rapid movement he threw his great bulk forward, and I found his body warm about mine, bumping and bustling me. Then, as suddenly, he retreated.

'Look!' he cried. 'How many more bunnies has thees funny man brought weeth him tonight?'

He held up another rabbit by the ears, and, when the audience saw the creature, to my mortification a great roar of laughter swelled up. I could have struck the man, big as he was, but Hennessy was between us, trying to conceal a smile, and saying, 'Now, now, Harry,' and the next thing I heard the strains of *God Save the Queen* being thumped out on the piano by the young person and the lusty bass of the conjurer drowning the voices of the singers in the hall.

I was in a shocking temper as I escorted Eileen home, and walked back to the hotel still full of resentment. As I passed through the hall I glanced into the commercial room and saw Mrs Marven seated with her elbows on the table, her hands clasped, gazing like a lovesick schoolgirl at Boldini. He was sitting opposite, a napkin at his throat, eating from the biggest dish of spaghetti I have ever seen.

I shall not easily forget the night of restlessness that followed the happenings at Boldini's first performance. After I had extinguished my candle I tossed and turned, and when at intervals I almost achieved the blessed unconsciousness I craved, I would jerk again into wakefulness at the recollection of the scurvy way I had been treated.

To have been the butt of Boldini's buffoonery was bad enough, but I was also deeply hurt by Eileen's behaviour and vexed that she should have publicly disclosed that she, my fiancée, had been wearing a ring given her by another man, and a trashy ring at that! I was ashamed of her unladylike action in rushing on the stage. Certainly, look at it in any light, she had treated me with very little courtesy and no consideration whatever.

As I lay staring into the dark, I remembered I had said as much while escorting her home, and she had replied that she was sorry. Her words, however, had lacked sincerity, and she was plainly distraught. As I parted with her I asked her permission to call the following evening.

'Oh,' she said, 'but we will be seeing Boldini again.'

I had not contemplated anything of the sort. 'I've seen quite enough of that gentleman,' I told her.

'You shouldn't get annoyed so easily,' she said. 'It was only his fun. Besides,' her voice fell, 'don't you wish to hear about Larry?'

'No, I don't,' I said with emphasis.

She appeared taken aback at my forthright answer.

'I think I understand,' she said. There was a little pause and I saw her chin set. 'But I want to know,' she went on with determination. 'I must go – even if I go alone.'

'That is nonsense,' I said. 'If you insist, of course I must take you. After all, you are my fiancée. But I think it is indiscreet. Ward is dead, and all this foolishness is – is wicked. People will be talking about you.'

She did not argue. She said simply, 'I *have* to go. I must know – for certain. I will explain to my father.'

'Very well,' I said with dignity. 'I shall call for you at a

quarter to eight, but I shall expect you to show me more consideration. We cannot afford to have a repetition of tonight's
happenings.'

She kissed me good night mechanically and unexpectedly.
It was the merest peck, and the intimacy was initiated by her. I
could not help suspecting that it was to forestall any advance
on my part, for the next moment she had gone and the door
had shut in my face. I had put up with a great deal that
evening and this curt dismissal was the last straw.

Tired of my tangled blankets, I rose early and went for a walk
before breakfast. I returned by way of the stables and rear
entrance to the hotel. Through the open kitchen window I
saw Rosie, the housemaid, with the cook and Mrs Marven,
gazing spellbound at Boldini.

About the capacious waist of the master mind-reader was
tied a ridiculously small kitchen apron, and he was standing
before a dish of freshly picked mushrooms. He was saying,
'You taka the mushroom – the beeg fellows, not thees leetle
squiffs, and you knock hees skin off – so! Then you scald heem
in the water weeth salt, please.'

As the cook hurried to obey, I moved out of sight, but lingered within hearing.

'Now, you bringa the baking pan. Grazie!' Boldini's voice
went on. 'Thees oil, I put heem in thees pan. Now we maka
the stuffing for thees big fellow mushrooms. Some bread, and
deep heem in the milk, so! and squeeze thees milky bread, so!
Eggs of the hen – two, and some cheeses to mince. I thank
you. And now the stalks of thees big chap mushrooms all
mince up together weeth the cheeses. Giva the pep and salt,
and, boila, thees stuffing iss did. Thees mushrooms we put in
thees pan. I put on the top a leetle more oil and, presto! you
bake heem half the hour – no, you bake heem only twenty-
seven minute, and you hava the stuffed mushroom à la Carlo
Boldini.'

I waited for no more.

The master mind, I reflected, was not neglecting his stomach. Somehow the knowledge comforted me. The fellow, after all, was only human. Viewed in the light of day his performance of the previous night lacked reality. I saw it as a conglomeration of audacious tricks played on a bumpkin audience he had lulled into a state of gullibility – tricks easy enough to fathom, no doubt, if you had the time and the inclination.

Boldini came in to breakfast, and Mrs Marven introduced us.

'I have met the gentleman,' I said coldly.

'Indeed!' Boldini actually affected surprise.

'I was at your little entertainment last night. I think you will remember.'

'Oh,' he said. 'Yes, now I remember. I theenk I see you, *signore*.'

'You saw me, all right, Boldini,' I said, 'and I want to tell you, here and now, that I resented your impertinence. I do not like being made the butt of anyone's buffoonery, especially in public.'

Boldini spread his hands.

'Ah, now I *do* remember,' he cried. 'Of *course*. My leetle trick weeth the rabbits! But, *signore*, it was the show. It was not a personal thing. It was for the laugh – to make the people laugh. It is good to laugh.'

'It didn't make me laugh,' I said curtly and sat down to my breakfast.

Mrs Marven had stood by, wringing her hands in great distress.

'Oh, please, Mr Ford,' she begged, rather tactlessly, 'I'm sure Signor Boldini didn't mean to make a fool of you. I heard all about it. It seemed as if it must have been awfully funny. Now have some mushrooms. Mr Boldini has gone to all sorts of trouble and prepared them for us himself in the Italian style.'

'Thank you,' I replied stiffly. 'I prefer the English way.'

'Oh, but please, *signore*,' Boldini said, 'the stomach she iss international. Iss it not so?' He appealed to Mrs Marven.

'Goodness, *signore*,' she replied, 'I wouldn't know. I like any kind of good food.'

I turned to Rosie, who was awaiting my order. 'Please bring me two lightly boiled eggs,' I said shortly, and brought an end to the discussion. I think I rather spoiled their breakfast for them. Anyway, everyone ate more or less in silence.

I left the table after a while, though I was still hungry. The mushrooms, which the bank fellow opposite was eating with such relish, had a tempting odour, and, as I stalked out, curiously enough, there flashed through my mind a vivid picture of an incident in my childhood. There had been a jam roly-poly, a dish of which I was inordinately fond, and by some oversight none was saved for me. I remembered how I had screamed the house down and the attempts of my mother to pacify me. Even the chocolates she gave me failed to soothe my outraged dignity and when I threw them under the table, she burst into tears.

My temper was by no means improved when, as I reached the hall, I heard Boldini say, 'Poor man. I think he iss in the high dudgeon. Yes?'

Mrs Marven giggled and said, 'Sh-h-h.'

That morning I was to learn something of the far-reaching effects of Boldini's cunning showmanship. Although his first performance had been only sparsely attended, that was due to the natural suspicion of the townsfolk, who never took visiting entertainers on trust. Astute entrepreneurs, who really had an interesting entertainment, invariably stayed two nights. The more reckless went to the first performance and, if it was good, advertised it greatly by word of mouth, so that the second show invariably attracted a larger attendance.

As letters were called for that day I realised that Boldini was the talk of the town and his second performance promised to be a big financial success. Each of my callers had an eager question or a more or less excited comment. Many reports of the show were grossly exaggerated, but I found to my annoyance that everyone had heard the story of the rabbits. Haggart, the draper, had the insufferable cheek to call through the delivery window in the presence of several people, 'Any rabbits – I mean any letters – today, Mr Ford?'

I ignored the impertinence, but my blood boiled. It was coming to something if this little country upstart thought he could poke fun at me. I handed him his mail.

'There are your letters, Haggart,' I said, deliberately putting him in his place by omitting the courtesy title.

He took them without a word to me but muttered something to those behind him on the verandah and there was subdued laughter. I retreated from the window so that none might see from my flushed face that I had overheard, but not before a stentorian voice called from the other side of the street, 'Hey, you fellows over there. Got any rabbits?'

I knew at once that Garnet Price had returned, and I also knew that he meant me to hear. I determined to make him pay for the insult.

As if the mountebank had not received sufficient free publicity, Hennessy needs must add to it. I heard the sound of marching feet and looked out to see the schoolmaster shepherding his pupils into the hall. They marked time outside the post office while Hennessy fussed about the entrance, and I learned that the whole school was going to see a special performance by Boldini. Old Plank came and stood by me, watching the youngsters.

'By gum, it makes you feel young again,' he declared. 'Boldini's giving the show to the kids for nix. I call that decent, danged if I don't.' All at once he began to laugh. 'By gum, Mr Ford,' he said, 'that was funny the way he took those rabbits off you.'

I turned my back on the old fool and went inside. During the next hour it was like Bedlam, because the hall was next door to the post office, and I could hear roar after roar of shrill, childish laughter, and then singing. Apparently Boldini was teaching them a song line by line. I could hear some of the words quite plainly:

> *I like rabbits 'cause rabbits don't drink,*
> *Rabbits don't drink at all ...*

It didn't improve my temper as I wondered whether it was meant for a further affront. I toyed with the idea of writing a letter to the Education Department (anonymously, of course, because I had no wish to lose Hennessy's friendship) protesting against precious school hours being wasted in such frivolity. My thoughts were interrupted by the unexpected arrival of Eileen.

Even now I seem to see her as I saw her that day. She made a very beautiful picture, framed in the little window, her colour heightened by the exercise of walking. She had, apparently, been hurrying, for she was breathless, and, as I noted the lovely line of her shoulders and the soft rise and fall of her breast, I felt an overwhelming desire to put out my arms and hold her to me.

'Oh, Harry,' she said eagerly, 'have you got the tickets for tonight?'

'Not yet, my dear,' I told her, all my resentment of the night before vanishing as, for the first time, I heard her use my baptismal name. 'There is no hurry.'

'Oh, but there is,' she urged. 'I've just come from Haggart's store and such a lot have been reserved already. Mr Haggart says the hall will be crowded.'

'Marvellous,' I said, and I could not keep the sarcasm from my voice. But she didn't notice.

'Yes, isn't it?' Her head lifted. 'Listen to those children. Isn't it lovely?'

'To tell the truth, my dear,' I said, hoping for a little sympathy, 'they have given me a headache.' I smiled wanly, but she turned away, still intrigued with the singing of the brats next door, who were again bawling the rabbit song; then, without another word, she left me and hurried towards the hall. I heard later that she had stood at the back and joined in the chorus.

The youngsters came romping out of the hall at last, making the air hideous with their screams, laughing without rhyme or reason, and pushing and shoving each other in an ecstasy of rowdyism. Hennessy came across to the post office and stood on the verandah watching them, making no effort to exert his authority but actually smiling as if they were behaving like little ladies and gentlemen rather than as a lot of noisy ragamuffins. He took his mail and said, 'You know, Harry, that was a rather wonderful thing Boldini did last night – about my dog, I mean.'

He told me that young Barmby had been on his mat before breakfast with the whole absurd story. He had risen at daybreak (he told the schoolmaster) on the day the dog had been found dead, and had gone to his father's workshop. They had had some trouble with rats and had set baits for them. His first job was to remove the dead rats, if any, but the creatures had cunningly avoided the food that had been temptingly set out. A copy of the *Boys' Own Paper* had come in the day before, and Barmby, Jr, was in the middle of an exciting adventure serial and so keen to read it that he forgot to remove the baits.

As he told it, he was far away in the world of romance when a slight sound attracted his attention and brought him back to earth, and he looked down to see Hennessy's dog eating one of the poisoned baits. The cur had taken most of it and ran away with the rest when Barmby rushed at him. After that, the boy told Hennessy, he became frightened. He wanted to confess but was afraid of his father and said nothing.

It was as simple as all that. Hennessy accepted his story and forgave him. 'I feel better about it now,' he told me. 'It's a nasty thing to think there might be a man in our midst who'd deliberately do a dastardly thing like that.'

He was always a sentimentalist.

The schoolmaster's wife was visiting friends that day, and he came along to Mrs Marven's for luncheon. As I strolled with him to the hotel, I wondered whether Joe Barmby might not have made a mistake. It was possible, but hardly likely. Helen Speek had not been at the hotel since the day I snatched from her hand the drink Mrs Marven had prepared for her, but, as I walked in with Hennessy, she was there, engaged in animated conversation with Garnet Price. It looked as if they had been arguing, for Price appeared almost angry. He jumped up as we came in, however, and, ignoring me, greeted Hennessy effusively.

'Good of you, Hennessy,' he cried. 'That must have been a great treat for the kids. What did it cost?'

The schoolmaster hesitated and looked embarrassed. 'Oh, practically nothing,' he said.

'That for a yarn,' Price persisted impudently. 'How much?'

'As a matter of fact,' Hennessy said, 'Boldini was very decent about it. He took his expenses only. Less than two pounds.'

'Fair enough,' Price cried, and thrusting his hand in his pocket pulled out a couple of sovereigns. 'There you are,' he said, 'and I'll bet it was worth every penny of it.'

'It's very decent of you, Price,' the schoolmaster began, but the other interjected, 'Never got better value for money in my life.' He looked at me slyly. 'Always get good value, my lad. Let's have a drink. I'll bet you need one, Ford.' The man was being deliberately rude and provocative, belittling me in front of my friends. I was tempted to retort but held my horses.

The luncheon passed off well enough. Boldini joined us, and he and Price and Hennessy were quickly on the best of terms and monopolising the conversation, for I could find little interest in their chatter. The bank clerk, however, seemed more or less spellbound, and Mrs Marven listened eagerly, her mouth open and expressing wonderment with an occasional, 'Did you ever, now?' They spoke of circuses and magic shows, past and present. Both the schoolmaster and Price were well informed, and Boldini appeared delighted to find two kindred spirits. Price had some story of training a pig to pick the ace of diamonds from a pack of cards. It was a manifest swindle on the audience and carried out so plausibly that I wondered how any showman could have had the effrontery to offer it as entertainment.

Boldini said, 'Ah, thees circus peoples iss clever. But you should not geeve them away. But, as we are all friends,' he went on, 'and weel not steal the business from each other, I weel tell you how to teach an oyster to smoke. First you must promise me that you weel not steala my trick. You promise?'

Price and Hennessy laughingly swore that come what may they would never divulge the secret.

'And you, Mrs Marven?' Boldini turned his big eyes on her.

'Goodness,' she said, 'I wouldn't dream of teaching an oyster anything even if I knew how. I like them to eat and don't mind how uneducated they are.'

'Splendid,' Boldini cried. 'I too like the oyster, cook and uncook. We could maka the double harness, Mrs Marven.'

To my surprise the landlady blushed quite prettily, and Price as usual was ready with some of his coarse wit. Boldini went on to explain the barefaced fraud practiced under the title of the 'Oyster which Smokes'. Audiences are shown an oyster smoking, puffing away at a pipe like a human being, and are taken down wholesale, for the thing, as I learned, is the shabbiest of swindles, and yet Boldini had the audacity to confess that he had made quite a lot of money out of the exhibition.

Once or twice, as Price related some circus incident or other, I noticed the magician watching him keenly, surprised no doubt that an outsider should know so much about the tricks of his unsavoury trade. Price said, 'But, as you say, Boldini, we shouldn't give the show away. Some of us may get hard up one day. Ford, for instance. Can't you see him going round the country exhibiting an educated pig?'

'It iss a good trick,' Boldini replied as if he actually thought it possible I could identify myself with such a project, 'and it iss a honest living.'

'As honest as mind-reading perhaps,' I said contemptuously.

Boldini surveyed me genially. 'Ah, that iss honest too,' he said, 'but there must be tricks, *signore*, even in mind-reading. It iss thees tricks that maka the fun, that geeve the interest. Without the leetle tricks the show he would be as dry as the dust. But' – his gaze wandered about the room – 'tonight you shall see something which iss not tricks.'

'At two and three shillings a time,' I sneered.

Boldini was not offended. 'Of course,' he said.

Price said, 'Boldini, I haven't seen your show but I bet it's great. And you're just as good off as on. You've got us guessing about tonight already. What's the idea?'

The mountebank looked meaningly at Hennessy before replying. 'You will see,' he said.

'I confess,' Hennessy said, 'that I believe you mesmerised that poor Barmby lad into telling what he knew about the dog. But give me tricks evey time. Look at those children this morning. You never saw such a happy bunch.' His brow clouded a moment and he added. 'I expected a full roll call but I didn't get it.'

'What is thees you say?' Boldini enquired. 'All thees little chil'ren they were not there?'

'All except five,' Hennessy said. 'One absence was unavoidable. Polly Garner's niece was sick. But the other four came with a note saying that they were to remain at their lessons and not to go with the others. I had to leave the poor little blighters in the schoolroom while we marched off.'

Mrs Marven raised her eyebrows. 'Barmby's?'

Hennessy nodded.

'But for why?' Boldini asked, frankly amazed.

'You don't know Luke Barmby,' Mrs Marven explained. 'He thinks all showmen come straight from the devil.'

Boldini exploded. 'I am of the devil?' he roared. 'Thees man weel not let hees leetle chil'ren come to see me taka the rabbit from the hat. He theenk it wicked that I do the magic to maka the kids laugh?'

'That's about it,' the schoolmaster admitted.

'*So!*' Boldini blew out his cheeks. 'Iss it possible?'

'Indeed it is,' Price said. 'I was surprised to hear that young Josephus was there last night. I think young Joe has been listening to some radical ideas.' He grinned meaningly at Mrs Marven.

'Why don't you change Luke into a goat or something?' the landlady suggested.

'Oh, I would like to, thees man!' Boldini cried with indignation.

'It *is* a bit thick,' Price said. 'It would have broken my heart to march the school off and leave those other kids gazing from the window.'

'It wasn't nice,' Hennessy admitted.

Price banged his fist on the table till the silver rattled. 'I tell you what,' he cried. 'We'll arrange a show for these kids. Come, Boldini, somewhere privately. What do you say? Tomorrow's Saturday. There's no school.'

Boldini agreed promptly. He shook Price pompously by the hand. '*Signore*,' he cried, 'I do heem.'

'Good,' Price cried. 'I'll foot the bill, whatever it is.'

Boldini spread his hands. 'No,' he said, 'no – no bill, please. This shall be a shout from Boldini.'

'We'll pretend it's Boldini's birthday,' Mrs Marven cried, quick as ever to enter into the spirit of anything unusual. 'I will make a cake.'

It disgusted me to see Boldini throw his great arms about her plump person and kiss her roundly on the cheek. 'What a woman!' he cried. 'I tell you what I do. I sella my principal wife and take you in my harem. Yes?'

'You and your harem!' Mrs Marven pushed him away, laughing but by no means displeased.

Together the four of them plotted their surprise performance, pledging Helen and me and the bank clerk to secrecy.

'Of course, we should invite the little Garner girl if she's better,' Hennessy said.

Mrs Marven agreed at once and offered to see Polly Garner. Dr Hansen popped in just then for a late lunch. There were lines about his eyes and mouth that I had not noticed before, and he was obviously a sick man sticking obstinately to his job, and Mrs Marven fussed around him like a mother hen.

Price introduced Boldini. The doctor shook hands gravely and said something in Italian.

For a moment Boldini looked puzzled; then he said loudly and with a laugh, 'Oh, come now, Doctor, please. No Italian. I lika practice my Engleeze.'

I glanced at him suspiciously, but he was again at his ease and the others were disinterested, while the doctor was too tired to pursue the matter further. He was initiated into the secret of the birthday party, and they were all very merry about it.

Hennessy left to return to his school, and I walked with him as far as the post office.

'By Jove, Ford,' he said, 'it's not such a bad world, is it?' and I was amazed that he could find pleasure in such trifles.

As Haggart predicted, the magician's second appearance attracted a crowded attendance. Before eight o'clock they were running down to the hotel and borrowing chairs and, as Eileen and I walked to our seats, I saw that Helen Speek, Garnet Price, Mrs Marven, and the bank clerk fellow had made a little party. This time our chairs were not next to the aisle. I had taken good care of that, for I was determined that I should not be exploited as on the previous evening.

While we were finding our way slowly to the front rows, somewhat to my embarrassment, Eileen stopped and spoke to Mrs Ringer. I meditated on the sympathy wasted on this woman who, for all her alleged hard life and difficulty in making a living in the most menial fashion, could nevertheless find the money to pay a second visit to Boldini's show.

Old Plank was also there for a second helping and even the Cotters, who were notoriously cheeseparing and definitely opposed to any movement that took money away from the town, had turned up in force, their interest in the promised revelation of their ex-grocery boy overcoming their scruples.

Young Josephus Barmby, resplendent in his Sunday clothes, was in an aisle seat in the very front row, and I wondered what sort of argument he was having with his father about his conduct in attending the performances. He looked over his shoulder and grinned amiably at Mrs Marven and a little foolishly at Eileen, but he seemed in no way abashed and was probably rather proud of himself.

The first half of the entertainment was merely a variation of the sleight-of-hand tricks and the mind-reading mummery of the previous night. Haggart was in the seat I had occupied at the first performance, and I was glad to see him singled out for ridicule. Boldini asked him to lend him his hat and, innocently, the fool passed it up. It was very amusing to see the expression upon his face when the conjurer broke three eggs into it.

I hoped it really was his hat and that the broken eggs were actually in it. Boldini went through the usual mumbo-jumbo and produced a duck from its interior, and then came into the audience, restored the hat to Haggart, and asked him to put it on. When he did so he pulled it off quickly and a pigeon flew out and over our heads to the stage, where the young person assisting the magician caught it on her wrist. Haggart's face was a picture, and I am afraid I roared with laughter. Eileen, I fancy, was really surprised to see me enjoying myself so much.

After the interval there were more 'mental experiments'. Haggart came in for more wigging as Boldini disclosed that, mentally, he saw the little draper buying jewellery from a city firm – jewellery that a '*signorina*' would wear. He even gave the name of the firm and whispered into Haggart's ear the name of the lady, and the little braggart blushed and grinned like a schoolboy caught with his first sweetheart.

Mrs Marven marched up, and he told her boldly he could see much happiness ahead of her. She had been very happy, he informed her, with one very big man and another big man was coming into her life. There were many others eager to hear something of themselves, but it was soon evident that most of the audience was eagerly awaiting the promised revelation about Larry Ward.

Eileen had been very restrained all evening and was apparently unable to enter fully into the spirit of the fun, and, while Boldini was making a speech about the supernatural and how little we really knew of the forces about us and such like tosh, I saw that she had her handkerchief in her hands and was alternately rolling and unrolling it in an effort to control her feelings. Suddenly, all the enjoyment of the evening was spoiled for me as I realised that her thoughts were still with Larry Ward.

I was apprehensive, but with an effort shook off the gloomy forebodings that had all at once flooded my mind. After all, what could this macaroni-eating mountebank say? What could he reveal? What *would* he reveal? I told myself it would be some declaration, highly dramatic in its effect, invested with plenty of mystic detail, but, carefully examined, entirely meaningless.

Boldini was saying, 'Many of you have come to hear something of Larry Ward.'

There was a stir in the hall.

'My friends,' Boldini went on, 'I aska you to be verra quiet when I make thees experiment. Whatever you may hear or see do not spik a word. Sit verra still in your seat or we shall not have the success.'

Already by his manner the man had invested the proceedings with an air of mystery, and the effect was heightened when he announced that the lights would be extinguished. Old Craven, the caretaker, and young Barmby stood up, prepared to help, and I wondered whether there was collusion between the lad and the mountebank. There was a buzz of conversation in the hall, and Boldini held up his hand enjoining silence.

'Before we maka the dark,' he said, 'Boldini would like two

peoples who knew thees young man verra well, two peoples who were hees verra good friends, to come on thees platform.'

Hennessy stood up immediately.

'Two,' said Boldini and looked down at Eileen. To my mortification she rose also.

'Thank you, *signorina*,' he said, and I thought his eyes wandered over her speculatively, taking in every detail of her dress. That night she had chosen to put on a dark material, altogether sombre and rather out of place for evening wear, though she had relieved the funereal effect by throwing over her shoulders a flowered silk shawl.

As she stood, there was a hum of interest from all over the hall and many curious glances were cast in my direction. I felt snubbed, but no one apparently was greatly concerned at my humiliation. I was only the poor fiancé. Why worry about *my* feelings? In a moment all eyes were directed upon Eileen as Boldini said, 'I would lika thees two peoples to come upon the stage.'

This was going too far. I made a gesture of protest, but Eileen swept by me as if I did not exist. She dropped her shawl on her chair and when, escorted by Hennessy, she walked up the steps, her appearance did not by any means do her justice, and I could imagine Helen Speek and Mrs Marven with their heads together pulling her to pieces in a way women have, commenting probably on her drabness, for, as she mounted to the platform, her black dress mingled with the dark drapings to produce an almost uncanny effect of a face floating in mid air.

Hennessy had submitted to Boldini's injunction to cover himself with a long black cape, which he wrapped about him in the manner of a stage Mephistopheles so that he, too, became no more than a face, while the conjurer himself, who had adopted a similar attire, would have been ludicrous at any other time; for his face was fat and pasty-looking and seemed to float through the air like a phantom pudding.

Boldini placed Eileen and Hennessy at opposite sides of

the stage. Then he said, 'Signorina Mahoney, Signor Hennessy! Weel you promise to do what I tell you?' They nodded and he went on. 'It iss well. Soon we weel put thees light out and, when he iss dark, you must not spik. You must not move – above all you must not move. In the audience, too, there must be the quiet absolute. No one must come in: no one must go out.'

He looked toward the rear of the hall, and Constable Burke, leaning against the door, called out, 'I will watch it, Professor.'

'Thank you,' Boldini said. 'And now, my friends, remember what I have said. No spik. No move. Please!' He glanced down to where young Barmby and Craven awaited their cue. 'Please to put out the lights.'

———

In a moment all was darkness. There was considerable shuffling and a little giggling until Boldini roared, 'Silence. You must be still.'

At once the murmuring ceased. I fixed my eyes on the spot where I knew Eileen was standing, but could see only blackness. The whole stage, the whole hall, had become as dark as pitch, and, suddenly, I was gripped by a presentiment that something unusual was about to happen – that out of that black void something would emerge that would startle and confound me. It was so still that I could hardly believe that every seat in that dark hall held a living being, sitting as tense as I, each contributing to the atmosphere of awe Boldini was cunningly contriving.

I tried to shake off the feeling of nervousness and project my thoughts into other channels. It was the old idea, of course, of reading a ghost story in the dark. The dark bred fearfulness. Deliberately I ceased to think of Boldini up there on the black stage doing heaven knows what, of Eileen trembling in the darkness. I thought of Boldini bent over a bowl, dribbling spaghetti – as a great, gross creature with a tiny kitchen apron spread about his prodigious middle. I told myself I would *not* be tricked.

But the feeling of uneasiness persisted and grew, and, all at once, I heard something. From the direction of the stage came the sound of stertorous breathing. Great gusts of breath appeared to be drawn in and slowly expelled, as if some giant had fallen into abrupt and heavy sleep. The sound accentuated the stillness around me and continued for some moments. Then I heard a voice. It was Boldini's, of course, but it was muffled and appeared to come from a great distance and the words came painfully as if each syllable cost an agony of effort.

'Lar-ry Wa-ard ... Lar-ry Wa-ard.' It was a moaning plea. 'Your friends are here. They wait for you ... Lar-ry Wa-ard.' The name was drawn out in a wailing lament and, as the notes died away, from somewhere far off I heard a voice echoing the words, a voice higher pitched but in the same dolorous strain.

Again there was silence; then, once more, the awful breathing went on until Boldini spoke from the blackness. His voice had acquired strength, and the words were uttered as a command. 'Larry Ward ... your friends are here. Listen ... Tell him, Richard Hennessy, that you are waiting.'

Hennessy spoke, and his voice sounded startlingly close.

'I am waiting, Larry.'

'And you, Eileen Mahoney. Tell him you also wait.'

I heard Eileen from the other side of the stage. There was a catch in her voice as she said, 'I am waiting, Larry – always.'

Once more that deathly silence, and, despite myself, I shared the suspense and horrible expectancy of those silent people around me – all waiting for a sign from a man who was dead. Again the heavy breathing and again Boldini's voice, but this time louder, carrying an agony of appeal.

'Larry Ward, living or dead, we wait for you ... wait for you ... wait for you ... Your friends are here ... Richard! ... Eileen! ... They wait for a sign, Larry Ward.'

The voice died away in a trailing moan. Someone near me drew in her breath with a slight, shuddering sound, and I felt a hand clutch my arm, and fingers dig into my flesh. And then I heard the notes of a mouth organ – just a few notes, softly played but perfectly clear and distinct.

'*Eileen ... alannah.*'

No one could mistake the air.

'*Eileen ... asthore.*'

I heard them as something played with the greatest diffi-culty; then, abruptly, the melody was interrupted by a high-pitched, hysterical laugh, and, for the life of me, I could not tell whence it came.

The music had gone, and from the stage a dull light shot over and past me. I craned my head and saw it writhe and twist, floating about the hall – a thing faintly glowing and moaning as it went, and I could have sworn it had a human face, but it was there no more than an instant before it shot back and dissolved in the inky blackness that enveloped the platform.

It did not reappear, but there came a short, sharp sound as if some small object had been dropped from a height, and a voice higher and clearer than Boldini's cried piercingly, 'Eileen ... wait ... *wait.*'

The next moment I heard a terrible groan, followed by a heavy thud, and Hennessy was shouting for lights.

They were lit at last, though the fingers of old Craven and Joe Barmby must have trembled, for they took long over their job. Hennessy and the young person who helped the conjurer were bending over the prostrate form of Boldini. I saw this in one swift glance, but my eyes were on Eileen. She was standing where Boldini had placed her, gazing downwards and pointing with a kind of awed fascination at something lying in the centre of the stage. Then her feet seemed to be giving under her. She began to sway, and Garnet Price leaped from his chair and was up the steps three at a time. He caught her as she fell.

Hennessy turned at the same moment and saw what she had been staring at. He took two rapid steps forward and, stooping, picked the thing from the floor.

It was a mouth organ, and, as he held it up for us to see, water dripped from it on the stage.

By the time I had forced my way onto the stage, they had taken Eileen to one of the little dressing-rooms where a number of women were fussing about her. They let me see quite plainly that I was not wanted, and it left me with a feeling of helplessness. Someone offered to drive her home, and in a little while she was assisted through the rear exit. Again the women were all about her, and I was ruthlessly shouldered out of the way as if I could be of no assistance and was of no consequence, anyway.

I found Hennessy at my side. 'Better leave her alone,' he said. 'You can do nothing just now.'

There was no sign of Boldini. I heard the caretaker urging people to leave the hall, but they clustered in small, excited groups, ignoring him. I saw Price and Helen, her arm in his, and Mrs Marven and Teecher, the bank clerk, moving towards the door. None of them looked at me and, by and by, Hennessy said, 'Good night.'

I felt frustrated as I walked home alone. When I reached the hotel, Boldini was in the commercial room, surrounded by a little crowd. They were holding glasses in their hands and fell silent as I passed, though all turned their eyes my way. No one invited me to join the party, and I continued my way up to bed. When I reached my room, I lit the candle and stood thinking, the lighted match dying in my hand.

It had all been hocus-pocus, of course. Some damned trick of Boldini's. And yet? Anyway, there was significance in the mouth organ dripping water. Surely it argued that Larry had been drowned. Ward was dead, and it was like this mountebank's impertinence to drag him from his watery grave after Eileen had begun to forget the fellow.

God alone knew what effect this evening of hysteria might have upon her. I had been powerless to prevent her making a public exhibition of herself, humiliated by Price going to help her before I could reach her, excluded from her society, and treated as if I were a social leper. I felt unutterably disgusted with everyone and everything.

I remember I kicked the iron bedpost.

While dressing in the morning I recollected that, towards

the end of his damned séance, Boldini had spoken good English. I smiled grimly to myself as I went to my chest of drawers and dug out an old bilingual textbook that had been lent to me in my college days. I had played with the idea of studying languages at one time, and, somehow, the little book had stuck by me.

I turned over the pages – English one side, Italian the other – looking for a suitable passage. Then I went downstairs and, in the deserted commercial room, copied it out carefully. This is what I wrote:

*Ma inutilmente. Per tre giorni si prolungo il lavoro; senonche l'acqua, scambio di scemare, aumentava. Tutti intendevano che quello non era piu un mezzo di salvezza, ma solo un prolungamento di agonia.*

I glanced at the translation of the Italian words:

*But it was in vain. For three days they toiled continuously; nevertheless the water increased instead of diminishing, and they all began to see that this was no means of salvation, but only a prolongation of agony.*

I smiled again as I closed the book on the innocuous passage. Putting the translation in my pocket I ran upstairs and stowed away the textbook. I went down to breakfast in a mood of happy anticipation.

Helen Speek was sitting with Mrs Marven and next to Garnet Price. It seemed that these two were throwing discretion to the winds. I thought Helen looked pale and a little distraught, but Price was hearty enough in all conscience, joking vulgarly with Rosie as she waited on table and in the presence of the other women. The bank clerk person was there early as usual, determined to get as much as he could for his board money, and Boldini came down when we were halfway through the meal, during which, by common consent, we avoided discussion of the events of the previous night. Price, as a matter of fact, pointedly ignored me, and Mrs Marven and the bank clerk did most of the talking.

I finished my breakfast, and, excusing myself, crossed to Boldini, who was waiting for his ham and eggs.

'I wonder, *signore*, whether you would do me a little favour.'

'Why, by all means,' he replied. 'If it iss possible.'

I took the few lines of Italian from my pocket. 'I have been reading a novel,' I said, 'and these few words in your language were interpolated, but without translation.' I held out the piece of paper and continued. 'I should be greatly obliged if you could tell me what they mean.'

He hesitated, but for an instant only; then he put out his hand and took the paper from me. He looked at me shrewdly as he did so and then began to study the words I had copied. There was silence in the room and everyone's eyes were on Boldini. Price wore a sardonic grin.

Boldini suddenly looked up and said sternly, 'What iss thees? You wanta I should read *thees*?' He tapped the paper with his fingers.

'Yes,' I said, 'if you can, please.'

He frowned at the paper.

'But, surely, *signore*. No – I cannot. Not before the ladies, *signore*.' He looked up at me. 'What book iss thees you have been reading?' He tapped the paper again. 'It iss most indelicate. No, *signore*, not now. Some time we are alone p'raps – but please, excusa before the ladies.'

He thrust the thing into my hands, leaving me thunderstruck at his implication. I couldn't speak. The blood rushed to my face. Mrs Marven looked at me in astonishment and then quickly dropped her eyes. I glanced appealingly at Helen, but she turned her head away, and the fool of a bank clerk sat staring with his mouth agape.

Boldini was busy thanking Rosie for bringing him ham and eggs as I flung furiously out of the room, Price's laugh ringing in my ears.

Dr Hansen was an early caller at the post office. Through the delivery window I saw him drive up in his ancient buggy and watched him climb out slowly. He came into the main office and smiled a pleasant good morning.

'I've just come from Mahoney's place,' he said as he took his mail. 'Thought I'd call and tell you, Ford, that girl of yours is all right after last night. Not wise for quiet people like her to indulge in that sort of excitement, though. Still, no harm done. Had a look at her after I saw her father, poor fellow.'

He was preparing to go and I was thinking to myself that he and Hennessy were the only two men in the town who didn't get my nerves on edge, though even Hennessy had caused me a little anxiety over his miserable dog, when he paused and came back.

'Bless my soul,' he exclaimed. 'Nearly forgot. I'm getting absent minded in my old age. Eileen gave me a letter for you.' He fished it out of his pocket.

'You ought to take a spell, Doctor,' I suggested as I took it.

'Spell?' he said. ''Fraid not, my boy. Too much to do. No rest for the wicked.' His eyes twinkled mischievously, and he added seriously, 'All the same, Ford, I think it might be a good thing for my patients if I had a long rest.'

He went out and I turned to Eileen's letter. An explanation, I supposed, of her reason for leaving me high and dry the previous evening; some sort of apology, perhaps. I opened the envelope.

The message was scribbled in pencil, and it was no apology.

As I read I recalled that other pencilled letter of Eileen's. There was the same evidence of haste so different from the dignified letter she had written me from the city after my proposal of marriage. 'I'm sorry I had to faint like that ... rushed away ... couldn't thank you ...' The scribble went on, 'I am so upset, but I know now, Mr Ford, that after last night, I cannot continue with our engagement. I know that ...' and then, at the very end of the page, as if to mock me, the same words she had written in her letter to Larry, 'the man I am going to marry is ...' I turned the page and read, 'Larry Ward, for I do still believe he is alive. I feel somehow that there's been some dreadful mistake.' Then there was something about not wishing to hurt me, 'but I want you to know at once and I am sending back your ring – '

It had fallen on the floor, and I let it lie there. My eyes filled with tears of rage and disappointment. After all I had done I was to be flung aside, made the laughingstock of the town, jilted by a penniless country wench. It was unbearable.

I looked up to see the Ringer creature grinning at me through the letter delivery window. I strode forward angrily and banged down the wooden shutter, and I heard her utter an exclamation of pain. I think it got her finger. I hoped it had. I wanted to hurt something.

I don't know how I coped with my official work during the next hour. There was a dull ache inside me. I talked to myself, seeking satisfaction in reviling myself, calling myself a fool for wasting my time on such a girl, spending money on her. I thought bitterly of the generous marriage settlement. I had been prepared to give her a thousand pounds, *a thousand pounds of my own money*. Didn't she realise that? Didn't she realise what she was throwing away?

I cursed Boldini for bringing this thing about. Going about the country ruining people's lives with his damnable hocus-pocus. Imposing on the credulous with his chicanery; wrecking careers for the sake of the wretched florins paid into his filthy ticket box. An Italian! A foreigner among decent English people. An Italian, forsooth, who couldn't speak his own language. An imposter! There should be prison for his kind.

I recalled his hateful moustache, his damned impertinence at the breakfast table. It was intolerable. It couldn't, it shouldn't, be countenanced. I picked Eileen's ring from the floor and locked it away carefully in the safe and ran out of the office. The post office should have remained open for business at that hour, but I didn't care. I'd given the government good service – years and years of it. It could afford to allow me a moment to settle my own affairs.

I was afraid Boldini might leave the town before I could wring from him a confession that his séance had been a cruel and deliberate fraud. When I remembered the generous financial arrangement I had made for Eileen, despite the fact that we could expect nothing from the penniless Mahoney, it seemed incredible that she would willingly give me up. It was her father's wish that she and I should marry. She had promised him as he lay dying. All I had to do was to erase from her mind the memory of that absurd séance, and, therefore, it was necessary, without delay, to compel Boldini to admit that it was a fake and that he knew nothing of Ward, dead or alive, other than what he had picked up since he arrived in the town, or gathered from Peter Gallagher's loose gossip as he drove him to Baloola.

There was no one in the hall except Craven, the caretaker, who was cleaning up, but I heard laughter and ascended the steps and crossed the stage, locating the sound in the shed at the rear. Through a window I saw the four Barmby kids and Polly Garner's brat seated about a deal table at the end of which Boldini stood in front of a huge cake with pink and white icing and innumerable candles.

As I watched, he blew out his cheeks and gave a mighty puff and the candles were extinguished at once. He darted forward with an exclamation and snatched a bunch of flowers from the smoking wicks and divided them into five posies, presenting one to each child. The Garner youngster roared with delight, while the Barmbys' mouths fell open till they looked absurdly like a row of dead fish.

I saw Helen Speek and Mrs Marven move into the picture and Boldini pick up a long knife and start to cut the cake. But I was in no mood for further delay and, walking to the door, strode in on them, Eileen's letter in my hand.

'I want a word with you, Boldini,' I said peremptorily.

He looked up in surprise, the big knife still in his hand, and I noted that Hennessy and Price were sitting in a corner, talking to Polly Garner. Price said impatiently, 'Oh, let it wait, Ford.'

'Keep out of this, Price,' I warned him and turned again on the mountebank. 'It can't wait *Mister* Boldini,' I said. 'I want an explanation here and now.'

'But, *signore*,' Boldini expostulated, 'we make the party.'

'Of course it can wait,' Price put in rudely. 'Go on, man, cut the cake.'

His tone irritated me to the point of fury.

'I warned you to stay out of this, Price,' I said. 'I can deal with you later.'

'Why, you – ' Price began rising quickly and coming toward me. Hennessy stepped between us.

Suddenly the Garner brat began to cry.

'I don't like that man,' she yelled, pointing a sticky finger at me. 'Make him go away.' Polly rose quickly to soothe her.

'You see,' Price said sardonically. 'The lady does not desire your presence.'

The youngster refused to be comforted and, taking their cue from her, the Barmby kids also began to snivel.

'Please, Ford,' Hennessy urged. 'You're spoiling everything. I wish you would go.'

'He's a wicked man,' the Garner child yelled.

'For heaven's sake keep your brat quiet,' I cried, turning furiously on Polly. I saw her face flame, but she said nothing to me. Instead she put her arm about the youngster.

'Hush, darling,' she said. 'You mustn't say such things.'

'But he is, he *is*,' the kid wailed. 'He's a wicked man. He opens people's letters.'

I was too stunned to speak. I suppose the youngster thought the silence her statement had produced presaged trouble for her. She turned and stared around her defiantly. 'I don't care,' she cried hysterically, 'he does, he *does*. I saw him.'

I don't know what was in my mind but I made a rush on

the brat. Hennessy grabbed me and held me in a grip of iron, while Price knelt down by the now sobbing child.

'Never mind now, Peggy,' he said. 'You shall tell us about it later. Wait outside now with Auntie and Boldini will bring the cake.'

Mrs Marven lifted the dish from the table and, gathering up the Barmby children, prepared to follow Polly Garner, who had led her youngster out, the brat glaring tearful defiance of me over her shoulder.

'Come on, Mr Boldini,' Mrs Marven called.

'Oh, no you don't,' I said, breaking away from Hennessy. 'Before you go, Boldini, I want you to confess that all that hanky-panky about Larry Ward was a fake – that you don't know anything at all about Larry Ward, dead or alive, and I insist that you come with me to Miss Mahoney at once and tell her so.'

'But, Ford,' Hennessy put in, 'why all this about Larry? What has he to do with it?'

'He'll know when he reads that,' I said, and pushed Eileen's letter into Boldini's hands. He took it with an air of surprise. 'Go on,' I urged him sarcastically, 'you can read it; it isn't in Italian.'

He scanned the scribbled lines. He read slowly and at length turned the page.

'You may as well all know,' I cried bitterly, 'that because of this man's craving for filthy lucre he hasn't hesitated to ruin my life. What's a little misery more or less to a creature like him, as long as he can make money? Yesterday I was to marry Eileen Mahoney. Today, because of this slimy swindler and his beastly séance, she has broken her engagement with me. Why in God's name,' I cried, addressing Boldini, 'couldn't you leave Larry Ward out of your damnable swindles? Ward is drowned – dead and in hell.'

Helen Speek uttered a little cry and covered her face with her hands. Hennessy turned on me.

'Stop it,' he cried. 'Ford, you're crazy.'

I ignored him. 'Well, master mind?'

With a slow movement Boldini returned me my letter and motioned to Mrs Marven, who was standing spellbound in the doorway, holding the cake, the children hanging to her skirts.

'Please, *signora*,' he said weakly, 'taka the chil'ren. I come soon and cutta the cake.' She turned and I was glad to see them out of the way. Boldini addressed me. 'I confess, *signore*,' he said. 'The séance was what you call heem – a fake.'

I smiled triumphantly at the others. 'You see,' I said, and then to Boldini, 'and now you will come with me to Miss Mahoney and confess your fraud.'

'I will come,' he said almost abjectly.

'You will tell her,' I ordered, 'that the whole affair was a mischievous fraud. You will tell her that Larry Ward was no more than a name to you – that you couldn't contact him by supernatural or any other means – that it was all a barefaced swindle – that you'd never even heard of him till you got here.'

'No, *signore*.'

'Oh, yes, you, you will,' I shouted at him.

'Oh, no, *signore*,' he said, 'I will not. I could not say that because it would not be true. I *had* heard of Larry Ward.'

'You'd heard he was drowned,' I cried, 'and so you engineered your beastly trick with the dripping mouth organ, raking up something that had been decently forgotten.'

'It was a trick,' he admitted, 'but I did not know then what I know now. You see, I had not only heard of Larry Ward before I came to this town. I had spoken to him, not in a séance, but in real life. Believe me, please, he is very much alive.'

The others were as stunned as I. No one spoke. At last Boldini turned to Hennessy and spread his hands apologetically. 'I am sorry, Mr Hennessy, that I tricked you.'

'It is a lie,' I shouted. 'It is more of your damned deceit.'

'No,' he repeated. 'It is quite true. I found Ward quite by chance – half drowned, almost delirious. He told me many things. He was very sick. I helped him. I am helping him now. He is quite safe.'

'I don't believe it,' I cried. 'You've lied and cheated, and you're lying now.'

Boldini's attitude suddenly changed. All his foreign mannerisms dropped from him, and he strode towards me. He still had the formidable knife in his hand and with his blazing eyes and big moustache he cut a menacing figure. I retreated precipitately.

'Why, you damned upstart!' he shouted, 'you paltry prig; you puffed-up peacock. I've stood all I'm going to stand from you. You've called me a liar, and I've stood it for the sake of peace, but now I'm going to wring your blasted neck, you – you cock-a-hoop.'

Hennessy was staring at him in surprise as he stooped to spring at me, but suddenly Price stepped forward and pushed him back with his open hand and began to laugh and laugh. We gazed at him in amazement as he continued to smack Boldini on the shoulder.

'Carlo Boldini,' he roared. 'Carlo Boldini!' and went off into another peal of laughter. 'Why, you old horse thief, you. You took me in, too.'

Boldini drew himself up to his full height. '*Signore*?' he said with dignity.

'Oh, come off it, *Charlie Baldwin*,' Price gasped.

For a second Boldini glared, then the ferocity died out of his eyes and into them came a little twinkle. His mouth opened in a wide grin.

'Oh, well, Mr Price,' he said, 'it was all right while it lasted. I knew you, but what made you recognise me?'

'When you lost your temper and called Ford here a cock-a-hoop,' Price explained, still spluttering with laughter. 'And by the way,' he added, 'you can put the knife down, Charlie, unless you'd like to carry on and cut the gentleman's throat. I won't object.'

I had stood by, fuming. When I spoke, I made my voice deliberately insolent. 'I have no doubt, Price, that it would suit you very well to have me out of the way.'

Price looked me up and down contemptuously. 'Listen, Ford,' he said slowly and very quietly for a man of his violent nature, 'as far as I'm concerned you're a louse. You're everything I think a man shouldn't be. You're a blackmailing swine, and if what the little Garner girl says is true, you're something else besides. For some inscrutable reason the law regards your life as of some value; otherwise I'd not be hanged for doing society a good turn and I'd slit your throat here and now and think it a damned good day's work.'

Helen Speek had risen while Price was speaking and seized his arm, striving in vain to restrain him. He had spoken with such studied insult that my blood boiled anew. Without thought of the consequences I shouted, 'And I'll tell you something, Price. You may be hanged, anyway.' Helen's face blanched as I went on, 'Yes, you and your paramour with you – from the same scaffold.'

Price hit me. So suddenly that I was taken unaware. He gave me no opportunity to defend myself. I fell backwards, and Hennessy was only just in time to prevent my falling. Boldini grabbed Price, and Helen sat down and began to cry. I was beside myself with rage and pain.

'You and your light-o'-love, there,' I screamed, struggling with Hennessy. I felt my mouth thicken with blood and the taste intensified my hate. I spat the words at Price. 'You poisoned Speek. You murdered him in cold blood – the two of you – so that you could carry on your filthy intrigue.'

'Why, you perjuring ...' Price cried and struggled to get at me as a shadow fell across the doorway, and, all at once, Constable Burke was in the shed, standing between us.

'Now, now, gentlemen,' he said ponderously. 'We can't have this, you know.' His stupid face turned from one to the other of us enquiringly; then he asked me, suddenly, as if the words had just registered in his mind, 'What was that you said about Speek, sir?'

'Nothing, nothing,' Hennessy interposed swiftly. 'It is best forgotten.'

Price said, 'Let the swine repeat it if he dare.'

'I dare all right, Price,' I said. 'You and your mistress there killed him.' I turned to Burke. 'They poisoned him in cold blood.'

The constable's eyes blinked.

'But, Mr Ford, sir,' he said, 'Mr Speek shot himself.'

I laughed hysterically. 'You have him up, Burke,' I cried. 'Get the blind man out of his grave and open him up. You'll find how he died, all right.'

Burke stared at me incredulously. The words at last penetrated his brain and he said heavily, 'That's a very serious accusation, Mr Ford. I think you had better come down to the station with me – that is,' he added, 'if you're not all having a joke with me.'

I laughed shortly. 'You fool,' I said, 'I'm saying that Price and his woman poisoned Speek. Is that plain enough for you?'

He considered it for a moment. 'I may be a fool, Mr Ford,' he admitted, unruffled, 'but I still can't understand how it could be. At the inquest the jury said he shot himself.'

'He was poisoned,' I insisted loudly.

'*You* say so, Mr Ford,' Burke said stubbornly, 'but that's not enough. You can't go and dig up graves to look for poison just on anyone's say-so. Especially,' he added, 'when a man committed suicide by shooting himself.'

Hennessy put in a word. 'I think it's all some ridiculous misunderstanding, Burke,' he said. 'Mr Ford has had some bad news and he is overwrought. I think it would be wise if we all forgot what we've heard here today.'

Burke shook his head. 'Begging your pardon, Mr Hennessy,' he said, 'but I don't think that's right, either. There's something going on here and I don't quite know what. It's making my head go round. People don't just go about making accusations about poison.'

'There are all sorts of people,' Price said. 'Ford is the sort that makes these wild, unsubstantiated statements – '

Burke seized on the word eagerly. 'That's it, sir,' he cried, and turning to me went on, 'It's not substantiated, Mr Ford. You couldn't get an exhumation just on a say-so.'

'If that's all you want,' I said, 'I'll soon fix that. Ask Miss Polly Garner to come back.'

Hennessy looked at me as if he thought I was mad, but Burke went to the door without comment and called, 'Miss Garner, would you mind stepping this way?'

She came at once, and I saw that she was frightened.

'Listen, Miss Polly,' I said quickly before anyone could speak. 'I release you from your promise. I want you to tell the constable that you saw Speek before he died and that he said, "Ward – poison".'

She looked wildly about her and would have run from the room, but I intercepted her.

'You heard Speek say, "Ward – poison".' I persisted, keeping my eyes fixed on hers. '*Didn't* you?'

'Oh,' she burst into tears. 'Mr Ford, please don't make me say it.' She sat down beside Helen and buried her face in her hands.

Burke's cowlike eyes followed her, but he said nothing. I don't think he could think of anything he could say, and Hennessy watched her in bewilderment. I turned to Price.

'There's a witness to hang you and your woman, Price,' I cried, 'because she saw Speek before he died. He was in agony and he said "Ward – poison" before he expired. He said that because you and Helen Speek had quarreled with him only a few moments before, and all the while you were present, because he was blind he imagined you were Larry Ward. Now, Burke, have you got *that* into your thick head?'

The constable rubbed his chin with stubby fingers.

'It's all very confusing,' he said, and just then there was a knock at the door and a man's voice called, 'Can I come in? They tell me I will find Mr Ford here?'

At the voice Polly Garner sat up, startled. We all turned and looked at the stranger. He was a middle-aged, well-knit, well- groomed, good-looking fellow with calm, clear eyes that swept from one to the other of us.

'This is Mr Ford,' Hennessy said with a gesture of his hand.

'Oh!' The newcomer came forward. He looked me up and down with annoying deliberation and without speaking. Then he went to Polly and to everyone's surprise she sprang up and threw her arms about him, sobbing on his shoulder.

'There, there, my dear,' he said, and standing with his arm about her he turned again, to me. 'My name is Wellday,' he said. 'I think you may remember it.'

Vaguely I recalled it.

'Yes,' I said curtly, 'but we are busy – '

'I think we should know each other, Mr Ford,' he said, unperturbed, and ignoring my words. 'I am sure you will be interested to know that my wife is dead. I have come here to marry Miss Polly Garner.'

I was unable to hide my surprise. Now I remembered the name. Wellday! The signature to Polly's registered letter and the cheque that came with it.

'Not only that, Mr Ford,' the man went on calmly. 'I have come for another reason – to be near my child and my fiancée and to protect them.' He led Polly to the door. 'I hope you'll remember that, Mr Ford,' he said over his shoulder as they walked out together.

When they had gone, Boldini spoke. I suppose he had forgotten his confession, for he relapsed into broken English. He said, 'If you will please excuse, I will go cutta the cake.'

Burke made no attempt to detain him.

Hennessy said, 'Well, Burke?'

'I don't know what to say,' the constable confessed. 'I'll have to think this over.'

'A very good idea,' the schoolmaster agreed. 'I think we should all go home and you can advise us what you wish us to do later.'

Burke went to the door and, pausing, addressed us ponderously. 'I hope you all understand that this looks a bit serious to me. It sounds fishy – though, if Speek shot himself, where does the poison come in?'

'It's a lot of nonsense, if you ask me,' Hennessy said.

'I wouldn't go so far as that, sir,' Burke said thoughtfully. 'No, I don't think it's nonsense, Mr Hennessy. Mind you, I don't say I believe it, but it's fishy. You see, you're all involved. All but Mr Hennessy, though even he's a witness to what Mr Ford has said about Mr Price and Mrs Speek. And there's Polly Garner.'

'And Larry Ward,' Hennessy added.

The constable blinked at him.

'Yes,' he said at length, 'his name's been dragged in. But we won't get much out of Larry, poor lad.'

'I think,' Hennessy said, 'that you should see Boldini, Burke, and let him tell you where Ward is. You see, Burke, Larry wasn't drowned. He's alive.'

I believe it was too much for the constable. He stared at Hennessy almost reproachfully for a second or two, then he turned without a word and walked wearily away.

My cut lip was smarting and the blood was still flowing. No one had attempted to help me. Price was leaning over Helen, comforting her and paying no attention to me.

'Are you coming, Hennessy?' I asked.

He said, 'Er, no, sorry, Ford, I have one or two things – ' He broke off in evident embarrassment.

Hennessy, too, I thought. So much for friendship!

I decided I would walk around to Dr Hansen's and get him to fix up my lip. There was, thank God, at least one decent person in the town. Outside, under the trees, I saw Mrs Marven and Boldini with the children. I heard them laugh at something Boldini said. The Garner brat turned her head and saw me and poked out her tongue.

Walking into the hall, I was passing one of the little dressing rooms and caught a glimpse of my disheveled self in a long mirror placed against the far wall.

As I stood regarding my reflection I heard a voice saying, 'I suppose you know you're looking into a lady's dressing room?' I had not noticed the presence of the young person who played the piano for Boldini and helped him in his tricks. She wore no dress and was standing, quite unabashed, in her petticoats, with one limb lifted to a high stool while she buttoned her kid boots.

'Why, you've got blood all over your pretty face,' she said. 'Come here.' Before I could protest, she had taken me by the arm, picked up a wet sponge, and, pushing me into a chair, was busy wiping my face.

'You're Mr Ford, aren't you?' she chattered. 'I'm Flossie La Rue – that's what Boldini calls me. My real name's Jinks. Ain't it awful?' She dried my face with a towel.

'There you are, Toots,' she said at length. 'Now you look something like a gentleman.'

I muttered some thanks.

'That's all right, Toots,' she said brazenly. 'Thank *you*,' and she tiptoed and kissed me roundly on the lips. I was staggered and turned hastily from her to see old Craven, the caretaker, standing outside the door, grinning at the scene and already anticipating with what relish he would retail the new and meaty scandal.

As I walked to the doctor's I felt mentally confused and physically sick. Hennessy, to whom I had always expected I might turn for sympathy and understanding, had failed me. I had been insulted by Boldini at the breakfast table, miserably jilted by Eileen Mahoney, and assaulted by Garnet Price, while this Wellday person had spoken to me in such a manner that I could regard it in no other light than a threat. On top of that there was the disturbing accusation of Polly Garner's detestable brat.

And Larry Ward was alive! God knows, I had had enough to put up with. The only kindness shown me that day had been by a painted trollop and even that would have repercussions when Craven began to wag his evil tongue.

I thought again of the man Wellday. In the letter he had written to Polly Garner there had been no mention of his wife's illness. Now, in that cursed provocative way women have, she must up and die, leaving him free to make an honest woman of this impossible *demi-vierge*. When I thought of Wellday, I could scarcely credit that a man of his apparent affluence and breeding could travel all the way to this town to marry a faded little thing like Polly Garner.

All said and done, there was no real obligation. His cheques had been sent regularly enough to keep her in comparative comfort. As I saw it, it was scarcely decent to rush from the funeral of one's wife to marry a past light-o'-love. Well, I considered, they would be leaving town. I had no intention of giving the show away and that would be the end of the *affaire Garner*.

The doctor was out when I called, but the woman who came in to tidy up and get him the few meals he took at his own house told me she expected him at any minute and asked me to wait in the drab parlour adjoining the surgery. The door of the surgery was open and to me, with my orderly mind, the room appeared to be in a chaotic state. The woman saw my look of distaste.

'You must excuse the untidiness, sir,' she said. 'The doctor never lets me go in there to clean up properly.'

I sat down and tried to forget my troubles by reading an out-of-date magazine but was relieved when Dr Hansen came in. He attended to my cut lip and asked no questions, but, as he finished, he took my hand and felt my pulse. He shook his head.

'Something wrong somewhere,' he said, and I wondered whether he'd learned of the happenings behind the hall. 'I'll mix you a tonic, Ford.' There was no chemist in the town in those days, and the doctor did all his own dispensing.

'Excuse the seeming chaos,' he said as he pushed a number of bottles away from his table and began to make up my medicine. 'Can't afford to let Mrs Bridgetts loose in here. Could never find anything again. No time to tidy up myself either. Here you are!'

He handed me the draught and I swallowed it in a gulp.

'That'll steady you,' he said, opening the door to his waiting room. He looked at me kindly enough, then, as I did not speak, he put his hand on my arm. 'All right,' he said, 'don't tell me if you'd rather not. Still, sometimes it helps.'

I suppose I was overwrought. Anyway, something snapped in me. All at once I sat down and cracked up. My throat choked and, burying my face in my arms, I began to cry.

He went quickly to the outer door and closed it, then he returned to me. 'Let it go, man,' he said, 'don't mind me.'

He waited until I had got control of myself and begun to talk and, as I did so, all my resentment returned. I spoke bitterly of Eileen's faithlessness. I told him of Price's illicit association with Helen Speek and of my accusation. I said I had suggested an exhumation.

'An exhumation?' he exclaimed.

'I know Speek was poisoned,' I said warmly.

'But this is fantastic, Ford,' he said. 'It's madness. The man was shot.'

'It sounds crazy,' I said, 'but I know you'll find poison in Speek's body.'

My story had shocked him. He sat down and wiped the perspiration from his forehead, though the day was far from hot. Then he leaned forward and spoke gently.

'Listen to me, Ford,' he said. 'You've had a lot to put up with. You're distraught. Why not rest up this afternoon? I'll mix up something and send it to you and you can take it before you lie down. It will steady you. Try and forget these awful things that you have got into your mind – about Speek, I mean. Isn't it just imagination?'

He paused and then went on slowly, 'Wouldn't it be better if you told Burke it was just imagination? It was a wild exaggeration in any case. You couldn't have seen Speek that night, could you, now? Remember, at the inquest you swore you had not. You didn't tell Burke you actually saw anything.' For a moment his eyes met mine searchingly; then he stood up.

'Take a doctor's advice. Forget it, Ford. Take it easy and be sure and take the draught.'

He closed the door after me and I walked away. I thought over what he had said about the oath I had taken at the inquest. And I suddenly remembered that I had not told him anything about Polly Garner's connection with the tragedy.

I wished that I had not brought her into the fracas that morning. It would have been easier to follow the doctor's advice. After all, Larry was alive, and, if Eileen should be foolish enough to prefer him and his penury to me and my thousand pounds, I would at least have the money entirely to myself. I would avoid all the wretched publicity and the filthy innuendoes a man like Price, with the legal assistance his wealth could buy, might drag into the case. In a little while I would be moved to my new position. Wellday would marry his light-o'-love and Garnet Price and his mistress could be left to stew in their own juice, frightened out of their lives by every knock at the door, terrified to open their letters because they would never know when I might be asking them to buy some more shares.

I had no appetite for lunch but I made myself eat, especially as Price and Helen had had the good taste to stay away. Mrs Marven appeared to be busy in the bar and did not come in either, but the bank clerk had apparently heard nothing and chattered away about a coming test match till my head ached.

After the meal I took the draught Hansen had sent round and rested for a while. Saturday was not a mail day, and it was seldom anyone came near the office, most people in the town going to watch the football. I took my time, therefore, and slept a little. When I awoke I felt refreshed. I lay on the bed thinking things over and decided to take the doctor's advice.

If Burke asked questions I'd tell him I'd spoken in the heat of the moment, as indeed I had. I doubted if the details had penetrated through his thick skull. He was an easy man to muddle, and I would offer to shake hands with Price and apologise to both these wretched people for losing my head, and Burke would be glad to rub the whole thing out. I wished to heaven, though, that I had not lost my temper and blurted things out. If only Price had not struck me!

I might as well have stayed away from the post office altogether, for no one came in till about four o'clock, when Burke appeared. I was surprised, because he was a football enthusiast and that day our town was playing a visiting team and there was more than ordinary interest in the match. I assumed a lightheartedness I was far from feeling.

'What!' I said. 'No football?'

'No, Mr Ford,' he replied and, without invitation, lifted the flap of the counter and came into the inner office. 'May I sit down?' he asked, and went on. 'I've been too worried to think about football.'

'That's a pity,' I said, 'It should be a good game. Do you think we'll win?'

He lifted his unwieldy head and looked at me with big, solemn eyes.

'Yes,' he replied, 'we've got a very good chance.' He shifted in his chair. 'About that affair this morning, Mr Ford,' he began.

'Oh, that!' I replied. 'Forget about it, Burke. Price and I got into holts. He hit me and I lost my head.'

He waited, considering my words, before answering. 'You made a very serious accusation, Mr Ford. I admit I'm still a bit at sea about it. I can't understand you saying a thing like that.'

'Hot blood,' I said. 'It runs in the family.'

'But,' he persisted. 'You didn't just blurt out things; you gave details. Place and time, and things like that.'

'Look here, Burke,' I cried, angered at his insistence. 'I tell you I was overwrought. I didn't know what I was saying. I hardly remember what I said. Whatever it was I withdraw it and I'll apologise to Price and Mrs Speek.'

'I'm glad of that, sir,' Burke said. 'That puts it up to them. As a matter of fact, I asked them to call in here so that I could see you all together.' He glanced at the big clock on the wall. 'They should be here now.'

I heard a step on the verandah as he spoke, and Helen Speek came in. Burke got up lumberingly and lifted the flap of the counter so that she could enter. He said, 'I'm glad you've come, Mrs Speek, because Mr Ford has withdrawn the accusations he made this morning and wants to apologise to you.'

It seemed to me that he watched her closely, noting her reaction. She was plainly taken aback.

'I'm sorry, Mrs Speek,' I said. 'I deeply regret whatever it was I said. I was beside myself. I humbly ask your pardon.' I held out my hand and she took it. Hers felt cold and limp, and, as we stood thus, Price walked in and stared. I turned to him at once.

'I'm sorry, Price,' I said, as he came behind the counter. 'I apologise for what I said this morning.' He gazed at me steadily, and I saw a speculative glitter in his black eyes, then their expression changed and he angrily struck aside my proffered hand.

'To hell with you, Ford,' he cried. 'Carry on with your beastly accusations. You've made your bed. You can rot in it.' And, turning to the constable, he went on, 'Look, Burke. You know what this town is. You know that stink sticks. You get Speek out of his grave and carve him up. I want him up, d'you hear? Let Ford here stick his nose into his stomach and smell out the poison – if he can. I not only welcome an exhumation, I demand it.'

I was astonished, but I intercepted Helen's quick look of alarm and I suspected that Price was bluffing.

Burke had got to his feet again and was saying, 'Now, Mr Price, that's not a nice way to talk.'

He turned to the counter as someone came in. It was Wringer Rosie, asking for a twopenny stamp. It didn't seem funny at the time, but I remember to this day the astonishment on the old woman's face as we sat still and silent and the constable gravely pulled open the drawer under the counter, tore a stamp from a sheet, and dropped the pennies into the till.

He followed her out without a word and, after she had gone, locked the door. When he returned, he slumped into a chair and with his thick fingers began to drum on the table, considering each of us in turn, frowning and solemn. We waited and it seemed to me that the infernal drumming continued for an age, driving me almost crazy. He said at last, 'I've never had a case like this before. I've never heard of one, either. I don't know what I ought to do.'

As nobody appeared to help him he went on, 'There's another thing. There's that bit about Polly Garner and poison and Larry Ward. Where does that fit in?'

He gazed at us bleakly, then turned his head slowly at a tapping on the delivery window. Rising heavily, he walked across the room and threw up the wooden shutter. Wellday was gazing through, stooping a little so that he could see into the office.

'Oh!' He was plainly surprised to find himself so close to Burke's moonface, but recovered his poise immediately. 'I was told you might be here, Constable,' he said. 'I thought it my duty to see you at once about what happened this morning.'

Burke said, 'Yes,' and waited.

'It seems,' Wellday said, and I am sure he meant his words to penetrate into the room so that we all might hear them, 'that something was said about an incident my future wife was unfortunate enough to witness. Miss Garner wants it made perfectly plain that, this morning, Mr Ford attempted to put words into her mouth. She did not hear Mr Speek, before he died, say, "Ward – poison." The words, she says, were, "Ford – poison."'

The two men continued to gaze steadfastly at each other through the little window, but presently Burke turned slowly and looked at me, and I felt the hair rise on the back of my neck, and then Price was laughing. Very significantly he began to swing his whip about in his hand. With a little jerk he made the thong writhe and twist and I saw he had made a loop like a hangman's noose.

Helen Speek sat very still, her hands clasped tightly in her lap, gazing at the floor, but Price was grinning as the constable closed the wooden shutter and heaved his great bulk on to a totally inadequate stool. He recommenced his irritating drumming on the counter, but after a while got to the floor with a grunt.

'I'll have to think about this quietly,' he informed us. 'We don't want the whole town to get wind of it either, so you'll all have to keep mum. It doesn't make sense to me, but there's something queer going on and I think it will be my duty to make a report. So you'd better come round to the station tonight at eight. Will that suit?'

'The earlier the better,' Price said.

'And you, Mrs Speek?' She nodded assent.

'Mr Ford?'

'Oh, all right,' I said impatiently, 'but I'm sick and tired of the whole business.'

The constable gazed at us mournfully.

'Very well,' he said. 'At eight.' As he unlocked the office door he called over his shoulder, 'I think, Mr Price, you'd better come along with me. I don't want any more arguments.'

Price laughed. 'Right you are, Burke,' he said cheerfully. 'I think Mr Ford agrees with you.' He paused as he held the flap of the counter, preparatory to leaving, and grinned at me maliciously. 'So long, Ford,' he said. 'See you on the scaffold.'

Helen Speek sat on after they had gone, her eyes still fixed on the floor, but now her fingers were intertwining nervously. Presently she said in a small voice, 'Why did you do it? I kept to the bargain.'

'I know,' I said. 'It was Price's fault. If he hadn't insulted me this would never have happened.'

She considered that. 'We mustn't have an exhumation.' She shuddered. 'It would be horrible.'

'Well,' I told her, 'I did my best. You bought my shares

and I was ready to play the game. I still am. Why don't you keep Price in order?'

'He is so headstrong,' she said, and after a bit she added, 'But now there is Polly Garner to consider, too. If she speaks, as I suppose she will, Burke may insist on the exhumation.'

'Possibly,' I said. 'I don't know. Exhumations are not so easy, though. The thing's too much for him, I think. As a matter of fact, it's too much for me.' I regarded her speculatively. 'Mrs Speek,' I asked, 'you did find your husband with the gun in his hand – dead, didn't you?'

She looked me straight in the eyes. 'Yes, of course,' she said.

'And Mrs Marven saw him with the gun in his hand – dead?'

'Yes.'

'And Dr Hansen and Burke himself?'

She nodded.

'And,' I continued, 'the jury said he'd shot himself. Then all this talk of poison will sound incredible to official ears. Believe me, government departments take a lot of rousing. After a coroner's jury with such evidence before it has brought in a verdict of suicide, they'll prefer to let sleeping dogs lie.'

The phrase was hardly an attractive one, but she was too preoccupied to notice. Her head was bent and she wore no hat and her pile of golden hair was caught by a beam of the late-afternoon sun. It was glorious hair, I thought, and considered the rest of her. She had a figure and, despite a certain sombreness, her features were good, especially her eyes. I had an inspiration.

'For your own sake, Mrs Speek,' I said, 'you must persuade Price to say no more about an exhumation and to fix Burke in some way. He's a poor man and Price should find it easy. If that fails, why you're a fine-looking woman, and Burke is a bachelor, isn't he? After all, even a policeman grows lonely in a little country town.'

She rose with an exclamation and faced me angrily.

'Why not?' I went on, unmoved. 'The alternative is not very pleasant.'

She went to the counter and lifted the heavy flap, slamming it down after she had passed through. She walked to the door and paused with her hand on the knob.

'You have the foulest mind,' she said, her face flaming.

'Come, now,' I retorted. 'There should be frankness between us. After all, there was Larry, and – er – poor Haggart, I believe. What's a constable more or less?'

She uttered an exclamation of impatience and flung out, slamming the door after her.

Well, at least I'd put the idea into her head! The only thing I knew of Burke's relations with women was his calflike devotion to Rosie, Mrs Marven's housemaid. She was a brunette. A blonde, especially a fine-looking woman like Helen Speek, would be a nice change. A chit like Rosie wouldn't stand much chance against an experienced woman like Helen. And it would save Burke such a lot of worry. With Burke ready to wash up the whole affair, I did not think Polly Garner would insist on coming forward. Wellday was sticking his nose in at present, advising her to tell what she knew, but he'd change his tune. After all, he was going to marry the woman and he'd scarcely risk involving her in the scandal I could loose if I chose to speak.

When Burke had served his purpose and compromised himself beyond recovery, Helen could go back to Price, of course. Women were like that. Faithless! Look at Eileen! You couldn't really trust any of them. I recalled the words of Gallagher, the mail driver, 'She'll be needing a husband pretty soon.' I thought of the names carved low down on the tree hidden by the undergrowth, the trumpery ring Larry Ward had given her, those words in her letter, 'After what happened this afternoon,' old Mahoney's desperate anxiety that the marriage settlement should be signed and the marriage hurried on, his cryptic remark about not condemning frailty in women.

Maybe I had been a fool all along. Men were usually fools

about women. But, even as these thoughts rioted through my mind, I knew that if Eileen came to me at that moment and begged my forgiveness I'd want her more than I'd wanted anything in the world.

I was surprised to see Mrs Marven at the police station when I arrived. Just after the evening meal I'd heard her talking to old Plank and his cronies in the public bar. She was telling one of her eternal stories, something about when she was a beautiful girl of sixteen going on a voyage in a brig and a big storm coming up and the captain calling the crew together on the main deck and telling them in a moving speech that she must be saved at all costs. I've forgotten the rest. It was a silly story, like all the stories she told, and the only reason I recall it, I suppose, is because it struck me as remarkable that she could be romancing like that one minute and the next sitting up in Constable Burke's office, quietly knitting, quite unperturbed by the fact that she was involved, however lightly, in this scandal regarding Timothy Speek.

Hennessy was there, too, sitting with Burke at the big table. Price was seated on the couch next to Helen and I took a chair opposite them.

The constable said, 'I asked Mrs Marven to come along tonight because, in a way, she's mixed up in this case, and I've asked Dr Hansen, but he won't be able to get here yet. I've invited Mr Hennessy, too, so he can help me. He's very kindly offered because, to tell the truth, I think this is going to be a bit beyond me, and if it comes to making a report, I'll be all at sea and it's no good pretending I won't, and the department won't be able to make head or tail of it.'

Hennessy said, 'Of course, I've no right to be here. If any of you object – '

We hastened to assure him, though I rather felt he had snubbed me during the morning and felt it would have been easier to deal with Burke alone.

'Hennessy's presence makes everything simple,' Price said. 'He heard it all this morning.'

'Just one moment, if you don't mind, sir,' Burke objected. 'I'd like to take this in the right order and quiet like. Now, as I see it, offically, the night that Mr Speek died this is what happened. I've been looking up the records of the inquest. Mrs Speek last saw her husband alive at about eight-thirty. No one saw him alive after that. At about twenty to eleven Mrs Speek found her husband dead.

'She ran to Dr Hansen's,' Burke went on monotonously. 'He wasn't home. She then went to the police station, but the officer in charge – that's me – was absent on flood duty, so she went to see Mrs Marven. Mrs Marven accompanied her to her home and testified that she found Speek lying in his chair, dead. They – that's Mrs Marven and Mrs Speek – then went back to the hotel and Mrs Marven made Mrs Speek go to bed and waited for the police officer to come, as he would have to pass her door on his way to the station.

'Later she – Mrs Marven – heard a buggy coming down the street. It was Dr Hansen's, and she took him to Speek's home. The doctor testified that he found the body lying in a big chair. Deceased had been shot through the head and the gun was clutched in his fingers. The police officer' – without pausing he touched his chest with his thumb – 'tesified that he had found a message pinned on his door and, following instructions in same, proceeded immediately to Speek's house, where he found deceased slumped in a chair. Dr Hansen said that Speek had been dead when he arrived and that he had not disturbed the body. The revolver was identi-fied as belonging to the deceased, and the coroner's jury brought in a verdict of suicide while temporarily insane.'

Burke stopped, a little out of breath, and looked owl-like about him.

'That's what the official record shows,' he explained.

'The record also shows that Ford had an appointment with Mr Speek for nine o'clock that night,' Price put in maliciously.

Burke turned over some papers and peered up over his spectacles.

'Yes,' he agreed, 'Mrs Speek testified to that, or rather that her husband said he expected Mr Ford to call at nine o'clock. But Mr Ford said he had no such appointment with Speek for that evening and, as a matter of fact, had promised to see Mr Hennessy at that hour.'

The schoolmaster nodded in confirmation. 'That's correct,' he said. 'I fixed the time myself and Ford kept the appointment punctually.'

Burke put down his pen and wiped his spectacles. 'That's all fair and square,' he said. 'We know where we are with that. But *now* we come to this other business.'

'I've told you,' I put in warmly, 'that I was hysterical. Price had struck me, and I made a wild statement for which I have already apologised.'

'What gets me,' Burke said solemnly, 'is why did you pick on poison? What made you think of that in particular, Mr Ford?'

'How do I know?' I asked heatedly. 'I said the first thing that came into my mind.'

'But, Mr Ford,' the constable persisted, 'you said you saw Mrs Speek and Mr Price together with Timothy Speek and they were – '

'No, Burke,' Hennessy interrupted quickly. 'I remember distinctly what Mr Ford said this morning. He did not say he *saw* anything or that he *heard* anything.'

Burke's mournful eyes blinked at the school teacher.

'That's correct, Mr Hennessy,' he agreed, and for the moment I thought he sounded somewhat relieved. 'But what I can't understand, Mr Ford, is why all that about Speek thinking Mr Price was Larry Ward. It doesn't sound like something you'd make up on the spur of the moment.'

'I've told you,' I said doggedly, 'I don't know why. I suppose I'd heard gossip about Larry Ward and – and Price and Mrs Speek. I didn't know what I was saying.'

There was a little silence before Burke said, 'I see.'

I could tell he didn't believe me.

A knock on the door preceded Dr Hansen. He nodded to us all in a friendly manner as he came in, and Burke went into another room and wheeled out a comfortable chair for him.

'There you are, Doc,' he said. 'Make yourself comfortable.'

'Thanks.' Dr Hansen did not sit down immediately, but, to my surprise, crossed to me. 'How are you feeling now, Ford?' he asked solicitously. 'Ought to be in bed, resting, by rights,' and before I could reply he had turned to the constable. 'I hope you haven't been worrying him, Burke. I think I ought to tell you that Ford's in a high state of nervous excitement. I advised him to rest, and he really should.' He looked about him and said with a grin, 'I'm not sure I shouldn't put him in a strait jacket. And, now, what's all this mystery?'

Burke's face became gloomier and his eyes rested on me as if appraising the reliability of the doctor's diagnosis.

'Mystery is right, Doc,' he said. 'I'm blowed if I can see daylight. It's like this.' He turned to his papers and, to my exasperation, went through the whole rigmarole about the inquest again.

Dr Hansen listened patiently, though he looked very seedy, and a man less stupid than Burke would have spared him the details. He shut his eyes so that, for all we knew, he had fallen asleep in his chair. None, I am sure, would have blamed him, for Burke's heavy monotone had a definitely somnolent effect.

The constable pushed the papers from him and removed his spectacles again. 'This morning, Doc,' he explained, as Hansen opened his eyes and blinked at him, 'Mr Ford here accused Mr Price and Mrs Speek of poisoning.'

'Stuff and nonsense. Poisoning who?'

'Timothy Speek.'

'Hallucinations!' the doctor said shortly. 'Speek was shot. Saw him.'

'He could have been poisoned first,' Burke said doggedly.

'Yes,' the doctor admitted, as if the idea had occurred to him for the first time. 'That is so. But why?'

'That is what I've got to find out,' Burke said. 'That is, if he *was* poisoned. Mr Ford even demanded an exhumation.'

'Ridiculous,' the doctor said quickly. 'I've told you the man's not himself. He must have been suffering from a brain storm. Hadn't the faintest idea what he was talking about.'

'That's what he says himself now,' Burke said slowly. 'But,' he continued, 'when he made his accusation he gave details, and he brought in Larry Ward's name.'

'Hysteria!' The doctor almost snorted.

'Beg pardon, sir,' Burke said simply, 'he was excited, but it didn't sound like hysteria to me.'

'But you would hardly be a competent judge,' Dr Hansen said with a touch of asperity, and the constable's cheeks reddened. He coughed to hide his discomfiture and turned to Mrs Marven.

'Mrs Marven,' he said, 'how long did you wait before the doctor came along – that is, after you'd sent Mrs Speek to bed at your hotel?'

She told him about half an hour. He turned to Dr Hansen again.

'You had been out to Dunbar's place that night, Doctor?'

Hansen had shut his eyes again. He nodded without opening them.

Burke said, 'Mrs Marven, when you ran out and saw the doctor's buggy, what did you do?'

'I stopped him, of course.'

'How?'

'I ran out on the road and called out. He was driving a little fast.'

'In which direction?'

Price burst in, 'For heaven's sake, Burke, where is this getting us?'

The constable's eyes rested on the interjector for a moment. He said, 'You must excuse me, sir. It's just to get a picture in my mind, as it were.'

He looked at Mrs Marven again. 'Was the doctor driving toward Speek's house?'

She hesitated and glanced at Hansen. 'I'm – I'm not sure. I believe he was. But I don't remember. I was so flustered.'

'That was going out of your way, sir, wasn't it?' Burke asked the doctor. 'I mean – away from the surgery?'

'Of course it was,' the doctor said testily. 'I wanted a drink. I was going to the hotel for a drink. Nothing wrong with that, is there?'

'No, no, of course not,' Burke replied hastily. 'I just wondered, sir. It was pretty late like. I wondered how you knew Mrs Marven would be up?'

'Why,' the doctor said, 'I forgot the time.'

'I see.' Burke waited a little and added apologetically, 'I'm sorry asking all these questions, doctor. I can see you're tired.'

'I am, Burke, rather,' Hansen confessed. 'I'd be glad if you'd speed things up a bit. I'd like to get home and rest.'

'There's only a little more, Doc. When you saw Mr Speek lying in his chair, how long do you think he had been dead?'

Hansen shifted in his chair and pursed his lips.

'I thought about an hour,' he said.

'That would make it about eleven when he shot himself.'

'More or less. One can't be definite, of course.'

'I was just wondering,' Burke said. 'Because this afternoon late I had a talk with Miss Polly Garner, and she says she saw Mr Ford come out of Speek's house at about half-past eight, and she saw Timothy Speek at a quarter to nine. He appeared to be in great agony. He was standing up and, when he heard her step, he half turned to the door and said, "Ford – poison," and then, Miss Polly says, he fell back in his chair and died. At a quarter to nine! If that is true, sir, I can't see how he could have shot himself at eleven.'

The doctor had been sitting a little forward in his chair as the constable spoke, his two hands gripping the sides, his knuckles white against the dark leather. I saw his face greying and his lips parted, and then he suddenly fell forward with a gasp, and Mrs Marven dropped her knitting and sprang from her chair. Price was beside her in a flash.

'Quick!' she cried. 'Warm water and brandy. Hold his head up, Garnet. It's his heart.'

---

We got the doctor to the hotel, eventually. Burke hung about looking a bit shamefaced. I wished he'd go away, but he sat down in the hall and waited till Mrs Marven was through with her ministrations. Helen Speek and Price had gone into the commercial room and, through the crack in the door, I could see them in earnest conversation. Price's face was very close to hers, and it appeared to me he was insisting on some point. Burke kept me talking. He switched the conversation to football and avoided all mention of the investigation he had been holding.

When Mrs Marven came downstairs, she said, 'I think we should have a little drink,' and led the way to the commercial room. 'I don't like the way he's shaping,' she told us. 'Mr Hennessy's stopping with him for a while. Poor man, he's worn his heart out.'

There was a general eulogy on Hansen's qualities till the drinks came, then Burke cleared his throat. 'I'm sorry this happened,' he said, 'but I've got my duty – '

'Now, wait, Burke,' Price said. 'I can't stomach any more preambles. Let's get down to business.' He swallowed the rest of his drink. He put the glass down on the table and spoke deliberately.

'Hysteria or no hysteria, Ford has made slanderous charges against Mrs Speek and myself. I'm damned if I let them go unchallenged. Polly Garner has indicated also that Speek may have been poisoned. That doesn't make things any nicer for Helen or me. She says she saw Ford come out of Speek's house a quarter of an hour before she saw Speek die. That doesn't make things so good for the estimable Mr Ford. If you ask me, Burke, I think what you're thinking in your slow official mind. You're thinking the whole thing is damned fishy. You're wondering what Ford meant this morning. You're wondering how the hell Speek really died. You're wondering if he poisoned himself first *and* shot himself afterwards, or whether he was poisoned by someone and later shot by the same or some other person.

'Mind you,' he went on, 'I think the man shot himself. But, because Helen and I have been dragged into this, we're not going to shelter behind Speek's corpse. You get right to work, Burke; see Cotter and get in touch with the right authorities and secure an exhumation order. Aren't I right, Helen?'

He turned to her where she sat on the couch, with every bit of colour drained from her face.

'Aren't I right?' he repeated. 'You must see it, Helen. It's the best way. You've nothing to fear, my dear. I swear it.' He took her hands. 'You do agree, don't you, Helen!'

Mrs Marven burst in, 'Helen, you can't, you mustn't agree. Garnet, you must be mad. It's – it's revolting.'

'Trust me, Helen,' Price said, ignoring the landlady.

Slowly she lifted her eyes to his, and they were wet with tears, but some of the fear had gone. She turned to the constable. 'I agree, Mr Burke,' she said, but her voice trembled. 'I ask for an exhumation.'

Price fell on his knees by her side as she burst into tears and folded her in his arms in front of us all. I saw Mrs Marven pour herself a stiff whisky and drink it neat. Burke blinked at us foolishly, while I was too astonished at Helen's submission to speak. Mrs Marven made a gesture over her shoulder, and we left them to themselves for, indeed, it appeared that they had forgotten us.

The constable refused another drink. He stood in the hall and said, 'I'd better go and see Cotter right away.' He sighed heavily. 'I'll have to go all over it again. Mr Cotter won't like it, especially at this time of night. He won't like it at all.'

I was long in getting to sleep that night. When at last I dozed off, my rest was disturbed by a ridiculous dream in which Eileen tapped upon the letter-delivery window and called my name. When I hastened to open it, I found to my surprise that she had left two magnificent apples. They were suspended in mid air, and, as I watched them with admiration, they began to slowly float away, and I rushed out of the office to seize them before they disappeared, for I was filled with an overwhelming desire to hold them in my hands and feel my lips against their rosiness.

But when I reached the verandah they were in a cupboard. I could see them through the heavy glass door on which was a tremendous lock with a huge bunch of keys. Frantically I tried key after key, but none would fit, and, in a rage, I began to beat my hands against the glass to get at them, and my mother came and said, 'There, there: we'll get you another,' and I turned, sobbing and indignant, to see Larry Ward sitting in the gutter with one of the apples in his hand and about to bite the other.

I beat my fists against my mother's breast and cried, 'Make him give them to me,' and she started kissing and fondling me and wiping the tears from my eyes, and suddenly I saw that it wasn't my mother at all but Boldini's trollop. I awoke with a sharp sense of disappointment and frustration and lay a long while, my mind in a tumult.

I wondered whether there would be an exhumation and if so how it would affect me. If they found poison, where did I stand? Price with his beastly innuendo had impressed upon Burke that I had been near Speek's house the night he died. Polly Garner had confirmed this. People might even think I had something to do with the man's death. It was absurd, of course. I had no motive. Why should I be suspect? Yet I felt a gnawing anxiety.

Suddenly a terrible thought flashed through my mind and sent a cold chill down my spine. Price might suggest a motive. He might say that I had attempted to blackmail Speek. He and Helen could easily cook up something between them. I wouldn't put it past them. The man was unscrupulous and would take all sorts of chances. He had a contempt for consequences. But he would set his trap cleverly. He would let the idea take root in Burke's slow-moving mind so that the constable would begin to imagine it was his own.

At first I had believed him to be bluffing about the exhumation. Now, I wasn't sure. Helen, I was reasonably certain, had agreed against her will, and Mrs Marven, who was her friend and perhaps in her confidence, had exclaimed loudly against the proposal. I felt worried and exhausted.

It was Sunday, but I rose early, although my usual custom was to sleep in. The ostler was standing by the horse trough in front of the hotel, gazing up the street. I followed his gaze and saw a buggy turn the corner near the post office and take the road to Baloola.

'Sam Cotter and the policeman,' he said. 'I wonder what they're up to?'

I could guess. Burke had lost no time in seeing the coroner, and together they were driving to Baloola for advice and authority. There was nothing to do about it. It was a nice enough morning and not yet time for breakfast. I went for a walk, and the air refreshed me and restored my spirits. I could think more clearly. Supposing I had to explain my testimony at the inquest. I had sworn I had not seen Speek on the night of his death. I could say that I entered Speek's gate at a quarter to nine, intending to call on him, but realised that he might delay me and make me late for my appointment with Hennessy. I had therefore changed my mind and gone into the street again and had run into Polly Garner. In the morning Agatha Garner had sent me a note asking me to call. I would tell the truth, repeating what Polly had said about seeing Speek and watching him die.

I would say that the two sisters were terror-stricken and begged my advice and that I told them that they must tell the truth when they were asked. Then I had learned that Speek had shot himself. I believed that Polly Garner had been mistaken in thinking she saw Speek die. That he had merely collapsed and recovered afterwards and got his gun and shot himself. When, later, the women had come to the post office for Polly's registered letter they had implored me to say nothing about the matter. They did not wish to be implicated on account of something in Polly's past life they feared would come out. They begged me to be silent. They called on my chivalry, and I had responded. Moreover, I had the natural reluctance of a gentleman to become involved even in the fringe of such a sordid affair. Neither the Garners nor I had anything to do with Speek's death. He meant nothing to us. We had done him no harm by remaining silent.

Surely any intelligent jury would believe me. I imagined it, listening gravely. I heard my counsel asking me questions, to which I replied with the utmost candour. I had my own code of morality, I told him. I had felt that a woman's honour was in my hands – every instinct of chivalry demanded that I respect the trust these frail little women had reposed in me.

As I strolled I could almost hear the approving murmur running through the crowded court – a murmur which even His Honour seemed loath to restrain.

Actually I felt much better. I began to feel hungry as I turned the corner into the deserted main street to see a man on the verandah of the post office behaving rather strangely. He was standing on the seat kept there for the convenience of passengers waiting for the Baloola mail buggy and peering over the top half of the window into my office. The bottom half of the window was frosted. He must have heard my steps as I drew level with the verandah, for he turned round. When he saw me he got slowly down and dusted his hands delicately.

It was Wellday. He said calmly, 'Good morning, Mr Ford,' and gestured to the window. 'Quite an interesting experiment. By standing on the seat one can see right into the office. Now, an active child, I believe, could quite easily balance herself on the high back of the seat. This would give her the extra height. Then she also could see into your office. You follow, Mr Ford?'

He did not wait for my answer, but continued, 'She could, in fact – supposing you were there, of course – actually see you at your desk. Objects might easily be discernible. These youngsters have such sharp eyes. She might, for instance, see a spirit kettle with steam issuing from its spout. And, just supposing anyone should be holding a letter over the kettle and steaming open the seal, she would be able to see that, too. Isn't that interesting?'

He waited, smiling urbanely.

'Well, well,' he said at length as I did not speak, 'I suppose it's nearing breakfast time.' He moved to leave, but added as if it had just occurred to him, 'By the way, Mr Ford, I wonder if you could advise me. Supposing someone, say one of Her Majesty's postal officials, for instance, became possessed of certain private information concerning, shall we say, a lady – information which could have come to him in no honest manner – would he be justified under *any* circumstances in divulging that information? It's a curious point. Personally I don't think he would be. Come to think of it, I'm sure he would find it much better for his peace of mind if he remained forever silent. But, there, you must forgive me for propounding my little problems at such an unorthodox hour. I'm quite hungry, Mr Ford. Your rural air, you know. Mustn't keep the ham and eggs waiting, eh? Good morning, Mr Ford.'

He smiled as if he had been saying pleasant things and walked briskly away.

I waited till he had gone some distance, then, assuring myself that nobody was in sight, I stood upon the seat and peered through the window into my office. After a moment's scrutiny I got down and walked meditatively to the hotel. The breakfast bell rang as I entered the front door, but my appetite had been spoiled.

My mood was somewhat improved when, later in the morning, I picked up the *Banner*. I was heartened to see the article I had written so long ago printed in full. I realised that I had been a little hasty with Fenton and decided I would send him a note of apology. He had given me full credit for my work and I had read it through a second time before I caught sight of a little paragraph immediately underneath the article which had taken up nearly a column. My heart stopped a beat, for there was no doubt whatever, though the language was somewhat veiled, that it referred to the company in which I had lost my money. The secretary, it seemed, had been apprehended and his defalcations made good by friends (anxious, no doubt, to secure some mitigation of the scoundrel's sentence), and there was a hint of some new endeavour by the company, the future of which was painted as rosy.

My sudden optimism was dampened almost immediately. The shares were no longer mine. I had always known that the thing was sound. Capital would turn it into a little gold mine. I wished I had not been so precipitate. It was damnable to think that I should have been the means of providing Helen with a gilt-edge investment she would never have even heard about.

Cotter and Burke returned from Baloola with the necessary authority for exhumation. The constable called on me with the news and told me that, in view of what had happened and the charges I had made, I might be present. He said it was possible that Price would be there, but no one else other than officials, and enjoined silence, as though I were likely to set bells ringing for a gruesome ceremony which, but for his obstinacy, need never have taken place. He did not offer to drive me to the cemetery, but suggested that Luke Barmby might give me a lift. I could hardly see myself riding in the town hearse, however, and was half inclined to ignore the whole thing. Curiosity overcame me. It would not be an alto-gether pleasant ceremony, but it would be interesting to watch Price's reaction.

The coroner had set the time for late afternoon, for he never, if possible, allowed his official duties to interfere with business, and, after closing the post office, I started on the two mile walk.

The cemetery was a few hundred yards off the main Baloola road, a fenced allotment with the wire broken in places and some of the posts rotten and collapsing; a desolate, treeless spot on which the summer sun beat relentlessly, withering the little garden plots which, in the first enthusiasms of grief, relatives planted over the resting places of their newly dead.

The pathways between the graves were overgrown with dry grass and some of the tombstones had toppled over. Apparently there was none interested enough to straighten them. Here and there, long-withered wreaths hung at rakish angles from small wooden crosses stuck, lopsided, into the heads of weed-grown, untidy mounds, and there were a few more ambitious monuments in stone against which leaned untidy black wooden boxes, their glass fronts revealing the stiff white artificial flowers within. It was a mournful vista of neglect born of necessity, for in those days of meagre facili-ties it was difficult enough to drop in on the living, let alone on the dead.

I came across the little mound covering the remains of Mrs Partridge's baby and, for a brief moment, my mind reverted to Boldini's mental experiments, and I wondered whether he had seen the inscription on the little cross. Speek's grave was alongside. I knew it, not because of any monument, but because of its newness.

The light appeared to be fading fast, and I looked up to see a sky leaden with that threat of rain those who had lived in the district had long since grown to disregard. Thunder clouds would gather, the air grow still, the farmer feel the faint flutter of hope in his heart, and then another night would pass without rain and the day dawn bright, the sun hot, and the earth as thirsty as ever.

Burke and Cotter and another man I did not know and who was evidently some official sent from the city walked through the gate and I recognised the Barmbys' horse jogging up the track from the main road, pulling the ancient buggy, in which Luke was seated alongside young Josephus.

There was a mutter of distant thunder as Garnet Price rode up. He did not tether his horse at the gate but cantered up the path between the graves and leaped lightly to the ground, letting the reins drop carelessly over a monument.

Cotter said testily to Barmby, 'Well, get on with it.'

Luke and Joe took off their coats and began to dig, and, with the first delve, there came a sudden lightning flash and a clap of thunder that so startled the younger man that his hat dropped from his head. Everybody looked sheepishly at his neighbour and removed his headgear – all except Price, who appeared not to notice, but kept walking nervously up and down, his hands thrust deep into his breeches pocket, the everlasting riding whip looped over his arm.

The clouds came oppressively low, and the atmosphere was so still that the sound of the Barmbys' labours seemed disproportionately loud. As they dug, the thunder rolled above us and passed on muttering, only to return with angry emphasis. The light faded so that at length Luke went to his buggy and brought the lamps and lit them and set one at each end of the grave, intensifying the surrounding gloom but illuminating his own and his son's perspiring features.

At last Speek's coffin was uncovered. Burke passed down the broad bands for lifting the casket, and Luke adjusted them. Price came over and peered down as the policeman and the official took one side and the Barmbys the other and lifted the coffin and swung it toward the end of the grave.

As they lowered it to the ground, Joe Barmby tripped and for a moment the casket was off balance. As it was righted we all heard a sharp bump. There was no doubt about the place of origin. The men hastily put their burden down, and Joe nervously wiped his mouth with the back of his hand.

'W-what was that?' he said, and answered his own question, trembling. 'It was something inside.'

'There be something wrong, Mr Cotter,' old Luke said.

Price peered over the shoulder of the constable, who was on his knees, his ear to the lid of the coffin.

'Don't be a damn fool, Burke,' he said. 'Get it open. There's only Speek there.'

'Of course,' Cotter spoke with weak authority. 'Mr Barmby – please.'

In a little while Luke had completed his task. With his son he lifted the lid and Burke and Cotter uttered an exclamation. The coffin was filled with stones.

In the light of the buggy lamps I saw bewilderment written on the constable's cowlike countenance. Cotter seemed to have grown greyer. Nobody spoke. Then Price broke the silence with a harsh laugh. He stooped and picked up a large piece of flint.

'Speek's heart,' he said contemptuously, and dropped it back into the coffin.

Before anyone could say anything he had swung on to his horse and was cantering towards the gate.

Nobody knew quite what to do. A few big drops of rain fell, and Cotter at length ordered the coffin to be screwed up again and replaced in the grave. Burke offered me a lift, for it looked as if the rain might really set in, but I preferred my own company and walked back to the town.

There was one sharp shower and I was rather damp by the time I got to the main street, and my feet were wet. I bethought myself of a pair of shoes I had had mended and left in my office and called in to get them. I removed my coat and hung it over a chair and sat down and took my boots off, and suddenly looked up to find that the young person who assisted Boldini had followed me into the office.

'I saw you come in,' she said brazenly. 'Every time I see you, you're in trouble.'

'Excuse me.' I rose, felling a little foolish without my coat and in my stockinged feet. 'What is it you want?'

'It isn't so much what *I* want, it's what *you* want, Toots,' she replied, 'and you want lots. Now sit down like a good boy and let me put on your shoes. Why, you don't know enough to come out of the wet!'

I was too astonished to speak, and she gently urged me back into the chair and, before I could protest, was kneeling at my feet. She was pretty in a bold, flashy sort of way and she looked up at me, smiling, and said, 'You can't travel with a mind-reader without learning a thing or two, Toots. I've been hearing lots about you and watching you and I feel a bit sorry you're so dumb, but I'm the only one who knows what's wrong with you, and if someone doesn't take you in hand soon, you'll grow up to be a nasty old man with no one to love you.'

She leaned on my knees disturbingly and went on more seriously. 'Let's you and me be friends, eh? A girl gets a bit lonely travelling round the bush.'

I could not resist saying, 'Lonely? What about Boldini?'

'Oh, *him*!' she said. 'All he thinks of is his show.' She looked up again and her lips parted provocatively. 'Aren't you going to kiss me?' she said.

'Good heavens,' I cried. 'I never heard of such a thing!'

'You've left it late, dearie,' she said, unabashed. 'Don't be afraid.'

Her arms were warm on my body and for a moment I weakened. But only for a moment. Then the absurdity of the situation brought me to my senses. This painted baggage and I! I almost laughed.

'You know, Toots,' she was saying earnestly. 'You and me's a bit alike. We're both alone in the world. Only, you don't know it and I do. I'd know how to look after you, Toots, really I would. I understand your sort. I wouldn't mind spoiling you.'

There was that in her eyes I had never seen in those of any other woman. But she was Boldini's trollop! A common player and God knows what besides! She and I! This thing whose real name was Jinks. It was ridiculous that she should imagine – It made me feel cheap.

I rose abruptly with an exclamation of disgust and pushed her away so roughly that she fell back and had to put out a hand to the floor to keep her balance. She was on her feet quickly, however, and must have read the contempt in my face, for her own flamed.

'Oh, you fool,' she cried, 'you blind fool.' The flap of the counter was up and she ran to the outer office. She was livid with rage as she turned and glared at me. Then she picked up a heavy directory from the counter and hurled it at me with all the force she could muster. It caught me near the eye.

'By God,' I cried. 'I'll give you in charge for this – '

But she was gone.

Hennessy met me as I entered the hotel and told me that Dr Hansen, who was still lying there under Mrs Marven's care, wished to see me.

'He's very low,' he informed me, 'and he's got something on his mind.'

I went at once to the sickroom and found Burke already there.

'Hello, Ford,' the doctor said weakly from his bed. 'Sorry to trouble you. Where's Price?'

Hennessy told him he'd sent for him, and a minute or two later Price came in. He shook hands with the doctor.

'I've got something important to say, Burke,' the doctor said, 'and I suggest you ask Hennessy to write it down to save time. Save my wind, too.'

As a matter of fact, he was having a good deal of difficulty with his breathing, and Mrs Marven, who was hovering around, suggested that, whatever it was he intended, it was taking too much out of him.

'No; can't wait,' Hansen said. 'Never know what's coming

with this business.' He tapped his heart. 'Or when,' he added. He smiled wanly at us. 'Better put things right while I can. Got your paper, Hennessy? Write this and I'll sign it.'

Hennessy seated himself at the bedside table and dipped his pen in ink. He was smoking his pipe.

Dr Hansen said calmly, 'I killed Timothy Speek.'

Mrs Marven caught her breath and for an instant I thought she was going to faint, but she took hold of the bed-post and steadied herself. None of us spoke, and Hennessy stared at the doctor, his pen suspended, his mouth open, as if he could not believe his ears.

Hansen nodded in confirmation. 'Write it down,' he said, and the schoolmaster bent to his task. I remember to this day the scratchy nib he used.

The doctor went on, 'It was an accident, of course. Speek came to me for a tonic. There was nothing whatever the matter with him, but he insisted that he needed something to invigorate him. I didn't like the man. Never did. I was annoyed with him for wasting my time. I had several things on my mind at the moment.

'I sent it round by one of Hennessy's boys who happened to be passing. I'd been busy dispensing and had made up a number of medicines and I had a busy night ahead of me, including a baby at Dunbar's. That's about six miles from here, Burke.'

The constable nodded. 'Nearer seven,' he said.

'The baby was obstinate. I had to hang about, and Paul Dunbar made me a cup of tea. While I sat drinking it, I began to think of all the things I had to do and the people I had to see. It's a habit of mine. I keep all my notes in my head. Bad, of course, but there you are. I began to run through the jobs I'd done that day, making a mental note of the ones I had to follow up. I thought of Speek and began to smile to myself as I recalled the harmless stuff I'd given him. Then suddenly my heart went cold. I believed I had made a terrible mistake in dispensing. I – '

Speaking slowly so that Hennessy should make no mistake, Dr Hansen explained what he had done. My mind flitted back to that chaotic surgery.

When the schoolmaster had the technical details to his satisfaction, Hansen went on, 'I make no excuse for my carelessness other than overwork, ill-health, what you will. I should have had a locum in a year ago, but country people are funny. They like their old doctors.' He shut his eyes a moment, and the flicker of a smile passed across his lip. 'I knew Speek was not a sick man and when he came to me and told me what he wanted, I confess I felt an utter contempt for him. He treated his wife shamefully. I suspected that when she came to me for help. Her nerves were all shot to pieces. She couldn't sleep. I hoped to God Speek had not taken the medicine I had given him. I'd made it foul enough, heaven knows, and some people don't, you know. But I had to get to him quickly; but, just then, the baby business started in earnest. It was necessary to see it through, and it wasn't easy and Dunbar was helpless. You know what a young man is with his first baby. And there was no one else.

'I tried to explain to him that he'd have to ride to town, but he just gibbered at me. He's not a clever man at any time and, just then, there was only room for one thought in his mind. He couldn't take it in. I was the doctor – the only one who could save his wife and baby – that's what he was thinking. My God, it's terrible the trust these people put in one.

'And as soon as I could, I drove back to town. I made Betsy gallop. For the first time in my life I put the whip about her – poor old thing. I was going straight to Speek's when Mrs Marven ran out into the road. She told me Speek had shot himself. I thought I knew why. The stuff I had given him would have caused excruciating agony. I'm glad he had the gun and the guts to use it. Got that, Hennessy? That's all.'

He shut his eyes as the schoolmaster scratched the last word. 'Give it to me and I'll sign it,' he said.

'Just a minute, sir,' Burke interrupted. 'How do you know Speek took your medicine?'

'Because,' Hansen replied wearily, 'I found the bottle in his bathroom. One dose had been taken. It was easy for me to slip the bottle into my pocket and destroy it later.'

'I see,' Burke said. 'I'd like you to put that in, sir.'

The doctor nodded to Hennessy, who wrote rapidly and handed the document to him. 'I'd better read it over to you first,' Burke said.

Hansen made a motion of assent. 'Hurry, please.'

Burke read in his dreary official manner and the doctor signed it. 'I'm sorry to have been such a trouble to you, Burke,' he said.

'What happened to Speek's – ' I began, but Price interrupted rudely.

'Shut up, Ford.'

Burke was busy at the table, looking over the document, while Hennessy dried the signature. I don't think the doctor even heard me, and then Mrs Marven began shushing us out of the room. The constable lingered behind and, as he put the document in his pocket, I heard him say, 'I'm not quite sure how I should act, sir,' and Hansen's voice, a little whimsical in reply, 'Don't worry too much, Burke. I think the problem will be settled for you – pretty soon.'

It was. He died that night.

At first Hansen's confession displeased me. Price was present when Mrs Marven came down and broke the news of his death and, after the commonplace condolences, he peeked at me sardonically. After Mrs Marven had gone he had the impudence to take my arm and lead me out onto the verandah.

He said, 'This rather puts you on a spot, Ford.'

'I don't know what you mean,' I said.

His horse was tethered to a post, and, as he threw the reins over its head and put his foot in the stirrup, he looked over his shoulder at me. 'Oh, yes you do,' he said. 'Remember I warned you.' He swung himself into the saddle. 'I wouldn't be in your shoes for a thousand pounds,' he said. 'You and your rotten shares, you blackmailing swindler.'

Before I could do anything, he had cantered off. Mrs Marven appeared at the door and sang out, 'Goodbye,' and he waved to her. Then he called, 'I'm going home, Ford, to think it out.'

I wondered what he had in mind and felt vaguely uneasy. You never knew with a man like Price. Fate was helping him at the moment and he was taking advantage of the situation to bluff me. Hansen's rank carelessness might have caused the death of the blind man, but I still believed Price and Helen had planned to put him out of the way. Otherwise their actions that night didn't make sense.

All the same, I was relieved to remember that I had conducted our little business in an orderly fashion. When I had signed the transfer note on the back of the scrip, I had dated the document earlier than the fateful day on which I had received the news of the secretary's defalcation. If ever there were any argument, it would be their word against mine, and I flattered myself I had always had a good record.

Still, Price was an unknown quantity. You couldn't trust him and his money gave him influence. Now that Hansen's carelessness and confession had cleared him and Helen, one couldn't tell what he might do. He was impulsive and he'd be vindictive. And he hated me. He would never have paid me that one thousand pounds. Not he. He'd have let Helen pay, let her take all the risk!

I began to feel a bit sorry for Helen and then I realised I could help her by buying the shares back. I determined to have a word with her at once. I had seen Price ride out of the town and made my preparations immediately. She received me in the room in which Speek had died, but it was a very different room. There were even a few flowers and some coloured cushions which, considering her recent widowhood, were hardly in good taste.

She was a little cool but plainly curious. We talked for a while about Dr Hansen and his confession, and I worked the conversation round till I could quote from the article I had written for the *Banner*.

'Perhaps you saw it,' I said.

She said, 'No, I haven't seen it. I rarely do. I must get a copy and read it.'

I knew then that she could not have seen the paragraph about the company and I said, 'I have really come here to apologise, Mrs Speek. Dr Hansen's confession puts such a different complexion on things. I feel embarrassed and thoroughly ashamed of myself for my unworthy suspicions. I feel I can only make amends by buying back the shares. I have brought a cheque with me. If you will let me have the scrip with the necessary signed transfers, we can complete the whole thing and forget all about it and I hope be friends once more.'

She said, 'I think you are making a very generous acknowledgment, Mr Ford. Appearances are very much against us at times. I shall be glad to accept your cheque in the spirit in which it is offered.'

She went away and returned with the scrip and signed the transfers on the very table from which I had seen her take the chocolate box away from her husband on the night of his death. I gave her the cheque, and we shook hands. She actually smiled as she said good night.

I felt easier in my mind. I didn't think Price would try any funny business or attempt to intimidate me now that his woman had her money back. Certainly Helen wouldn't want any further probing into the wretched business. We were all back from where we started, and Price could go to blazes. Later he'd find that I'd had the laugh on him.

All said and done, perhaps Hansen's confession was to the good. The police, I supposed, would go on looking for Speek's body, though doubtless they would come to the conclusion that the doctor himself had removed it, in which case the secret of its hiding place might never be discovered. In conversation with Burke, the constable led me to believe that that was what he thought had happened, and the doctor had certainly more opportunities than most for stowing a body away, for he was forever coming and going at all hours and none would have dreamed of questioning him.

I wondered whether Eileen had recovered from the shock she had received at Boldini's séance, and I determined to see her. I could no longer bring myself to believe that she would throw me over for a penniless ne'er-do-well. I had already written her a dignified note deploring her decision and her action in returning my ring, and had asked her to reconsider the matter in the light of the promise she had made over the bed of her dying father. I asked her not to throw away her life and face a future of poverty when she had only to say the word and I would freely forgive everything.

She had not replied to that and, as I walked to her home, I supposed she was ashamed of herself. I made up my mind, come what might, I would not rebuke her. I would be kindness itself and, if Larry returned, I determined to meet him generously, without rancour, and hold out the hand of friendship. There was no reason, I would explain to Eileen, why the three of us should not be friends. After all, I told myself, almost as soon as we were married, we would be in the midst of a whirlwind of farewell festivities incidental to my leaving town. There would be the usual illuminated address, I supposed. Speeches to prepare. Little farewell dinners to attend. She wouldn't have much time to see Larry. Then we would leave the place forever and I would see and hear the last of the fellow.

Thank heaven I had destroyed the letter Eileen had written to him. If he were puzzled and brought the matter up, it would merely confirm what I had suggested – that the day he received it he had been drinking. I couldn't be expected to remember all the letters I handed through my window. The sooner the Garner kid was out of the way, the better, though.

I am not a vindictive man, but I found myself wishing the brat would develop diphtheria.

Eileen was not at home when I arrived. Agatha Garner was looking after Mahoney and gave me a cold greeting before ushering me into the sick-room. Perhaps, I thought, it was just as well I was seeing Mahoney first. He, at least, was on my side, and I could frighten him a little by pretending to accept Eileen's behaviour at its face value. He looked much better than when I last saw him, and the idea that he might have wilfully exaggerated his ailments in order to hook a good husband for his daughter flitted unpleasantly through my mind. He was in quite a happy mood.

'I'm glad you've come, Ford,' he said. 'Sorry, of course, about you and Eileen, but, you know – love's young dream.'

'I am quite ready to overlook everything, Mr Mahoney,' I said, rather at a loss to understand his words. 'That is, if Eileen has come to her senses.'

He looked up at me shrewdly and pursed his lips.

'Um,' he said, putting the tips of his skinny fingers together. 'I'm afraid it is not as easy as all that. You see, Larry turning up has invested him with an air of romance and, well, you know, Mr Ford, what young girls are. Not much romance about penny stamps and postcards, eh? I'm afraid you must take your gruel, old man.'

'Are you trying to tell me,' I asked, beginning to fume inwardly, 'that Eileen is really going to marry Ward?'

"Fraid so, Ford,' he said. "Fraid so, my boy. Hot-blooded youth, you know. Parents haven't much say these days.'

'Do you mean you'll permit your daughter to wed this pauper?' My anger and indignation were mounting.

'Oh, come now, Ford,' he said. 'Larry's a nice boy. We all have to make a beginning. He'll do all right.'

I couldn't understand his attitude. He had whined to me about deathbeds and the fear of leaving his daughter penniless, and now, apparently, he was content to die and leave her to the mercy of a man with neither a shilling in his pocket nor a prospect in the world. I picked up my hat and bade him a curt good evening. He held out a thin hand, but I ignored it and, without bothering the Garner woman, let myself out and walked away in a towering rage.

My cup of bitterness was not yet full, however, for I met Garnet Price on the verandah of the hotel. He stopped me with a show of friendliness.

'Ah, there you are, Ford,' he cried. 'I wanted to see you. Helen has told me about you buying the shares back. I'm glad you've done the decent thing.'

I resented his implication and was in no mood to talk.

'After Hansen's confession, it just seemed the right thing to do,' I said.

He regarded me curiously. 'Of course, of course,' he said. 'Still, it pleased Helen and me, too, if that means anything to you.' He smacked his leg lightly with his riding whip and looked down and for a moment I thought he was actually confused. He said, 'Thought I'd tell you that Helen and I are to be married.' He waited, evidently expecting me to blurt out something congratulatory. When I didn't he looked up and said almost belligerently, 'I've got ample means, thank God, to keep her in comfort, so the money doesn't really mean much to her. She's decided not to keep any of Speek's money. She's making it all over to the Blind Asylum, I think. All except the money you paid her back for the shares. She's giving that to Eileen Mahoney for a wedding present. That'll give Eileen and Larry a good start.'

For a second I reeled, but I managed to say contemptuously, 'So Ward is going to live on a woman?'

'Oh, no,' he said quite genially, 'as a matter of fact, after the honeymoon, he's going to look after a place of mine. When he's married to a fine girl like Eileen he'll settle down, all right. There's good stuff in that boy. Besides, you wouldn't know, of course, but he's going to do a little tour with Boldini – playing his mouth organ with the show and making those phonograph-record things. The old scoundrel says there's quite a pot of money in it. That's why he kept the lad under his wing after he'd fished him out of the river. Well' – he placed his abominable hand on my shoulder – 'thought you'd like to know. So long, old man.'

Even then I never suspected the black heart of the man. When the mail came in next day there was a letter for me. When I opened it, I felt as I had done on that day when I received news of my ruin, for this was a communication from the company in liquidation dated the day before and making it plain beyond a shadow of a doubt that there was not one chance in a hundred million of the company ever re-establishing. The damn secretary was still at large and likely to be. All at once I knew, just as if he'd told me, that Price had wangled that paragraph in the *Banner*, astutely putting it under my article to make sure I'd see it. Like a fool I'd fallen for it.

I made a desperate effort to get my own back. I ran out, slamming the office door after me, pushing Haggart, who was about to come in, out of my path. I was breathless when I got to the bank. I asked Teecher whether my cheque had been presented.

'Oh, hours ago,' he said lightly. 'As soon as we opened, in fact. Is anything wrong?'

'Wrong?' I said, and noted he was staring at me curiously. 'No, why, what should be wrong?'

I got back to the office somehow and remember serving stamps to someone, quite mechanically. Haggart's voice floated to me from across the street. 'Good day, Mr Price. Great weather.'

And Garnet Price's answering bellow, 'A great day, Haggart. It's good to be alive.'

Something surged up inside of me and with all my force I kicked the leg of the office table. Though I did not feel it then I found later I had broken a toe. Wringer Rosie was peering through the letter window. Something in my face must have frightened her, for she said, 'Oh, goodness,' and fled.

I slammed the window as if by doing so I could shut this damnable town forever from my sight.

I never saw Eileen or Larry again. In a little while I left the place. I said goodbye to Mrs Marven but to none other.

As I sat in the mail buggy outside the post office, waiting for it to start on its journey to Baloola, the two Misses Garner passed, Wellday's brat walking between them. The women ignored me but, as the horses moved off, the youngster turned and stared at me rudely. Then she put her thumb to her nose and extended her fingers.

It was my farewell to the town.

Fifty years ago! And yet I remember it as yesterday. Old Gallagher flicking his grey horses with his whip; Sam Cotter, an apron about his waist, coming to the door of his grocery store to see who was going out in the mail buggy; Haggart picking his teeth in the doorway of his draper's shop; smoke rising from the chimney of Mahoney's cottage.

This morning the nurse was gossiping and giggling outside my door, and I rang the bell sharply. I find laughing near a sick-room intolerable, and I shall have to complain again, though I suppose as usual nothing will be done.

The nurse answered promptly enough, but I let her see that I was annoyed. She was quite unperturbed, however, and I have to confess I find a certain calm efficiency in her movements difficult to reconcile with her shaped eyebrows and scarlet lips. There is something about her that makes her more endurable than her predecessors.

As she smoothed my pillows she said, 'Now, how about seeing that old lady? It will do you good to talk to somebody.'

'What lady?' It was the first I had heard of it.

'Why, the one I told you about.'

She hadn't, of course, but I let it pass.

'What is her name?' I asked testily. I was afraid it might be some hospital visitor.

'Why,' she exclaimed. 'Don't you remember? I told you,

Mrs Baldwin.'

'I know no Mrs Baldwin.'

'She knows you, Mr Ford,' the girl persisted, 'at least she used to know you, ever so long ago, she says.'

I grunted. 'She's made a mistake.'

'I don't think so. She asked her nurse to find out your full name. It's Henry Xavier Ford, isn't it?'

'What of it?'

'Why, she recognised it at once. She said there couldn't possibly be two like you. Her name used to be Marven.'

Mrs Marven! After all these years! And this girl chattering away!

'I remember,' I told the nurse. 'What's she here for?'

The girl lost her smile. 'She won't be here long, Mr Ford,' she said, and knew by her tone what she meant. 'She's a dear old thing and quite resigned, though. She'll come and see you, if you'll let her. We could wheel her in.' She seemed quite eager.

Well, why not, I thought, why not? It would be interesting to see the old dame after all these years. She'd be pretty frail, I suspected, but if she were tiresome I could get rid of her.

She came. I had expected them to wheel in a feeble old creature, wrinkled and withered, and I could scarcely believe that this plumpish woman beaming at me with alert eyes, whose hair had not decently greyed with the years, was actually older than I. It was hardly credible that she should be nearing the end of her days.

With a twinge of jealousy I noted that she wore no glasses and had in her lap a novel with an appallingly gay cover.

'*Well*!' She said brightly. 'Mr Ford!'

'How are you, Mrs Marven?' I asked her when I had recovered from my first surprise.

'Not Marven, Mr Ford. I married that old scamp, Boldini. His real name was Baldwin, you remember.'

I hadn't, but I said, 'Indeed. I hope you have been happy.'

'Oh, it was a great success,' she told me, and her eyes

twinkled. 'You see, we both liked the same things to eat. You should remember that, my dear,' she added to my nurse. 'The way to a man's heart is through his digestive organs. Kissing goes a long way, but a great deal can be done with a beef-steak pudding.' She turned to me again. 'We fell in love with each other's cooking. We had a wonderful honeymoon, dashing from restaurant to restaurant. I never ate so much in my life.'

The nurse left us, and I asked, 'You gave up your hotel?'

'I sold it to that nice Mr Butters. Perhaps you remember him? He used to go ahead of Boldini's show and gather up all the bits and pieces of gossip so that Charlie could memorise them and work them into his mind-reading, the old scamp. Mr Butters was the man who planted the half sovereign where Wringer Rosie could find it.'

I saw her memory for the old things was as keen as mine. 'So everything your husband did at his show was deceit from beginning to end,' I said and, although it happened so long ago, I could still feel the bitterness of the thing.

'Of course!' She actually smiled. 'That Boldini was an awful cheat. And yet, when he was dying, he'd quite made up his mind he was going to heaven. He said to me, "Listen, my dear, I'll be waiting for you always and when you come along and knock at the golden gate I'll say, 'Who's there?' and you answer, 'Polyanthus.' That'll be a sort of password. Then I'll say, 'Polyanthus who?' and you'll say, 'Polyanthus the door,' and then I'll know it's really you at last, my dear." They were almost the last words he spoke.'

I am afraid she noted my displeasure. In these later years my thoughts have turned more and more to religion and this ribald revelation savoured of blasphemy.

'Oh, dear,' she cried. 'I believe I've shocked you. Do you know, Mr Ford, I always had the idea you were shocked too easily. And you were so stiff-necked and proper in your young days! And so self-important. I do hope you've improved. It won't do any good being collar-proud up aloft.'

She raised her eyes in irreverent indication of the here-after, for there was in them humour rather than humility. It was not a nice way to talk, and I almost asked her to go, but somehow I didn't. I wanted to know things and such a few people come to see me these days.

'And you were so suspicious, too. You thought I was trying to poison Helen, now didn't you?'

It embarrassed me to be so directly questioned, but she smiled and gaily went on, 'I did have to laugh at that. I never could understand what gave you the idea.'

'Strange things were happening,' I replied. 'It was better to be on the safe side.'

'Of course,' she said. 'That's what I say. I'm very careful about medicines, though – ever since the night I gave Rosie the seidlitz instead of the headache powder. Poor lass, it did upset her. After that I always wrote a warning note on the outside of the packets, like "Take care", or, "Watch your step", or something like that.'

I changed the subject. I said maliciously, 'And Marven? I suppose Boldini made you forget all about your first husband?'

She was not in the least offended. She shut her eyes and shook her head very slowly and smiled. It struck me as absurd that a woman of her age should be so pretty.

'Dear old fat Jim,' she said softly. 'I often lie in bed and wonder how he's getting on with the old rogue, Charlie. I think of them sitting together on the bottom step of the golden stairs, waiting to carry me up. I wonder how ever they've fixed things! Jim was always such a simple soul, Boldini's sure to put one over him.'

She actually giggled.

'It's really dreadful,' she went on, 'to think of all the people that man fooled. Do you remember the night we all sat in the dark and got ourselves all worked up when a light floated about our heads and the thing moaned like a lost soul?'

I remembered it all too vividly.

'That old rogue,' she said, 'did that with a guitar and a phosphorescent face tied to the end of a lariat. He stood in the dark and spun the lariat over our heads and that made the guitar whine. He was wonderful with the lariat. He used to threaten me that if I ever served him a bad dinner he'd cut my throat with a whip at twenty paces.

'Larry Ward had told him all about sitting in the tree with the flood all about him, playing his mouth organ, so he easily faked that bit. That nice young girl he used to do tricks with played "Eileen Alannah" in the dark and sent the message to Eileen Mahoney. Do you remember her? She was an understanding little thing, I always thought.'

I said nothing. She regarded me quizzically and said, 'I'll bet, Mr Ford, you've spent a lifetime wondering what really happened to that blind man.'

'Speek?'

'Who else? I thought you'd like to know before you died.'

It wasn't a nice way of putting it. After all, many men have lived to a hundred.

'Of course,' she said, 'I'm a very old woman with a very wonky inside, so it doesn't matter who knows now.'

'I'm sorry to hear you're so sick,' I said.

'Oh,' she replied lightly, 'you only die once so you might as well make the best of it. Jim used to say, "Really, Marvie, it's only like going away to some place where there are no mails, like you might be having a holiday in some nice resort with grand scenery and good cooking, where you come on lots of old cobbers. And then you get word that your sweetheart's coming to join you, and you spruce yourself up and go and meet her so you can show her all the grand sights and stick out your chest, and say, I told you you'd like this place, lovey!"'

All right, I supposed, if one had a wife – and cobbers.

Mrs Marven went on, 'You remember that Helen Speek ran to me when her husband died. She'd found him dead in his chair, but he wasn't shot. She was terrified. Poor girl, she thought she'd done it. That silly man, Haggart – a draper, wasn't he? – imagined he was in love with her and sent her some chocolates. Speek had been in a wicked mood for a week. He was supicious of everyone, jealous of every move she made. He was bullying her and terrifying her, and, of course, she was in love with Garnet Price. Speek couldn't watch her, Mr Ford, but he listened to her every movement. He was uncanny that way.

'On the day he died he taunted her. He said he was going to alter his will. She thought he was going to cut her out of it, but she wasn't worrying about that. She was worrying how she could get to see Garnet. She desperately wanted to see him that night, for she was terribly in love. When you're in love you do the silliest things, don't you?' She paused to wipe her eyes with a silly little lace handkerchief.

'Well, Helen took a sleeping powder Dr Hansen had given her and she cut some of Haggart's chocolates in halves and mixed the cream inside with the powder and closed the chocolates up again. She put the chocolates where her husband woud find them. He was a real glutton for sweets. He found them, all right. Poor Helen! She thought he would just sleep heavily till morning and she would be able to slip out and see Garnet. When she found him dead, she thought she had given him an overdose and killed him. Price thought so, too. He'd known what she intended about the sleeping draught, but he was a bit afraid of it. He tried to persuade her against it, but, naturally, he stuck to her when things went wrong. He was very worried about the exhumation. That's why he stole Speek's body.'

'He stole Speek's body?'

'Yes,' she continued in a matter-of-fact way. 'Didn't you guess? He took it away one night.'

'Where?'

'Oh, somewhere. He told me he'd put it in quite a pleasant place – much nicer than that dreadful cemetery. I'm sure even Speek would have thought it a nice change. And they never found it. There were so many places round that town where you could hide a body in those days, weren't there?'

'I don't know,' I told her. 'It has not been my habit to interfere with the dead.'

'Price must have found it awfully exciting,' she said, quite unperturbed. 'After Helen found her husband dead, she came straight to me. She didn't go to Dr Hansen's. She didn't even go to the policeman's. She'd lost her head. She told me everything, and I put her to bed in my room.'

'I remember,' I said. 'I heard her crying.'

Mrs Marven went on, 'I went to her home and looked at Speek as he lay in his armchair. He was not pretty, Mr Ford, with froth over his black beard and his big teeth showing, and those awful eyes. I could hardly bear to look at him. His chair was alongside a little table and a drawer was partly open.

'I pulled it right out, and there were some papers and, on top of them, his will, and pinned loosely to the will a piece of paper with some scribbling. And this is what the scribble said – I remember it because it has always seemed to me a terrible thing that a man should wish to carry hate beyond the grave. It said:

*Memo for Mr Ford: Fix up codicil to will so that all still goes to my wife to be disposed of according to her own ideas, provided she enters a religious order within one month and spends the rest of her life praying for me.*

'That was a terrible codicil, not only for what it contemplated, but because of the hate that prompted it. I thought, My goodness, if they find out he was going to do this thing, they'll think Helen poisoned him before he had time to alter his will. It would have been stupid, of course, because Helen would have married Garnet, and he had pots of money.

'I thought how bad things were going to be for Helen without anything being known about the codicil, and I did a very wicked thing. I hid the piece of scribble in my shoe and carried it home. But before I went I put the will back in the drawer, and, as I did so, I saw Speek's revolver. I nearly fainted. I'm terrified of guns. I'm not afraid of many things, Mr Ford – mice, for instance, I think are rather dear little creatures, if one could only get to know them better.

'But I saw a chance to help Helen and I just *made* myself pick the gun up. I hoped it would be loaded. I pushed the muzzle against Speek's mouth till I felt it hard against his teeth, and I pulled the trigger. I was terrified someone would come, but no one did. Then I forced the gun into his hand. I pressed his fingers round the trigger thing, and held the arm up with the gun against his mouth just as it had been when I fired the shot, and I let his hand drop. When it did I was glad to see it still held the gun.'

She fumbled a moment under the rug which covered her legs and pulled out some woollen thing and began knitting.

'I often sit and think,' she said, 'what a blessing it was that it all happened before that French policeman invented finger-prints.'

The twinkle came back into her eyes.

'Just fancy,' she said. 'I might have been in the waxworks!'

She dwelt on that for a moment, knitting silently, then went on.

'What was I saying? Oh, yes. I went back to the hotel and told Helen what I had done, and I told her exactly what to tell Burke when he came to ask questions. Then I slipped to the constable's place and pinned a message on his door. I was worried afterwards that he might recognise my writing, but he never did, poor man, though he did rise to be a sergeant. Many a little drink I had with him and Rosie after he married the best housemaid I ever had.'

'And the draft of the codicil?' I said impatiently. 'What did you do with that?'

'I burned the nasty thing,' she said.

She smiled at me from her wheeled chair.

'It was an awful night and such a rush, and, when I'd

finished and got everything straightened out, you'll never guess what I did.'

'What?'

Mrs Marven began to giggle.

'I've often laughed at myself since,' she said. 'I went outside and sat in the gutter and had a good vomit.'

She was always a vulgar woman.

Mrs Marven – I cannot bother with her new name – visits me every day. I find I can put up with her. And no one else ever comes! Considering what is before her, however, I wonder that she can still find time for frivolity. Yesterday she actually said to the nurse, 'What sort of lipstick do you use, dearie?'

It seems the stuff is called Kissproof.

'I'd love to try it,' Mrs Marven said. I could scarcely credit I had heard aright, but in a flash Jane was smearing the paint on her lips. She looked at herself in a tiny mirror set in a little case the nurse lent her.

Jane said, 'Why, it's wonderful. You don't look a day over forty.'

The old lady gave her a playful push.

'You little flatterer,' she said. 'I'm forty-five.' She turned to me and there was mischief in her eye. 'I think it improves me, don't you, Mr Ford?' she asked, and was handing the little case back to the girl when she paused, reading the initials engraved upon it. 'E.W.,' she read aloud. 'What does that stand for, dear?'

'Eileen Ward,' the nurse told her. 'It's a present from the boyfriend.'

Mrs Marven did not speak at once but looked across at me where I lay propped up on my pillows.

'Why, what's the matter?' Jane asked.

Mrs Marven began to laugh softly. 'Nothing, my dear,' she said. 'Only it would be awfully funny if it were true. Were you named after your mother, dear?'

The nurse shook her head. 'After gran,' she said. 'She was a dear old thing. Dad's name was Larry after *his* dad, so there just naturally had to be an Eileen in the family.'

I have at last decided what to do about my will. I shall leave the money to Jane. She might as well have it as anyone, and charities would only fritter it away. I shall tell her what I am doing and she should be grateful. I should get better attention. In any case, there is only a thousand pounds, and I shall probably live for many years.

If she doesn't behave herself I can easily alter it.

**THE END**

In 1885 Archibald Edward (A.E.) Martin was born in Adelaide at the Scotch Thistle Hotel (now the Cathedral Hotel). He grew up in the small South Australian country town of Orroroo, where his father had the Imperial Hotel, and attended Prince Alfred College in Adelaide. On leaving school, he worked for a time on the *Adelaide Critic*, where he met the humorous poet C.J. Dennis. The pair founded a notorious parish-pump paper, the *Gadfly*, and at eighteen Martin not only co-owned a weekly newspaper, but also wrote for it satirical prose and verse of such quality that readers were often left guessing whether Dennis or Martin was the author.

A cast of talented youths gathered at the *Gadfly*, including its society columnist Alice Rosman ('Aunt Tabatha'), who later became a successful romantic novelist; political journalist Geoff Burgoyne, who set up a Labor paper in Western Australia; Beaumont Smith, entrepreneur and maker of some of Australia's earliest films; and artists, illustrators and cartoonists Ruby Lindsay, Will Dyson and Will Donald.

The *Gadfly* folded in 1909 and in 1912 Martin left to ramble around the fairgrounds of Europe, where Houdini became his mentor. He brought back to Australia 'The Wonder Show', a circus featuring freak acts such as 'The Fat Man', Edgar Crane, who weighed in at fifty-two stone, prizefighters and stars. The show opened in Adelaide in a heatwave that followed it to Melbourne. Martin was left broke after he had paid the artists' passages home. He moved to Sydney to work as advance publicity scout for Beau Smith's 'Tiny Town', a touring sideshow of midgets.

In 1915 Martin and Smith took the play *Seven Little Australians* to New Zealand. Martin returned to Sydney and worked as publicity agent for First National Pictures and then for the Fuller brothers' vaudeville show. In the early 1920s he became the publicist for J.C. Williamson, and worked for them until about 1934, promoting many great acts, including Anna Pavlova.

During the 1920s Martin took some time off to travel again to Europe, where he bought the Australian rights to movies such as the German health-and-skin flick *The Golden Road* and another about venereal disease. Martin, or the authorities, or perhaps the two in collusion, were careful to alert Australian audiences that a qualified nurse would be in attendance at the single-sex viewings.

In the later 1930s, Martin established The Women's Weekly Travel Agency, which offered overseas package tours, until the was forced its closure. He then wrote and published magazines for soldiers and children's comics, often working with the artist Brodie Mack. He began his career as a novelist and also wrote books about Australian place-names for the New South Wales Bookstall Company.

Martin had a wealth of life experience behind him when, in 1942, *The Australian Women's Weekly* announced a £1,000 prize for an unpublished novel. Encouraged by one of his sons, and needing money, Martin set to work and wrote two novels in six months: *Sinners Never Die* and *Common People*. Consolidated Press considered each to be worthy of the award, but finally plumped for *Common People*, which was early serialised in the *Weekly*. 'Old Sinners Never Die' was the title under which the other was serialised, considerably later, 30 December 1944 to 17 March 1945, with illustrations by Wynne W. Davies.

A.E. Martin's son, Jim, for whose help the series editors

are much indebted, is unsure how the books were picked up by the American publisher Simon and Schuster. *Sinners Never Die* was released in the States to fabulous reviews, being listed as among the 'Ten Best' in 1944 by every major mystery reviewer. Both books were later published in Britain by Nimmo and, in 1955, *Common People* was filmed in the UK as *The Glass Cage* and released as a Hammer production.

The text of this edition of *Sinners Never Die* is based on that issued by the NSW Bookstall Company in Sydney, 1945, which is a lithograph of the first edition by Simon & Schuster (New York, 1944).

The London edition from Nimmo, Hay & Mitchell, undated but published in 1947, was followed by an abridged edition, also undated, from Bestseller Mystery. It was translated, at least into Swedish and Danish.

The author adapted the book for radio in fifty-two quarter-hour episodes, at the behest of George Edwards (of 'Dad & Dave' fame). He went on to do more radio scripts for Edwards, including an adaptation of his own *Death in the Limelight* and several original fifty-two episode serials (they paid better than the novels).

It is clear from this cursory account of A.E. Martin's life that his autobiography would have been sensational, although he himself, as his spruiker character Pel Pelham in *Common People* and *The Bridal Bed Murders* suggests, was notably self-effacing. Carlo Boldini of *Sinners Never Die* owes much to Martin's vaudeville experience. His birthplace, Orroroo, in the mid-north of South Australia, was the model for the small town. Its post master, so the joke runs, only ever had to deal with two addressed letters. Jim Martin remembers how they used to say in Orroroo, when the post master was late opening his little window, it was because he was reading all the postcards.

*Sinners Never Die* is a remarkable novel, able to hold its own in company with any of the well-known mainsteam classics of

Australian fiction. Its bleak tone and savage irony are reminiscent most immediately of Jim Thompson. There is also something of the dark humour of Twain here. You could only complain that the author's irony is somewhat too pervasive: hardly anyone is spared in this cynical masterpiece, but hardly anyone is not some sort of sinner.

The implicit question of the title is somewhat like that of its contemporary, *Common People*. Who is to judge? The principal sinner in the book, Harry Ford, regards himself as more sinned against than sinning and, if you could measure it, he might be right. Another of those who survives to 'fade away' in a nursing hospital, Mrs Marven, 'always a vulgar woman' in Harry's book, committed several crimes, including that of burning the draft codicil to a will. Readers of the book may regard Mrs Marven as salt of the earth. Jim Martin tells us she was the author's mother, who died in 1912.

Although Harry Ford's snobbery may not compel readers to despise Mrs Marven, the fact that he is the one presenting the story surely has its effect in other cases. It is, for instance, difficult not to hate cordially the melodramatic swaggerer Garnet Price, cushioned by his wealth and strength from the consequences of his cavalier behaviour, and seemingly always equipped with that infernal riding whip. And 'Wellday's brat' certainly deserves the opprobrious epithet. Harry Ford strikes us as essentially sound on dogs and small children, yet he is denied even the small triumph of poisoning one of them.

A more interesting case is Boldini's young assistant. Very astutely, Martin has Ford refer to her the first time as a 'person': 'The young person who did the ushering', 'the young person at the piano' or 'the young person, who, with miraculous speed, had changed from her tawdry evening gown into the garb of a pageboy'. Only after several of these circumlocutions does he refer to her outright as 'the girl'. It is much later, on a chance encounter, that she is allowed a name, and then she has to provide it herself and it is doubly unsuitable: 'I'm Flossie La Rue – that's what

Boldini calls me. My real name's Jinks. Ain't it awful?'
Besides that, she refers to him as 'Toots'.

If the story is that of 'The Ordeal of Harry Ford', and
deals with whether an inveterate snob is ruined by his
mother from achieving the liberating recognition that he
too belongs to the human race, then this young person
called Jinks represents Harry's last chance to prove himself.
The astonishing scene in which this brazen hussy, this
'painted baggage', offers Ford the precious gift of an affec-
tionate friendship almost unfreezes him: 'Her arms were
warm on my body and for a moment I weakened. But only
for a moment.' We never get to know this young person
well enough to tell whether she is one of the angels or the
Becky Sharps of this world: certainly, she has all of Becky's
energy in her parting gesture of hurling a 'heavy directory'
at the one insensible to her real qualities. Ironically, Ford
threatens to put her in for assaulting him and another sinner
fades out of his self-righteous little life. Possibly she would
have been very bad for Harry: the dream he has of his
mother transformed into Boldini's trollop has horrible
implications. Mrs Marven is more objective. She comments:
'That nice young girl' is 'an understanding little thing'.

Ford, however, would not wish to think of Flossie La Rue
as an attractive young woman, and by reducing her to a mere
'person' he does his best to neuter her. Those who, in the
interests of feminism, prefer to be known as 'persons', will
consider Ford's usage instructive. Harry does not think of
Eileen Mahony, the woman he 'had chosen for his mate', in
such terms; rather, he has leaped to the opposite fault, having
set her, he tells us, on a 'pedestal of Christian virtue and
maidenly modesty'. For Harry, a person is a woman whose
sexuality has been prudishly repressed; a maiden is a woman
whose sexuality has been jealously appropriated. The kiss he
gets from Eileen and the one given him by Jinks are nicely
juxtaposed. It is a question whether Eileen's is not the more
mercenary of the two. She is, after all, only the daughter of

her father, one of the most odious characters in the book. That Harry is still carrying a torch for Eileen is, in retrospect, indicated on the novel's first page: nurse Eileen is promptly renamed Jane.

If Thackeray might have been proud to father Jinks, Dickens would not have disdained the great Carlo Boldini. Most of Boldini's conjuring tricks may appear fit only for late nineteenth-century yokels to sophisticated modern readers, but everyone must appreciate the skill with which Martin works them in the two big performances. He seems to have deliberately kept the pace slow and set the key low in these sequences that are to bring such life to the latter part of the book, in order better to spring his surprises. For the narrator, they are scenes, primarily, of excruciating embarrassment. Such scenes are very dangerous for an author, the danger being that the reader will feel more for the victim (here, Harry Ford) than is proper. But Ford is so consistently set on being a prat, on being Malvolio, that he fails to acknowledge his own degrading equality with Boldini's more cheerful victims. Before breakfast on the morning after the first performance, while Boldini is demonstrating his culinary expertise, Ford is busy reconstructing his own superiority:

The master mind, I reflected, was not neglecting his stomach. Somehow the knowledge comforted me. The fellow, after all, was only human. Viewed in the cold light of day his performance of the previous night lacked reality. I saw it as a conglomeration of audacious tricks played upon a bumpkin audience he had lulled into a state of gullibility – tricks easy enough to fathom, no doubt, if one had the time and the inclination.

Ford is entirely right, though he does not draw the correct inference. It is one of the rare moments of disappointment in the narrative when Ford suddenly gets the opportunity to confront Boldini with his inability to translate Italian and fails to follow through when Boldini weakly pretends that the text is 'indelicate'. The irresolute Ford would never have been a match for the bold Boldini, but perhaps he should not have been quite so easily disarmed.

*Sinners Never Die* is so much more than a genre novel that it is easy to forget that its principal character is a blackmailer and that the occasion of blackmail was, apparently, a murder. Both the murder and the blackmail are quite sufficiently well motivated. The murder victim, Timothy Speek, is cruel and jealous. The blackmail victims can well afford the demand made upon them, and it would never have been made had it not been for another criminal's embezzlement of Harry's funds. According to Ford's lights, Helen Speek's reputation is such, from the beginning, that she does not deserve to be considered in the same light as a virtuous lady – I refer to what he describes as the 'mild flirtation' on the occasion when he gives her a package outside office hours. That action, although it amounts to no more than an insinuation and putting his hand on her arm, is as callous a piece of blackmailing harassment as what he later offers to her when he thinks she is a cold-blooded poisoner. Ford's harassment of the reluctant Eileen is one of a piece with this behaviour. We can see why Martin thought it desirable to set the novel in the Victorian era.

The plotting, despite its reliance on coincidence such as the similarity between the names Larry Ward and Harry Ford and the business with Polly Garner, as well as the dog poisoning, is brilliant in its provision of surprises and fresh mysteries. These mysteries are not all resolved until the end, back in the frame story, for Constable Burke's resources were never going to be sufficient to cope with them, once the corpse had disappeared, another reason for the Victorian setting of the main action.

The final coincidence, the identity of Harry's nurse, leads to an ending that could be considered romantic in some lights were it not for Harry's saving cynicism that, by leaving her the thousand pounds (the exact amount he once thought he needed to buy her grandmother with), and telling her about the legacy, he 'should get better attention'.

A.E. Martin's extraordinary book repays close reading. In an interview for the *Australian Women's Weekly* of 3 September 1949, A.E. Martin said he got a nasty shock when he saw the dust-jacket of the American edition and found that it (like the Australian edition) showed a gravestone with his name inscribed: 'Luckily I'm not a superstitious man. The English edition carried on with the gravestone motif, but I was relieved to find that the artist had handled the author's name in a more conventional way.' There must be many an author alive today who would be only too glad to have the title of a book of the calibre of *Sinners Never Die* inscribed on their gravestone.

MICHAEL J. TOLLEY AND PETER MOSS

**WAKEFIELD CRIME CLASSICS**

Peter Moss and Michael J. Tolley, general editors of the Wakefield Crime Classics series, are colleagues at the University of Adelaide. Late in 1988, they began assembling a series of Australian 'classic' crime fiction and soon realised that the problem was not going to be one of finding sufficient works of high quality, but of finding a bold enough publisher fired with the same vision.

This series revives forgotten or neglected gems of crime and mystery fiction by Australian authors. Many of the writers have established international reputations but are little known in Australia. In the wake of the excitement generated by the new wave of Australian crime fiction writers, we hope that the achievements of earlier days can be justly celebrated.

If you wish to be informed about new books as they are released in the Wakefield Crime Classics series, send your name and address to Wakefield Press, Box 2266, Kent Town, South Australia 5071, phone (08) 362 8800, fax (08) 362 7592.

———

A dead man alive at Melbourne's Festival Hall ... a merino- shaped lake ... a stolen copy of Thoreau's *Walden* ... ASIO's wall of silence.

Sandy Carmichael can pick up the jigsaw pieces, but to fit them together, he needs to risk his life.

*Ligny's Lake* is a puzzling story of suspense that weirdly echoes the disappearance of Prime Minister Harold Holt.

'S.H. Courtier is unjustly neglected. His works show a good narrative style, ingenious plots, and integral settings that are powerfully atmospheric.'
*Whodunit?*